"A GIFTED WRITER OF FICTION . . . Mrs. Dew can convey, with a skill matched by few writers today. the quick, peculiar shifts in feelings that we experience, moment to moment, day to day—how in an instant love can sour into irritation; anxiety dissolve into affection, attraction subside into nostalgia. And in *The Time of Her Life*, she uses this ability to map out the ambiguities of the Parks' marriage, and to show the devastating consequences that this unstable alliance has on their daughter."

Michiko Kakutani
The New York Times

"Dew is the most generous sort of writer. She takes the time and the care to share whatever is important in her characters' lives without skimping on the hard parts. . . . In the last chapter, it's Christmas day and, scene by scene, the family drama heightens amid ribbons and champagne and twinkling lights. Dew knows just how to hold us, spellbound, through these scenes. And, when the time is right, she also know show to let us go. The novel ends with the image of splintering glass, and Dew leaves us dazzled among the shards."

USA Today

"Like Virginia Woolf, Dew charts the big changes that can be set off by small actions— a glance, a turned back, a tone of voice. These changes in mood which happen so imperceptibly in life that we often don't know what's come over us, are part of the terrain that Dew slows down and examines second by second in this moving novel."

Glamour

THE TIME OF HER LIFE

"Her most striking talent is for getting inside the mind of a child. This talent . . . makes this novel come alive. The passages describing Jane's thoughts, attitudes and emotional responses are brilliant and convey perfectly the awful, racking struggle for psychological survival children go through when their parents split up. . . . The conveying of emotional pain through the medium of a child can not only be deeply moving, but if it is as well done as it is here, it can be illuminating."

New York Times Book Review

"*The Time of Her Life* has every nuance right—the botched good intentions, the casual cruelties, the horrible comedy of family life gone wrong. It is a powerful and disturbing book, and only a writer with Robb Forman Dew's deft touch could have brought it off."

Anne Tyler

"An accomplished, chilling, and memorable book, one that establishes Dew as a novelist of the first rank . . . In a skillfully constructed narrative, she gives us a couple who have never passed the stage of emotional adolescence, and the crushing responsibilities they unwittingly inflict on their 11-year-old daughter."

Publishers Weekly

ROBB FORMAN DEW

"Robb Forman Dew has a marvelous seismograph that allows her to pick up otherwise undetectable shifts and rumbles of the heart. She can remark nearly invisible fault lines in the terrain of relationships; she can detect the movement of emotions in a seemingly placid domestic still-life. . . . *The Time of Her Life*, she again puts her sensitive ear to a family's heart. And again she comes up with a beautiful, personal language with which to describe its pulse. . . . Dew works with small, fine strokes, heartbeat by heartbeat, thoroughly mapping the interior life. And her delicate work pays off in an ending of surprising and disturbing violence, as feelings long in turbulent disarray finally make themselves known. . . . this book is an achievement."

The Detroit News

"Writing like Robb Forman Dew's is more than a miracle of luck. It is the sure sign of a hard-working major talent."

Houston Post

"Robb Forman Dew has a wonderful sense of the most subtle shifts and shades of feeling and a wonderful sense of the depth and complexity of human relations. She seems to have been born with insights that most novelists spend a lifetime trying to learn. She is that rare bird—a fascinating tale-teller and a true artist."

Robert Penn Warren

THE TIME OF HER LIFE

Robb Forman Dew

BALLANTINE BOOKS • NEW YORK

Copyright © 1984 by Robb Forman Dew

All rights reserved under International and Pan-American Copyright Conventions. No part of this book may be reproduced or utilized in any form or by any means, electronic or mechanical, including photocopying, recording or by any information storage and retrieval system, without permission in writing from the Publisher. Published in the United States by Ballantine Books, a division of Random House, Inc., New York, and simultaneously in Canada by Random House of Canada Limited, Toronto.

Library of Congress Catalog Card Number: 84-4665

ISBN 0-345-32542-7

This edition published by arrangement with William Morrow and Co., Inc.

The first chapter of this novel originally appeared, in slightly different form, in *The New Yorker*.

Grateful acknowledgment is made for permission to reprint the following:

On page 188, lines from the song "Tell Laura I Love Her," by Jeff Barry and Ben Raleigh, copyright © 1960, Edward B. Marks Music Company, used by permission, all rights reserved.

On page 184, lines from the song "Twilight Time," lyric by Buck Ram; music by Morty Nevins & Al Nevins. TRO, copyright 1944 and renewed 1972, Devon Music, Inc., New York, N.Y. Used by permission. The correct words of the song are: "Heavenly shades of night are falling,/ It's twilight time. Out in the mist your voice is calling,/ It's twilight time. . . ."

Manufactured in the United States of America

First Ballantine Books Edition: November 1985

For Charles,
". . . my cause, my proper heat and center."
—JOHN CROWE RANSOM
"Winter Remembered"

1

Once every summer a mass of humid air settled over Lunsbury, Missouri. For perhaps ten days in July or August a muggy silence predominated, and everyone became short-tempered and uneasy in the still heat. Otherwise during the year there was a pervasive susurration of wind that rustled through the streets and down the alleys, across the golf course and between the houses, moving the light objects—Frisbees, aluminum lawn chairs, a scarf—from one place to another in any backyard where they had been left behind. An open door would soon slam shut. Papers on a desk near an open window would drift away and lie in trembling, shifting disarray across the floor. There was always something afoot, afloat, in motion. Sometimes the weather was severe, but from day to day it was more often tame. Since Lunsbury was a settlement of sixty thousand people, with many good-sized buildings and sycamore trees planted strategically in long rows of windbreaks, the force of the air that shifted from the Pacific coast across the plains was divided and channeled through the maze of the community.

The movement of the trees was whispery in this season. It was autumn, and the dried leaves stirred in the

1

full-blown heads of the old trees or rolled and spun across the grass in turmoil. In the summer, when the leaves were full of sap, there was a tender, fleshy chafing. When winter came, there would be the creaking of the bare, abrasive branches, and then again, with spring, the softer sigh of young leaves and the tall, spurred grasses that grew in the meadows, in the ditches, and untended patches of real estate.

All of the residents enclosed within their own quiet rooms had more than an ordinary sense of security. When they shut their windows and went to bed they had an unusual knowledge of being protected from the elements. And those prevailing westerly winds were some part of the reason that—against all odds on this Saturday morning—Claudia Parks came out of sleep in her closed and silent house in a state of optimism. She awoke as though she had been out running; her body was loose and warm, and she was carried along into the day on an early surge of animation that led her mildly to consider good will, good luck, new chances. Her turn of mind so early-on had the same frail and opalescent quality as the crescent moon that hung late in the first light.

Before she went down to fix breakfast, she brushed her short hair until it was full of static electricity and stood out around her head like a cloud. It had no sheen, and her hair didn't curl so much as curve in soft brown puffs against her cheeks. It bobbed as she moved around the kitchen but then settled around her head once more when she came to rest. Electrified wisps and tendrils frizzled outward against the backlighting of morning windows, softening the outline of her image in the white kitchen.

Claudia had drawn her eyes all the way around with dark pencil that was artfully smudged, and she had exaggerated the pale wedge of her face by blending a little pink color beneath her cheekbones so that they bore the strength of her looks in a wide, gleaming winglike span above her fox-pointed chin. But she had left off there and wandered into the kitchen, and in the fluorescent light the triangle of her face was shadowed into a pinched and haggard look by her uncolored mouth and darkened eyes that seemed huge and hollow-socketed beneath her indistinct and unpenciled brows.

Claudia had on her scarlet robe that billowed and undulated around her ankles with each step. It was a finely made robe that descended in long tucks to the waist, where its fullness was released, and the sleeves were also pleated from the shoulder and then let loose in exorbitant width to be caught up again in more banded pleats and a pearl button at the wrist. Her movements as she broke eggs into a blue bowl and took dishes from the shelves were as red and startling as the flight of a male cardinal in the snow. However, that robe was three years old, and it was by the force of her own complicated vision that she didn't notice that the elbows were worn thin as gauze. She almost never remembered to run the robe through the lingerie cycle of the wash, and the cuffs were darkly edged and fraying slightly. All down the front were strewn tiny scattered holes where ashes from her cigarettes had flown and caught as she swung her arm in an expansive gesture. "Oh, well. Don't worry," she would say as she brushed at the tiny flickers where the cinders smoldered, "ashes keep the moths out."

Her daughter, Jane, sat at the table and paid sullen attention while her mother fixed breakfast and talked to her. Claudia transferred the milk to a pitcher and the jam to a crystal dish, and she put the silver down on woven mats with matching cloth napkins. But she put the mats down on a table gritty with scattered sugar that had spilled during some other meal. She stood at the counter staring out the window as she waited for the toast to pop up, and she put her cigarette on the windowsill as she poured out orange juice. She forgot it there, and later in the day she would be surprised to find the dark burn it had left on the white paint. The sunlight fell across her face and bright red robe with a shaft of light that caught her in its narrow beam and enhanced the peculiar tension that was Claudia's alone; she had a waveringly suppressed and dramatic energy that was with her rain or shine.

"I don't know if I should do it or not," she said to Jane, about a class she might take. "Maggie wants me to, but I don't know. . . . You know how she wears you down. They don't teach it here. I'd have to commute to Kansas City, and I don't have any sense of direction. And in the winter . . ." She told Jane all about her plans, new things that had occurred to her. She talked and chatted while she moved dreamlike around the room, stepping over their dog, Nellie, without seeing her, reaching automatically for the things she needed, without alacrity, just a lazy uncurling of her sleepy muscles when she reached or stirred. It was the urgency of her new ideas that made Claudia appear languorous as she moved around the counters. It was dazzling to her, the things that were possible, and in the morning her musings were entirely visionary and hopeful. She gave Jane some toast and juice and settled at the table across from her daughter with her own breakfast, but then she elbowed her plate slightly to one side and lit another cigarette, idly breaking her toast into pieces with her other hand.

"And this is the last pack, Jane. I swear it! It really is," she turned to her daughter to say, gesturing with the cigarette she was smoking. Claudia's gestures were fluid and poignant with earnestness, and she was impressed, herself, with her own sincerity.

Jane was looking out the window in the direction of the Tunbridges' house which could be glimpsed through the trees far away down the hill, and her mute nod of acknowledgment was so peremptory, so casual, when Claudia meant never—*never*—to buy another pack of cigarettes, that Claudia slowly took in the presence of her daughter with a tinge of resentment that colored her early ebullience. It was the first bruise on what she had chosen to see as the perfect apple of her day. Claudia looked down the hill, too, at Maggie's house, and was agitated all at once by the things in this day that she meant to get done. She was disturbed by the idea of order and efficiency that always eluded her at the last minute. She almost got things right. She just missed by a hair.

"Jane, you've got to get your things ready to go to Diana's tonight." This was a command, but in her sudden uneasiness Claudia's voice was faintly tentative. She was offering a small bit of instruction, a slight complaint. These days she had constantly to remind Jane of the obligations of Jane's own social life, but all at once this year Jane's face had elongated and become narrow and stern, so that compelling her to do this thing or that was a risky business.

"I might not be going," Jane said.

"Well, Jane. Please remember to tell me these things. Would that be too much trouble?" Her tone was light with injury. "I thought it was all planned. When I talked to Maggie yesterday, she said Diana was counting on it. I thought you were going over this morning and staying overnight."

"I'm not sure I want to go, though," Jane said.

Claudia sipped her coffee and let the conversation become vague in her mind. "I don't want you to hurt Diana's feelings," she said, but her wishes dispersed into the warm, scented kitchen air.

Jane finished her toast but still sat at the table, moving her juice glass in tight circles that blurred the ring of condensation beneath it. "Did Dad come home?" she asked.

Claudia made a dismissive gesture with her hand and gave her daughter a nod, but in spite of herself a sudden weight of accountability plummeted through her in that instant, making her lethargic, her arms and legs heavy with despair. Thirty-two years and the responsibility for them. Claudia had never thought that life would demand any effort on her part; she had assumed it had its own momentum. She had never even thought she would be thirty-two. The whole business had taken her by surprise.

"He's still asleep," she said to Jane. That's where she had meant to leave Avery for the moment—stuporously asleep in their bed—and she was irritated at Jane, because here he was now, in the forefront of her mind. She wasn't pleased to disturb herself this morning, in her favorite, mellow hour.

Claudia and Avery had gone to a party at the Tunbridges' the night before, and now Claudia lost all track of her thoughts about the class she might take. The idea of herself in her blue car driving along I-70, sure of her destination, crisp in nice clothes, passing by the idling traffic while she drove straight on to Kansas City to be on time—that soothing image—became a kind of low hum of a thought to fall back on. It was a bit of theater, really; she enjoyed watching the idea work itself out, but she would never have taken the action. She was irritated, though, because she didn't want to think about the night before, not any part of it at all, and here it was, surfacing in her mind.

At the party Maggie had been explaining how disappointed she had been after meeting and entertaining the convocation speaker, a writer whose books she had reviewed several times. "It's ruined his writing for me. He's a whiner," she had said, drawing one foot up on the couch and clasping her arms around her knee. It had gotten late, and only eight or nine people were still ranged around the room in various stages of party fatigue. Eight or so acquaintances who lingered on. "He's insinuating. In a sneaky way," Maggie went on, "he's really trying too hard to convince you how humble and amusing he is."

"You were not impressed," said Vince, who had been sitting in a chair across from his wife. He summed this up. It was only a statement, but Avery waved his hand impatiently at this comment.

"Oh, Maggie. You were impressed. I know you. I know you were impressed. Think of what that man has achieved!" There was a nasty note to Avery's voice; there was a challenge in his tone, and the whole group turned to him, surprised. He had said very little for some time.

This was a group of people—the ones who remained in the long living room—of some note. They had a little fame one way or another or, like Claudia, were married to persons of some limited renown. But they were not necessarily fond of each other; they simply tended to congregate because they had that much in common, and they were all there was.

Vince watched Avery for a moment. "Well, all right, Avery. What about you? Who would impress you? Living or dead?" Avery's face lost its sardonic expression and became momentarily reflective, so Vince pressed on. "Any single person. Who would you like to meet? And why?" Vince added. "Why would you like to meet whoever you'd like to meet?"

Avery had become quite solemn, and he took some time thinking about this. "I would be"—Avery spoke slowly and raised one hand to emphasize his words—"I believe I would be impressed by Lincoln. Abraham Lincoln."

There was a small collective sigh of disappointment, and Avery raised his hand a little higher to retain their attention, but he kept gazing morosely ahead of himself. His solemnity had become a kind of maudlin petulance. "No," he said. "No. I mean it. The language. He had the language. . . . He could write. But his terrible melancholy . . ." Avery was sinking into a slow-witted and boozy sentimentality.

Vince moved right along, turning away from him. "Okay. Maggie? We're stuck with early American. Who would you want to meet?"

Maggie had finally come up with Elizabeth Cady Stanton, an early feminist, and Evan Price, a young architect, had gone with Thomas Jefferson. Vince himself had chosen Stephen A. Douglas. Then he had turned to Claudia.

"Oh, I'll pass," she said. "This isn't my kind of game."

Avery sat up straight and leaned toward her in irritation. All at once he was disconcertingly alert. "You can't think of *anyone*?" he asked her much too loudly. "Not a single human being who ever lived?" He made a great show of incredulity.

"I don't want to play this game," Claudia had said very mildly. She didn't seem to notice Avery's immense irritation, but he wouldn't let the subject drop.

"Okay. Okay. What about Aaron Burr? Aaron Burr. Now he would interest you. Wouldn't he? You really would like to meet Aaron Burr, wouldn't you?" Avery was becoming increasingly unpleasant, but Claudia looked across at him with no expression or response at all.

"Oh, come on. Make Avery happy, Claudia," said Vince. "You can come up with someone."

At the same moment Avery had risen with difficulty from the deep wing chair in which he had been sitting. He had risen laboriously and storklike, waving an arm to quiet Vince.

"No, no, no, Vince. No, there is nobody," Avery said, "nobody at all who could ever possibly impress my wife. Not a single, solitary person who ever existed. And it's because what she really is . . . what Claudia really is is a nihilist. A real one. The real thing," he said ponderously, and he drank down more of his drink. "And ultimately . . . *ultimately* that's just boring. Tedious! Tedious!"

No one said anything at all. No one had realized how drunk Avery had become. But Claudia was calm and irritated. "For God's sake, Avery, don't be such a fool. I'd never describe myself as a nihilist."

"But it's exactly what you are! God damn it! That's what you are." The whole group tried hard to pretend that there was no menace in Avery's voice, but Claudia was not in the least intimidated. Instead she was unwisely cross. She disliked being spoken for and having herself categorized in this sophomoric conversation.

"For Christ's sake, Avery! Will you drop it? I certainly don't believe in nothing." She paused for a moment, and then she smiled slightly so that all the force of her tremendous and ingenuous charm came across her face. "It's just that there's nothing much that I believe in." And the whole gathering broke into mild and relieved laughter. All, of course, but Avery.

Avery was still standing above them, and he looked around the room. "What you don't understand . . ." Then he stopped in the center of the room, resting the hand of his uplifted arm on the top of his head. He stood alone, looking angular and puzzled as if he had forgotten what it was that he did understand. But the room remained attentive, and he continued. "What *you* don't know, and *you* don't know, and *you* don't know," he said, turning in a slow arc and lowering his raised arm at one person and then another in accusation and inebriated slow motion. "What no one seems to see is that what Claudia thinks of all of you is that you're just a *dot*! That's it! Just a dot . . ." He was too drunk to get the right tone; it fell short of sarcasm into a furious slurring. "A dot on the great big blackboard of life!" He had meant this as a little witticism, but there was only silence in the room, and this time Claudia had frowned. She hadn't replied. After a moment he dropped his arm and smiled in huge pleasure at having transmitted this message, and he wandered out of the room, not choosing to elaborate.

Claudia heard him leave through the front door, and when conversation started up again, she went and got their coats without saying anything to anyone at all. Maggie came over to her, though, moving among her guests discreetly so as not to interrupt them, and with a slight tipping back of her head, a conspiratorial downglance, had said to her, "Call me if you want. Later. Or tomorrow." She had spoken so softly that Claudia wondered afterward if she had actually said the words or mouthed them in a silent pantomime of solidarity. Claudia had gone outside and found Avery sitting in the passenger seat of their car, looking smug. He was pleased and quiet, and Claudia drove home.

By the time they were home, however, Avery had so

much to talk about, and he was insistent that someone listen to him. He put the dog out, coaxing her because she didn't like the dark. "Go *on*, now, Nellie! You cowardly hound. Go out, now, go on out!" While he waited to let her back in he roamed around the living room studying his own bookshelves, the pictures on his walls, as though there were something there of which he was suspicious, something out of kilter, put there behind his back. At last he said, "I'll go check on Jane," while he was still on the move around the room, and he was away in a flash. He was quick, and he was sly; Claudia had been heading in the other direction to hang up their coats.

"Damn it! Avery, don't wake her up! It's almost one o'clock." By then, though, Avery was leaning against Jane's doorframe, talking to her. Talking and talking. Asking her opinion. Wheedling and cajoling. What fools people were, weren't they? he said. Her teachers . . . "There is no one more intelligent than you are, Janie. That's the thing. Now, knowledge. They might have you there. But, still, if you always know that you've got one up on them"—and he tapped the side of his head with his forefinger in a pretense of jest—"then you can be sure of a lot of things. Not *happy* all the time. That's not the point. But you can always be absolutely sure that you know what you know." And he rambled on in a sweet muttering. The pleasure of his own voice was there, full in his throat, as he lifted the sound persuasively up and down the scale, alternatingly soft and firm in tone. A joy in the night. He emitted a sound so charming it would lure the birds right out of the trees. For a little while it always mesmerized Claudia. That's how he could be when he chose. But he grew tired there in the doorway and followed Claudia to the kitchen, where he fixed himself another drink. He always came home late from long conversations and then had more to say. He could not *finish* talking, and his voice altered and became a deep, insistent whine. He was distressed all at once.

"Your real talent, Claudia, is that you suffer fools graciously! Christ! Fools. God, they're fools. All the people we see. How can you stand it? Why do you make these plans? How can I live with a woman who laughs at Evan Price's jokes? He's mentally five years old! How can I *live* with a woman who laughs at bathroom humor? Did you know that? He's five years old!" With the last two sentences he had pounded the wall each time for emphasis, shouting now at Claudia, while she moved around the kitchen clearing up the dishes Jane had left and emptying the ashtrays. When he had thought she wasn't paying attention, he had put his drink down and gone slowly toward her and taken hold of her lower arms between the wrist and elbow so that she had to stand in one place and watch him. "How can I live with someone who would ever, ever laugh at Evan Price? How can I?"

"I didn't laugh, Avery," she said to him. "Evan's your friend." Claudia always tried to explain herself whenever Avery began wondering how he could live with her. Always, at that point, her irritation became a soft fear that would arouse her own defensive anger. "You wanted to go. I hate those parties." Her own voice rose, although he was holding her arms very tightly and shaking her when he spoke so that she was swayed from side to side.

Avery had let her go and turned aside, arching slightly over himself in a protective and sorrowful attitude. He was quiet with his own woefulness for a moment, but then he arrowed straight up again and pounded the wall once more in frustration and to keep her attention directed at himself. "Shit!" he said. "Holy shit!"

She never understood that there was nothing at all that he wanted to hear her say. She never understood that she was only incidental to these moods of existential and profoundly insightful despair that swept over him because of all the things he believed he knew and his experience in the world. He was passionately agonized. He smashed his fist again against the wall, and it

11

went right through the thin Sheetrock. Upon impact tiny particles of paperboard and insulation exploded into the room, powdering his face into a sandy look of less ferocity. Claudia and Avery stood there motionless a moment until finally Claudia laughed at him, but Jane was standing in the center of the room tense and pale in her seersucker pajamas with happy panda bears printed in rows upon the faded blue cloth.

"Stop it! Stop it! Stop it!" she said over and over until Avery perceived the noise she was making and where it was coming from and turned to her, enraged.

"Don't you ever get out of bed this late at night and interrupt your mother and me when we're discussing something. You aren't supposed to be out of bed, are you?" His voice was not loud so much as it was suddenly voluminous with rage. "None of this is your business. You don't have any idea about our privacy. You seem to think that you're an awfully grown-up little girl. You seem to think you can do just about anything you want to, don't you? Maybe it never occurred to you that your mother and I have something to talk about. By ourselves! Just go back to bed!" He started to move in her direction for two or three steps, but he had never touched Jane when he was angry, and she stood her ground right where she was, shaking her clenched fists by her sides with each word.

"No, I said stop it! Stop! Just stop it!" And she wasn't quiet until Avery left the house in a fury, slamming the door and roaring out of the driveway at two-thirty in the morning.

Now, the next morning, in the kitchen and the sunlight, sitting across from Jane, Claudia undid the buttons at her wrists and pushed back her full sleeves. She held out her arms to see that, in fact, they were smudged with bruises where Avery had held onto her. She turned her hands palm up and studied the marks on the pale white underside of her arms with curiosity.

"Oh, well," she said to Jane with vague irritation, "I just don't think that should have happened! Look at my arms! Damn! That just shouldn't have happened." Jane was looking out the window again, and Claudia was mostly musing to herself in any case. She rested her elbow on the table, settling her chin into her hand, and gazed and gazed at nothing. One corner of her mouth twitched downward in an expression of distaste. With this first dissipation of her slippery morning expectancy, disappointment grew apparent in all her movements, especially in the subtle hooding of her large, wide eyes. Her appearance was as susceptible to disillusionment as a morning glory that wilts with fragile translucency when the light fades.

Jane had moved to the counter to make herself more toast when her father came in, and Claudia was still leaning into her hand, absorbed in her own thoughts; she didn't look up right away. Jane put two more pieces of bread in the four-slice toaster and poured another glass of juice to give to her father.

Avery was disheveled. Even in his handsome green robe and still crisply creased pajamas he had an air of being askew, and he was not quite sober from the night before. But he was not uncivil. He was hesitant and quiet; he came into the room as though he might immediately back out of it. Avery was a man, this morning, to be pitied, and he wouldn't shun pity. That was how he looked. He carried his injury with him. It defined him for this day, although it didn't make him less pitiful; it only made his abjection less savory. He didn't have much to say when he sat down at the table; he gave only a halfhearted nod of greeting. When Jane put some toast and juice down in front of him, he was careful to thank her with elaborate courtesy.

Claudia did not acknowledge him at all except to raise one eyebrow in an expression that Jane had often practiced in the mirror. Her mother didn't aim this expression at her father; it was a comment she was making strictly to herself. Disdain. It was superb disdain, and only a light sigh accompanied that look as she very deliberately cleared her place and rinsed her cup and saucer. She swirled her robe out of the way—flicking it to one side or the other with a twitch of her hand—to avoid catching it on Avery's chair, which was in the way now that he had drawn it out from the table to sit down. She even wiped the residue of jam and sugar from the counters and shook out her place mat, making a swipe beneath it with a cloth to clean the table.

"I'm going to get dressed," she said out into the room with no inflection. Perhaps it was a bit of information just meant to float upon the air, and she left the room with a final sweep of her robe and impressive urgency. Finally Jane went to get dressed, too, while Avery remained at the table, solemnly eating a piece of toast.

Avery was writing a book, and he took a second cup of coffee into his study and sat down at his long bleached oak table, so spare and functional, which was laden with neat piles of research notes across its surface. He turned on his draftsman's lamp and sipped his coffee and studied the tidy stacks of paper. He needed to bring all his wits to bear on this book in order to make it interesting. He had grasped hold of an idea that was just beginning to be tossed around with great seriousness now that discussions of the greenhouse effect had finally filtered down to the cocktail party level. His book would be an investigation of the notion that the more civilized a culture, the less adaptable it is to environmental and climactic changes. He knew so much to say about it. He would reexamine the ancient cultures—the Anasazi Indians in particular—and bring the narrative forward to encompass humankind in the space age. And he knew how to string his words together in pages full of wit and grace so that the message unfolded with an ease that assured him of a large audience. It would require great concentration to get the arrangement of information just right.

He swiveled his chair to one side and looked out the tall window that flanked his table on the left. There was nothing there to see except the long slope of the hill above the house and the autumn trees wound around with trumpet vine. He missed their orange flowers, which he had looked out upon through the summer. He turned from his window to his papers and then to the window again. He moved some notes from one pile to another, and he thought about this and that. He sat still and quiet and now and then picked up a pencil and twirled it thoughtfully between his thumb and forefinger, occasionally leaning over to jot a note to himself on his legal pad. And what he had decided by late morning was to make some of his homemade chili for lunch. He left his study, still dressed in his pajamas and robe, and called up the stairs to Claudia and Jane.

"I think I'll make some chili for lunch. Hot, this time. Hey, I'm going to make some chili for lunch."

In the kitchen he was very busy; and Claudia and Jane hovered about. It was irresistible; they came in and out. It was quite a production when Avery made chili. Jane opened and drained and rinsed the beans, and Claudia leaned over a counter where the chessboard had been set up and studied the chess puzzle taped to the wall above it. Avery opened a beer and sipped it from the can while he stirred and seasoned the meat, and then he joined Claudia and they argued about the solution to the chess problem. Avery put forward only gentle disagreements, while Claudia was adamant and went to find the book that had the answer.

Jane saved the chili every time. She stirred the meat up from the bottom whenever she smelled it beginning to scorch. Her parents were absorbed, now, in their board game. Avery opened another beer, and Claudia looked around the kitchen for the pack of cigarettes she had hidden from herself the day before so she wouldn't be tempted.

"Now, look, if you'll just think about it, Avery," she said when she came back to the board, "you'll see what I mean." She bent over to peer at the little chess pieces, and she pushed her hair straight back from her forehead in exasperation, holding it there abstractedly, so that her chin was aimed like a pencil point at the game laid out in front of her. There was nothing coy about Claudia; she was intense at every moment.

Jane added the beans and tomatoes to the chili but then turned the heat down under it and left it to simmer. She went out of the kitchen to her own room to read a book. She had a book report due Monday, and Claudia and Avery were still peacefully debating some point of chess.

Avery drank some red wine with his chili and poured a glass for Claudia, too, and they sat at the table to eat with the chessboard between them and the puzzle Claudia had taken down from the wall and laid out to one side. Jane didn't join them for lunch, and they didn't notice. The Parks never worried much about meals; as far as eating went, it was mostly catch as catch can.

Avery carried his wine with him after lunch, and followed Claudia into the living room, where she pulled her chess books from the shelves. She took down Byrne and Reshevsky, but she had stacked them beside her chair and was leafing through *Bobby Fischer's Best Games*. She bent over the book and began making a diagram in the margin with her pencil, and Avery stretched out full length on the sofa, in his robe and slippers. He was very pleased to have his wife there, his dog there. Five hours into the day he could still think of his drinking as a tender undertaking, only enhancing the precision of his thoughts. And he dazzled Claudia in the afternoon with his pleasant verbosity. He was so nice to look at, long and lean, with his features charmingly uneven. Every day about this time Claudia let any sense of foreboding drift loose from the moment because for a little while Avery was so pleased with the idea of his work, pleased with his house, glad to have her as his wife.

"Look at this dog's head, Claudia! Look at Nellie's head!" Nellie had curled up on the floor next to Avery on the couch. "Now, I knew the first time I saw her that she was a good dog. An exceptional dog." He put his wineglass down so that he could ruffle Nellie's collie coat all up and down her back, and the dog leaned into his arm, fawning and arching her neck. "She has a wide forehead. You see that! Look at that head! They've bred the brains right out of most collies. Christ! Have you seen those dogs? Heads like needles." He paused to think this over and was satisfied for a moment. "This Nellie is no needlehead!" It was a wonderful thought. "No needle is Nellie!"

Only when Avery became suddenly imperative like this did Claudia become the first little bit uneasy, and she was also cross at Jane, who had finally come downstairs to get lunch after the kitchen had already been cleaned up. She came into the living room, and she was restless and agitated, moving around the room from chair to chair, interrupting her father.

"Are you going to drive me to Diana's, Dad? Will you fix me a cheese sandwich first? The chili's almost gone. It really is awfully spicy, too. Would you make me a sandwich? The kind you do in a skillet?"

Avery's attention wandered over to her. He studied her serious face, and he planned carefully in his mind the cheese sandwich he would fix for his daughter: rye bread with two slices of cheese and a piece of ham between. He was quiet while he considered this sandwich. He would sauté it slowly on both sides until it was golden brown. A prize.

"Jane, for God's sake," Claudia said. "I can fix you a cheese sandwich. And there's plenty of chili left, anyway." She had closed her book and had been enjoying Avery—his good humor. She liked watching him this afternoon.

Claudia didn't think ahead; her day unfolded however it might and almost always in unexpected ways. And in fact, she was unaware now that she had disturbed the image Avery was constructing, because she had snatched away from him the delectable offering he was mentally preparing for his own daughter, and a rather hazy irritation began brewing in his head.

He looked at his wife, who had moved over to the

window and wasn't even remembering that she had spoken. She was never turned out exactly right, but her lack of style was a style unto itself. Her failure to have ever made a concentrated decision about the way she would dress produced an effect that appeared to be studiously haphazard. Today she was wearing boots that Avery thought must be intended for the outside since they turned down around the calf in a sheepskin cuff. She also wore a long purple skirt and a wheat-colored sweater belted at the waist. The whole outfit was somehow a little off, and besides, it was a style for which she was too full-blown, too buxom. Avery watched her profile against the light, the delineation of her waist and full hips. He begrudged her every single thing, just then, in an almost sibling petulance. He resented the fact that in the elegant room he had designed she was amazingly sexual, untidy, blatantly female.

"You could never do it," he said. "You could never possibly make that sandwich the way I can. Your own daughter knows it. It's not an easy, simple sort of sandwich. That's what Jane knows. It takes concentration!" He was quite angry. "The cheese oozes out of a sandwich like that if you're not careful. You would just burn it. It takes timing. How do you think you could ever do that? You won't even bother to buy the right kind of food. Not once—not *once*—have you ever come back from the store with anything but processed American cheese and that slick-tasting ham in little square packages that says 'water added.' Can't you ever stop at the deli? Even Janie knows not to ask you to make her a sandwich, don't you, Janie?" He considered it all for a moment, a trifle calmer. "It's a sensual sandwich," he said, and he liked that phrase.

"I don't really need a sandwich," Jane said. "I'm really not all that hungry."

Claudia turned as she did at some point in each day to look at Avery in surprise. Jane saw it as an eternal motion, a profound movement her mother would make time and again. Jane hoped desperately that her mother

18

would not try to explain that she could, indeed, make a toasted ham and cheese sandwich. But all Claudia did was look back out the window, and then she came to sudden attention.

"Oh, God!" she said. "Look! The exterminator's here. What's he doing here on Saturday? I haven't even made the bed. Did you make your bed, Jane? Avery, don't you want to get dressed? He's going to be spraying in here first. Don't you want to change your clothes, Avery?"

Avery was quite comfortable just the way he was, and he stayed right there on the couch. It was Jane who left the room when her mother opened the door for the Orkin man. She went to the kitchen and made herself a cheese sandwich.

The exterminator was a burly, bearded man who was wearing rubber surgical gloves and holding the nozzle end of a long piece of tubing that wound its way over his shoulder where it was attached to a cylinder he wore strapped to his back. He was very careful to stamp any debris from his shoes before he stepped into their living room. Avery liked him right away, and he was entertained for a little while, listening to Claudia speak with him and watching the precision with which the man fitted the nozzle against the baseboard heaters in order to spray behind them from his canister of insecticide. As the Orkin man moved slowly along the edges of the room, releasing the poison, its sweet, pungent odor filled the air. It was the scent of bubble gum.

"Ah," said Avery, "it's bubble gum. Dubble Bubble. Why would they scent insecticide like bubble gum?"

But the Orkin man seemed not to know that Avery was speaking to him. He continued to move deliberately along the wall. Avery was slighted, and he spoke a little louder this time. "Do you know," he said, "that roaches are as clean as their environment?" There was no slur to any word, only the sly, wide vowels that could rivet Jane's attention from two rooms' distance. In fact, she came into the room now with her sandwich on a plate.

"Janie, your father hates it when you bring food in here," Claudia said, but Jane stayed where she was, taking note of the descending scale of her mother's tone that might soon drop right off into anger. The Orkin man only turned to Avery and nodded. He was intent on what he was doing.

"I read that in *World* magazine, Dad," Jane said. "They've taken roaches from the slums . . ." She tried to hold her father's attention, but he wasn't looking in her direction; he was interested in getting his point across to this bearded man who was paying so little notice to what he was saying.

"No, now that's the truth," Avery went on, running right over Jane's words, although he spoke with great cordiality.

"Is that right?" the exterminator finally replied, but he didn't turn around. He was moving the nozzle along the edges of the bookcase beside the fireplace.

"Absolutely. That's absolutely right." Avery closed his eyes for a moment, but then he looked again at the industrious man moving around his living room.

"Now this house. We're very clean. Not obsessive. Not obsessively clean. Not *tidy*. I'm neat as a pin myself. My wife believes more in sanitation. Basic cleanliness. She lines the shelves in the door of the refrigerator with aluminum foil." Avery paused once more, this time long enough so that the exterminator shot him a polite glance.

"Uh-huh," he said.

"Even in the refrigerator we are clean. We are clean right down to the bone around here. The roaches in this house are paragons of insect sanitation. A credit to their species."

"Well," the exterminator said, "this stuff kills all your silverfish, too. And beetles." He settled back on his haunches as he came to the bottom of the bookcase and looked over at Avery. "It kills spiders. Your small bugs. Those little centipedes. The ones people call doodlebugs."

"Spiders," Avery said. "Good. That's fine. That's okay. But what about the flies? Who will kill the flies?" He closed his eyes in a long pause. "We have a lot of flies here in the summer."

The Orkin man was readjusting his canister so that he could lower himself enough to reach up into the fireplace. He didn't say anything as he adjusted the harness that held the cylinder in place. "I don't know much about flies," he said with some effort as he peered up into the vast fieldstone chimney. He drew his head back out of the fireplace. "I just started this job. I got laid off at the printworks. They just don't have the business they used to."

"That's too bad," Claudia said. "I'm so sorry." It was all there was to say, but it made her daughter flinch. Avery lay back on the couch again while the exterminator reinserted his torso as far as it would reach into their chimney.

No one in the room said anything more. But then the Orkin man called out from inside the chimney. "Hey," he said, "do you know what's in here?" They watched him as he put down his canister and slowly backed into the room with Avery's hunting rifle. He brought it down into the room with a puzzled expression and held it out mutely to show the three of them. He had found it on the inside ledge of the fireplace where Claudia had hidden it some long time past. The winter before, she had taken the gun from Avery's closet and slipped it in among his golf clubs, but when spring had come and the golf course reopened, she had remembered to move it. She had forgotten all about it after that, however, and Avery had never missed it, or never said so.

All three members of the Parks family stared back silently at the exterminator. All of them were at an absolute loss until Avery gestured broadly in Jane's direction. "You have to keep those things away from children, you know," he instructed the man earnestly, but the man gazed back at him a moment without comprehension, and he turned to Jane with curiosity. She was a tall girl for an eleven-year-old, not really a child anymore.

Avery noticed that glance and gave the Orkin man a secretive, melancholy look, twisting his mouth to one side and cocking his head. He gestured again toward Jane, a small indication, just a sad turning of his hand. "Not quite right, you know," he said in a parody of a whisper. "Doesn't have both oars in the water, if you know what I mean." By now Avery was almost leering with intrigue, and he turned sideways to Jane and gave her a slow wink.

The Orkin man looked on at Avery for a moment, and he still held the gun flat out in front of him in his two hands. Finally, with a good deal of trouble, he maneuvered himself back into the fireplace and replaced the rifle where he had found it, then left the room to spray the kitchen.

Jane studied her half-eaten sandwich. When she did look up, she saw her parents each catch the other's eye and quickly look away. Both their faces were strained with an effort toward nonchalance. Jane's parents looked off blandly into separate distances in a tremendous effort to cover that shock of recognition. They had been terribly jolted precisely when their eyes met for that one second in their insect-free living room. They didn't glance at Jane. They didn't say a word to her or to each other, and the three of them stayed still and silent while the man sprayed insecticide around the kitchen cabinets and underneath the stove.

Claudia and Avery were entirely overcome with the fact that two people such as they had been forced to such lengths. They were each separately astonished at their own vulnerability and their escape from humiliation, and they didn't think to say anything to Jane when she left the room with her own face closed down in rage—her mouth tucked in at the corners and the skin over her forehead and cheekbones pale and taut with fury and terrible embarrassment. And there they sat, in odd solemnity, when she came down to tell them that she had packed her overnight things and was walking over to Diana's. She had decided to spend the night out after all.

2

In the night a severe cold front from
Canada slipped under the warmer air lying over
the central United States, and the dense chill penetrated
any small crack or fissure in the buildings in Lunsbury
in the same way a heavy fog cannot be kept entirely out
of doors. The thermostats all over town had clicked on,
and the houses were heated well enough, but Claudia
and Avery awoke simultaneously in their darkened bedroom. They lay side by side like gingerbread cookies,
their arms and legs lying flat on the bed, their faces
staring straight up at the ceiling. It was unusual, because
Avery generally slept late and roused himself only with
great difficulty. There was an eerie quiet within the
room that had alerted them both, and they woke up into
instant attention.

They lay there like that for a while, each knowing that
the other was awake. Claudia was selective enough in
her attention to the details of her life that when Avery
finally spoke out loud, she didn't take note of the words
he was saying; she heard only the unfamiliar tautness of
his sober voice.

"We aren't going to be able to do it, are we? There's
no way to work this out. It's just not going to work."

They both lay quite still, and neither of them spoke for a moment. Nellie had heard their voices, and she came shambling into the room and put her head across Claudia's arm while her feathery tail swept across the floor in a soft whoosh.

"If I can't get hold of myself pretty soon, I think we'll all sink." He raised his arm up and let it slowly fall back to the mattress in illustration. "Right on down," he said. "Right down to the bottom."

For a few easy moments what Avery was saying was just a noise alive in the room, radiating out into the thick air to break the peculiarly claustrophobic silence. Slowly, though, the energy Claudia thrived on early in the day slipped away from her. She was so careful in the morning to have nothing in her mind but hopefulness, and as Avery's words came together in their intention, she silently squared off against them: I do work hard at the days. I work hard to make the days go by.

She really did believe it, too. She was quite certain that in her life there was a connection between the passing of time and her need for it to pass. During any of the days when the pall of Avery's rage or drunkenness hung over the hours, she had the stray notion in the back of her mind that all the dreary time would pass them by. She had the idea that they were going through something and would one day get to something else. If she had not thought she could force the pace of the days along, sorrow would have caught her up for sure.

"I've got to get myself in shape, Claudia." He crooked his arm over his face to cover it; he was so sorrowful, but Claudia didn't trust his sorrow to be in any way beneficial to herself. Besides, she never credited Avery with all the regrets he claimed. She had known him too well for too long. And to possess so many regrets, she suspected, was an evasive kind of self-indulgence. Claudia didn't pity him at all; he was talking about going away from her.

She tried to see his expression, but only the sharp planes and angles of his turned head shone palely in the dark room, giving him a frail and skeletal look. He was self-deprecating even in the way he drew himself aside, as though she might find his presence offensive. He lay deliberately apart from her, so careful to enforce dignity upon this situation. It was all Claudia could do not to roll over on top of him, spreading herself across him like a blanket over a horse, her thighs embracing his hips.

When he was six years old and she was four, at least once he had bent his head down between her legs and nuzzled her—a gentle touch of his lips brushing down the vulnerable ridge of her prepubescent genitals, a sweet familiarization. Surely *more* than once during the many hours in closets, locked bathrooms, someone's garage when they had each explored the other and Claudia had splayed herself out open-legged and urgent with the need to have Avery see her and touch her. Avery had been the boy next door, but there had always been more between them than the ordinary curiosity of childhood. They had experienced a thorough lust for the other one as soon as they had grown old enough to realize that they were two separate people sitting in the communal sand-box in their adjoining backyards. There was no telling about this sort of thing. It had been an impulse that overtook them so completely and so young that Claudia was sure it wouldn't have mattered if they had been male and female or the same sex; that impulse to know the other would have been as strong in either case.

If she threw herself over him now, with her gown hiked up around her waist, he would have to reach his hands around her and stroke her thighs. His cautious separation from her in their own bed made her angry. She lay quite still while Avery talked. She knew what he was saying. She knew all about him. In fact, as far as personal knowledge went—her subjective perception of a thing—he might be the sum total of hers. She had expanded all her senses in comprehension of Avery.

When they were growing up in Mississippi, in the summer afternoons, there hadn't been any turbulent weather. The heat and heavy scent of flowers were a condition of life. In Mississippi in the summer afternoons, there always used to be girls sitting on porches waiting in the dusk. At Claudia's house they sat and watched the boys in Avery's driveway playing basketball until the game was given up, and some of those boys drifted over and sat down, sweaty, beside a girl and perhaps touched her arm so that at her age, in high school, and in the soft-edged muted surroundings, a sensation as riveting as an electric current would pass through her, galvanizing her to the moment. The girls Claudia had known, and she herself, had been more persistent in their young lust than the boys. It was ever with them, the idea of it, in classrooms, when they were in gym playing volleyball, away at summer camp. Those girls wouldn't have chosen to put aside that overwhelming absorption for a quick game of pickup basketball.

Claudia and her friends had become ill with desire about age twelve. They were, most of them, obsessed with the need to be kissed and caressed and touched and fondled, and by necessity they spent a great deal of their time consumed with interest in all the games and contests of the compellingly awkward teenaged boys. But not one of those girls cared much one way or another about the contests; they simply longed for proximity to those male bodies hot and damp from football practice or a baseball game. And those girls grew disheartened when they became sadly aware of the peculiar nature of the lust of those same boys. That intoxicating, lovely, and longed-for male interest turned out to be not much more than a flashlight beam falling over them in a darkened room. A narrow illumination might linger on them for a while but was then diverted to another object with the very same concentration—basketball, tennis, golf, poker. It was then that the girls began channeling their own passion in other directions, but the nature of society in that town would have been quite different if the girls had not had to adapt so absolutely to the customs of men. It was the beginning of their anger, because this was the difference: Those Mississippi boys were genuinely interested in other abstractions and brutalities of everyday life, while for the girls their social diversions and intellectual devotions were first born of frustration and, in the beginning of their adolescence, were a second-best concern.

One afternoon when a group of girls collected on Claudia's porch with glasses of Coke, Annie Dobbs, who was going with Avery that year, had suddenly let out a little laugh. "I don't know," she said, "I hope I don't end up still in love with Avery." They were all a little in love with Avery no matter whom he singled out. "He's not ever going to be all that easy to get along with. You know what I mean?"

Claudia liked Annie Dobbs, who was a year older than she was, but she already had known, anyway, who was going to end up with Avery. In fact, she ended up with him every weekend after he had taken Annie home. He came drunkenly across the backyard and through a window into her bedroom on the first floor. Upstairs Claudia's father lay partially paralyzed and perhaps oblivious since his stroke, and her mother lay in her separate bedroom sedated into sleep.

The first night he had appeared at her window she had been undressing from her own date, and she had gone over to unlatch the screen wearing just her slip and bra and pants. He had stumbled in and lain down beside her on the bed fully dressed, too drunk to go home to his parents, who were still up and about. The following weekend she came home early from a party out on the Natchez Trace, leaving her date behind and catching a ride with another couple. She put on a pretty cotton nightgown. Once again, though, Avery just lay down beside her, cupping her shoulders companionably toward him until he got up to go several hours later. The next Saturday, not at all sure what she was doing, she had fumbled with his clothes while he lay there next to her, coming out of an alcoholic haze. At last he had turned to face her and then moved over her and they had made love briefly, and she had lost her virginity with no regrets.

Claudia had suffered a good bit, though, during the rest of the years in high school when so many pretty, gluttonous girls were available to Avery. He went on to Tulane, and two years later Claudia followed him to New Orleans and went to Sophie Newcomb. They were married by the time Avery began graduate school at Chapel Hill. Claudia had been immensely relieved when they moved to Lunsbury and finally settled right in the middle of the country, where there was such blustery weather but an atmosphere that didn't weigh so heavily on the senses.

But this morning Avery's sobriety intruded on Claudia's expectations, which, lately, were only that the three of them who made up her family would get up that day and lead a regular life. She had begun to covet a small degree of boredom. She had begun to hope that if nothing else, their three lives would take on the calm, carefully planned pattern of the house Avery had designed for them. But Avery was going too far. His sober self was alarming in its determination, and Claudia realized that Jane was becoming more and more like him.

Claudia wasn't ever apt to make up her mind entirely. From any one formulated idea that might be an opinion she had, there trailed little wisps of "maybes." Qualifications drifted around the things Claudia was almost sure of, the way the plastic grass had straggled out of Jane's basket on the Easter mornings when she was very young. Her daughter was steadfast. Once she had a grudge or could place the blame it was a thing done, an emotion made, and Avery was like that, too, when he was sober. Claudia lay in bed and didn't say anything at all. She had the sudden illusion that any word she spoke would start the doleful cranking out of all the minutes in the time ahead of her.

"I can't live with you anymore. We're coming to pieces," Avery said. "This time we've really got to do it. I've rented one of those unfurnished apartments near campus. We have the two cars." He was talking out loud in the same puzzling way as the tree that falls in the forest when no one is there to hear it; maybe his words didn't exist, so little did Claudia show any reaction. He talked on, with his arm still half covering his face to shield the world from the full force of his meaning, and Claudia knew that his efforts at rationalization were meant to convince her that his leaving was not to be taken personally. She also realized that she had been waiting for some time for the moment when he would decide to go, although her senses were leaden with the knowledge that they had once again come to this terrifying state of departure from the other. Always before, however, Avery had stayed in hotels or with friends, places designed solely for temporary inhabitance, so that the very circumstances forced him to come home.

She traced her hand along the pattern of the bedspread and was surprised by a brief, secret surge of anticipation. Whatever else this was, it was at least a new development, a dramatic variation of their days. But it was a truant sensation, because she was also so sad that it was as if she had fallen flat and knocked her breath out. She had always been with Avery, and he with her. They would be orphans in the world without the other; she knew that, and she was struck through with trepidation. Nevertheless, an initial gleefulness overtook her for a moment. Even while Avery was speaking, she felt that same excitement, that same fugitive upswing of the spirit, that she had felt for a second as a child when her mother had told her that her father had died after he had been sick for so long. She felt that momentary exhilaration because so many new possibilities lay ahead. Although even upon that very instant of curious elation, Claudia became despondently reflective once again. She knew that it was shameful to be so passive in her own life.

Claudia's tendency in the mornings to get on with the time ahead was irrepressible, so that she felt a peculiar responsibility for Avery's success at getting said what he was saying, at getting done what he was doing. She wanted to know what quality his absence would have when she and Jane were left behind. He should have gone before they built their clever little house.

"Annie Dobbs said one time that you would be hard to end up with," Claudia said mildly, stopping Avery in mid-sentence. He turned for a moment to stare at her and then went on explaining. Claudia was wishing they were still in the first house they had bought when they moved to Lunsbury, when Jane was still an infant. Each house along that street had had a different façade, but inside there were the same three split levels, the same efficient plumbing at the core, the same three bedrooms replicated in all the other houses—two windows to each room. Those rooms were designed to accommodate transience, and she thought that it would have been an easier thing to be left behind there, because that had never been a house that would bespeak loss, and she had enjoyed the homogenized neighborhood. Now they lived in what had become an intellectual ghetto. Their nearest neighbors were the Tunbridges, who were a mile away across the meadows and at least three miles around along the unpaved, rural roads. She had never admitted that she preferred living in their middle-class suburban tract house.

One morning in that other house Avery had come downstairs to find her watching the family across the street dismantle the columns on their front porch—their house was a Southern Colonial—and then hose them off inside and out before reestablishing them beneath their second-floor balcony. Claudia had been standing at the window, gazing across the street, watching their neighbor heft the hollow columns with one hand and carry them around to the side of the house, one by one, where the hose was attached. His wife had detached the capitals and immersed them in a dishpan of soapy water and worked at them with a cloth. Claudia had liked the look of the house without its columns; it had taken on a guise of tough vulnerability, a Mae West posture, and she had stood for a long time leaning against the windowsill and looking out, while Jane, who was just walking, hung around her knees and whined.

Avery had been beside himself. "Doesn't it ever occur to you to be anything but curious? I mean, you're interested! And that's it. That's all you are. I mean, for God's sake, those people think their house is beautiful! I don't even know if you know the difference. You look at everything as if it were in a museum."

These nine years later she thought he might be right in thinking that her perception was trapped in an ingenuous misunderstanding of the human condition. She had a hard time making the kind of distinctions he expected intelligent people to make, and she was still trying to develop a correct sense of discernment. She was trying as hard as she could to learn how to be judgmental in the right way.

Avery was still talking, telling her all his plans, and finally she said, "What about Jane?" But before he even answered she got out of bed. Her question was only what was expected, only a wistful kite tail trailing off beyond their reach. He didn't know any more about Jane than she did. The two of them loved their daughter unconditionally, but they loved her as the third person among the three of them, and they loved her as the only one among them not complicated by sexuality. They didn't know that it was not like the love of other parents for their children; what Avery and Claudia felt for Jane was an extreme *regard*.

Avery did tell her what he planned for Jane, though. When Claudia went to the kitchen to fix coffee, he followed right behind her. Jane was old enough to go back and forth between them. He intended to follow through with her violin lessons. It was he, after all, who had struggled along with her during the first year of her Suzuki class, and it was he who had discovered Alice Jessup, her private teacher. Through all these words Claudia could not escape the fact that he had been thinking about this for some time.

"You know, Claudia," he said, "that the last thing I have in mind is to make you or Janie unhappy."

Claudia believed that, but she didn't believe it in the spirit in which it was said. She had her own idea of the shiny thing that Avery sought. He needed to take some action that would translate into goodness and rightness and perfection and immediacy—a reflection of his own life upon the earth. And, truly, in Claudia's estimation that was a frivolous and childish desire, but she had never said that to him when he was sober. In her mind it seemed reasonable to accept certain things as givens and then to love the people you have to love and live out the life you have to live. One might *strive* for this or that but never hope for it. Striving was what humans had come up with to pass the years.

Avery pulled back the kitchen curtains while he still had his head turned to talk to her, so she noticed before he did the white light that filled the room in a way that made the surfaces glisten as though they were covered with cellophane. The windows were glazed with ice so smooth that it was like old glass, only a little flawed and bubbled. Ice covered their road, their driveway, the leaves on the trees, so that each one of them hung gleaming orange or red under a frozen crust.

They both stood at the window to look, and Claudia put her lips against the glass and slowly exhaled. The warmth of her breath made the ice crack into a chrysanthemum of feathery splinters that crept outward across the pane from the round circle of the most concentrated heat. She stepped back and observed the world through the pattern she had made. It was very much like looking out through a kaleidoscope filled with clear crystals. When the wind blew, the ice was shaken from the trees in an unnerving shower that rattled like buckshot onto the brittle lawn below.

They turned on the radio and found out that all the town was frozen. When they listened to the explanation that a freakish Canadian air mass had settled over the region, Avery thought it was very likely that he could see it accurately in his imagination. Heavy and dark and silent, slipping in low over the gentle hills of southern Missouri, displacing the warmer, friendly, humid air in just the way a cold despondency closed in on him and unsettled the pleased good humor induced by a drink or two. He never expected it, was never prepared.

The moisture in the upper air had condensed into rain which froze on its way to earth, and the ice had accumulated so quickly that cars were frozen in place, and city equipment couldn't move. The announcer read out long lists of cancellations and warnings. Walking was hazardous; driving was impossible, and people would have to make do with whatever supplies they had on hand.

Maggie phoned while they were sitting in the kitchen, and she assured Claudia that Jane could stay—must stay—until the ice could be navigated. She was crisp and chipper, unlike any grown-up Claudia had ever known as a child. Maggie was admirably adult and sure, so Claudia stifled the sudden pang of longing she had for her daughter to be here, at home with her while Avery took his leave.

"Is Jane all right? Can she borrow some things from Diana?" Claudia said.

There was a brief pause on the other end of the phone, and Claudia instinctively turned and curled the cord halfway around herself in an attitude of self-protection.

"The thing is," Maggie said, with the efficient sound she made of defining her *G*'s at the end of a word in a little drawl, "are you both all right? I meant to call you yesterday. I should have noticed that Avery had had so much to drink. I should have served coffee." She didn't say any more. Maggie took the blame upon herself; she could be counted on for discretion. Even so, Claudia didn't like it much, to be asked anything about herself; she didn't confide in anyone but her daughter and her husband. She didn't have Avery's knack of camaraderie.

"We're fine. We have milk and eggs and plenty of food," she answered, and she was met with another brief pause before she got a reply. It was clear that in some way she had insulted Maggie with her reticence, and they hung up on a brisk note: Jane would spend the night again at the Tunbridges', and they would get in touch in the morning.

For the next four days Lunsbury was frozen inside its buildings. The wind had stripped the trees of their heavy leaves, and it blew in gusts between the houses, carrying frozen debris that sandpapered the shiny surfaces outside until the world took on a matte finish. Claudia stood for long spells staring out the windows. With Avery halted in mid-departure, she was enclosed in a curious last-ditch frenzy of lustful imagination. When they sat in the kitchen listening to the radio, she let her gaze brood over Avery's body. She watched his hands with an intensity detached from herself, not connected with anything she was doing or saying at the moment. Nothing was clear to her in that time, neither elation nor despair; the waiting had muddled her ideas. There was nothing to drink in the house, and they were solemn and sober and quiet. They listened with attention to the news. A state of emergency had been declared, and the weather was discussed at great length. But Claudia was bemused by the phenomenon of the ice. It disconcerted her more than she would have expected, and there was still no way to get Jane home.

Claudia and Avery spent those long days going through the house room by room, packing and sorting until Avery would be able to leave. They argued about the shoe racks or the china without passion. It was Claudia who said that he should take those things, speaking out mostly for the sake of having noise in the house. He could come get them anytime, of course, and he was indifferent; he pretended boredom. She would not be able to extend any influence into his life that he planned to lead from now on. And he was ill at ease. Avery disliked being detained. He had always fidgeted at stoplights, become embarrassingly irritable in checkout lines, bemoaned editorial delays. When they heard on the radio that barge traffic was frozen to a standstill in St. Louis, at the confluence of the Missouri and Mississippi rivers, he had got up and walked around the kitchen in frustration. He had taken a package of pecans out of the freezer, where Claudia was saving them for Christmas, and stood at the window, staring out, eating the frozen nuts one by one and musing.

"I can't believe that," he said. "We can go to the moon. We can play golf on the moon—idiots!—but a frozen river is going to cause grain shortages."

"I know," said Claudia, although most of the puzzles in the world, natural or engendered by mankind, did not surprise her, and she was wise enough not to point out that this strange quirk of weather that paralyzed the region strengthened the theories that Avery was currently expounding in his book.

The ice outside heaved and exploded randomly across the yard and road and up their front steps during the day, and then by morning it would have frozen once more into new patterns of webs and craters. Claudia experienced sympathetic and random implosions of lust while she watched Avery move among the boxes. The haggardness of his enforced sobriety was erotic; it would be a pleasure to soothe him. At night she would dwell on this and imagine that they were immobilized by unconsummated desire, not ice, in this abnormally frozen season. Those musings would be half dream, and she would fall asleep restless with the idea of Avery touching her when, in fact, they took care not even to brush fingers when they handed boxes back and forth.

Once Avery had been standing behind her while she sorted through a closet, and when she turned around, she was startled into sudden irritation to find him so quietly nearby. She put her hands against his chest and lightly pushed him backward.

"I can do this myself. I know what you need to take. Please leave me alone!"

He stood there in front of her looking slightly baffled,

and then he raised his hands against her in the same way she had just shoved him away. He didn't push her; he only placed a hand lightly over each of her breasts for a moment, long enough so that she felt the warmth through her blouse. Then he dropped his hands to his sides and moved away. Claudia stood in the doorway of the closet alert and tingling with the sensation of having been passed over by the ghost of a gesture, and she shuddered involuntarily from head to toe out of sheer yearning.

Later that same day Avery was wrestling one of the twin-bed mattresses from the guest room down the spiral staircase just as she was coming up the steps. They stopped, both of them embarrassed; a mattress is a final thing. Avery was taking it into the garage, where he was gathering his belongings until he could leave. All at once he sat down on the steps, clasping the cumbersome mattress, and began to weep without a sound. She sat down beside him.

"I don't know how you expected this to be," she said after a moment.

"Shit!" Avery said. "Fucking shit! It's not all my fault, you know." And he paused, shaking his head in a loose, downward motion as though he were trying to jolt into his mind the words that would be what he meant. "It's just not all my fault! We really aren't good for each other. We aren't any help to each other. It isn't all because I drink!"

Claudia looked at the mattress and wondered if Avery would rent a U-Haul. She had never thought that this had anything to do with the fact that he drank. She knew that however they were together was really beside the point. Being good for each other or not being good for each other—in their case those things were incidental. She was thinking of a maxim she had had to memorize in her seventh-grade science class. Mrs.Greenfield had made them learn this fact: Adhesion and cohesion are the two molecular forces of the earth. Without adhesion and cohesion everything would fly out into space.

This was a principle of the natural world that Claudia

had never doubted for a minute, and it had never crossed her mind that within that principle lay choice. The two of them were a unit, coherent each unto himself, and adherent one to the other. The universe yawned implacably infinite now that one particle of that entity was breaking the bond. It defied her imagination to picture what would become of them. She thought they might be lost forever, that they might, indeed, just float out into space.

3

On that Saturday afternoon before the ice and while the exterminator was still roaming around her house, Jane phoned Diana Tunbridge to tell her that she was coming over after all. They arranged to meet halfway across the meadow so that they could walk back together to Diana's. By the time she collected her things and packed her backpack she was overtaken once again by that familiar dolefulness that assailed her whenever she deserted her mother and father. It worried her to leave them to their own devices even when she was angry at them. They were still sitting quietly in the living room when she came downstairs, and she stopped in the doorway to say good-bye, but both Avery and Claudia were abstracted, and her mother was a little irritable.

"All right, then, Janie. You are going?" Claudia raised her hand in a listless dismissal. "We'll see you tomorrow. Have a nice time." This was not a wish for Jane, or encouragement. It was what her mother said by rote while her mind was working on something else entirely, and as always, when Jane stepped outside her doorway, she was swept through and through with a peculiar kind of loneliness. She suffered a paring away and sparseness at the very core of herself that left her unhappily disburdened.

She set out through the meadow, and as she wound down the path through the grass, she saw Diana already waiting under the cluster of trees where they always met. Without considering it Jane slowed her approach to allow some substance of the day to fill her a little. Besides, this was not just any piece of land between two houses; she had invented this terrain at age eight, when her parents had bought four acres from the Tunbridges' and built their house. The steep path between her house and the Tunbridges' was of her own making, and it wound narrowly through the high grass. Diana was sitting beneath the Four Trees—four great pin oaks that formed a hollow square. Summer before last she and Diana had buried a cache of candles and matches and a flashlight there in two layers of Zip-loc bags and a larger plastic bag enclosing those and fastened with a twist-tie.

They had marked the turnoff to the Troubled Rocks with a handful of assorted stones that they had arranged to look as if those various pebbles had merely rolled into place there along the main path. Only one or the other of the girls could detect that separate trail so subtly marked through the head-high weeds, and they could find their way along it to a large boulder and some other good-sized rocks that lay in an inexplicable clearing. Jane had gone there alone, now and then, willing herself to sit among those stones even when the low-moving clouds threw her into deep shadow beyond which she could see the sunshine. At a moment like that she would press herself flat back against the boulder, because such a selective darkening of her environment opened out before her an abyss of desolation so extreme that she lost any faith in her surroundings. Most days, though, she was sure that that large boulder brimmed with serenity and that she could draw some of it into herself merely by her own proximity to it.

"I don't think we should call them the *troubled* rocks," Diana had said when Jane first led her to them. They had spent arduous hours debating these points, naming their landmarks. "I think it would be better to call them the Rocks of Trouble. Because we can come here if *we're* in trouble, or if we're depressed or something. I mean, the *rocks* can't be troubled, Jane. What about the Comfort Rocks?"

Jane had disliked the meter. "No, Diana. That just doesn't have the right sound." And she had drawn her straight pale eyebrows together in an unchallengeable expression. Privately she invested those few stones with an ability to suffer or give solace. Pummeled as they were, mute and exposed, tossed into this space by some ancient force—Jane believed in them. When Jane gave herself over to this landscape, she extended the connection between reality and sentiment. Each facet of this world that she had named had personal significance, and she would move through the meadow in a state of exquisite melancholy that was a permutation of nostalgia. Here was order. Here was control. Here was peace, and here was she; she was known.

Farther on across the meadow was the Secret Feather River, which was a drainage ditch that, over the years, had cut deep, grassy banks down the hill. Two miles away water streamed off the carefully laid planes of the golf course, running off the greens and fairways into unobtrusively placed red clay pipes, through which it was channeled into a cement tunnel and carried along underground, until it poured out into the culvert at the top of the hill and flowed beautifully clear all the way to the Lunsbury Sand and Gravel Works and into the Missouri River. When Jane and Diana had first discovered this stream, it, too, had been hard to name. Jane had first said to Diana that it was the River of Paradise, but that had been met with such condescension on Diana's part—she had not even acknowledged it as a serious notion—that for a while it had been the Blue Feather River. Diana had suggested that one day when she had found a jay's feathers strewn mysteriously along the

bank. It was a good name, but Jane was always cha-
grined to give any amount of control to her best friend.

"If we just call it The Secret Feather," she said,
"then no one would even have any idea that it's a river
or anything. It would be a code, you see?"

"Why 'secret'?" Diana had said, and Jane had taken
that chance to use impatience to get her way.

"Because, Diana, it's *our* secret that it's a river!"
And that had been all right.

Along the banks of The Secret Feather, Jane and
Diana were sometimes early settlers. They stored pro-
visions in the high coves, and Jane took charge because
she had read *Little House on the Prairie* and the other
Wilder books, too. She assured Diana that the television
show was simplistic and revoltingly sentimental.

"It's really just awful," she said. "My father calls it
Little Shack." She instructed Diana in ways of gathering
wood for winter and berries and nuts. Of course, when
winter came, the land died; the grass was flattened under the weight of snow, and Jane and Diana traveled to
each other's houses in the front seats of their parents'
cars, driving the three miles around.

But on that Saturday in late fall, before the ice storm,
as Jane entered her own territory and spotted Diana
waiting in the meadow, a slight expansion of herself
took place. When she saw her friend sitting patiently
under the Four Trees waiting for her, she began to have
weight in the world, and will, and determination of a
sort. There remained a persistent sullenness within her,
but by the time she reached Diana sitting there on the
grass, Jane had begun to get a picture of her own self in
her mind. She was so much a part of what her parents
were as a couple that when she was within her own
house, it was almost as if she were entirely erased,
although this concept manifested itself only as a feeling
she had; it was not a clear thought. Now there ran a
picture in her head of herself walking down the hill while
Diana waited. In this picture all the future—all the moments which she could see falling one upon another like

a line of dominoes—was dependent just upon her own actions, on what she would do next. She was filled for one instant with an enormous sense of power and importance in the scheme of things. She continued to walk toward Diana, but she moved now with more intention, and Diana saw her and got up to meet her.

They made an interesting twosome. Separately neither one of them was particularly remarkable. They were young girls of an indeterminate age. When they were side by side, Jane looked quite awkward and bony, and Diana looked like a miniature adult. All the parents in Lunsbury with children in this age-group said to each other that Diana would be a beauty, and she was such a nice girl, too, and smart. But when Jane and Diana were together, it was instinctively to Jane that people addressed a collective question: "What can I do for you girls?" "What flavor ice cream cone do you two want?"

It was to Jane with her stern, slender face and sensibly cut hair that people became attuned to, as people do with a constant, subliminal sensoring. It was an unreasonable attention Jane attracted. Who could tell about her? Her schoolwork was erratic, but her teachers admired her. Her clothes weren't always coordinated; her tongue was unreliably sharp; her honesty was questionable. She was a puzzle to the parents of children in her orbit because she *was* stellar. She was a puzzle and perhaps a threat, although grudgingly they, too, admired her. And those baffled grown-ups courted her on behalf of their daughters and even coveted her approval for themselves, as much as they thought about such things.

Diana brushed grass and debris from the legs of her jeans and walked along beside Jane, attending her in the way any two children can be observed as leader and devotee. They had known each other since kindergarten, and they knew each other's moods. Diana recognized at once, on that Saturday afternoon, that Jane had about her a bleakness that might transform itself at any moment into mild contempt for Diana or any of her plans. To the west the sky lowered toward them, gray and gloomy. Diana wanted Jane to cheer up; she wanted the sleepover to be fun; she wanted to engage her friend's interest.

"Did you see what happened in math lab yesterday?" Diana said, leaning around to observe Jane's face as they walked. She chatted on, knowing not to wait for a reply. "God! It was Chris Barraclough. Didn't you see what he did? I couldn't believe it. I had on my plaid wraparound skirt. You know. That ties in back. He was already sitting down at the back of the room when I came in, and when I went by his desk, he took hold of one end of the bow!" She paused but got no reaction from Jane. "And then he keeps saying, 'Diana, you're in my way. Come on, Diana, I can't see. What're you standing around for? Aren't you going to sit down?' " She had imitated Chris Barraclough's singsong of mockery. Now her voice dropped back into its regular scale. "He really did! What do you think that means?"

Jane only glanced at Diana with a quick frown of disparagement.

"Well, Jane! I couldn't move or my skirt would have come untied and just fallen off. I mean, it was tied in a plain bow. And I couldn't do anything, because you know how Mrs. Dehaven is. Oh, my God. I was so mad."

Jane still didn't say anything, and they walked a little farther before Diana tried again. "Have you finished *The Secret Garden* for Great Books? We have to have a report on it by Monday."

"*The Secret Garbage*," Jane said.

"I know," said Diana. "Well, are you reading *The Summer Birds* instead? I started it, but it was really strange."

"*The Secret Garbage* and *The Summer Turds*," Jane said. "Christ!"

"Oh, come on, Jane!" Diana was finally irritated. Jane could be so tiresome. "Maggie said that *The Secret Garden* was her favorite book when she was growing up."

Jane's attention was completely engaged for a moment. She so much admired the familiarity of the Tunbridge family, in which the parents were not Mom and Dad but Maggie and Vince, their real names. By an unasked-for and special dispensation she, too, as Diana's closest friend, had been urged to address them by their first names, and she did this often and with gusto, especially if she was with them in public. It seemed to her that such an intimacy conferred upon her a superior status.

Diana was in front of Jane on the path now, where it narrowed on the steepest part of the hill, and they continued down the slope without any more conversation, each one mulling over one thing or another. When they drew abreast, though, Jane was more animated.

"Your hair looks good like that," she said to Diana in the cautious way she gave compliments. Diana's mother had carefully braided her daughter's hair in a single thick brown rope that intertwined luxuriously from the crown of her head to the middle of her back. Green grosgrain ribbons were woven through it to match Diana's green sweater.

"It's a French braid. I really wanted to try it, but it takes hours. I'll never be able to wear it to school like this." Diana wasn't at all worried about that, really, because at the moment she was simply glad that Jane had cheered up.

They went on to talk about their teachers and their friends and their enemies. To a great extent it was school that shaped their lives and how they spent them, and that was what they were discussing, not frivolously. As their conversation wound out, they became more intense, bending their heads close together, chins down in contemplation. The subtleties and complications of the days at school were endless and delicate.

And in any case, here were two children who watched the news with attention every night, who knew all the nations of the world and their capitals and their forms of government. Those two girls were beginning to fall in and out of love on a minor scale; they took computer science every other day; they did posters supporting a nuclear freeze for their art project; they were on the verge of having reproductive ability. It might be that they said any number of things that had been said time and time before. They might have a conversation that would bore any thoughtful adult, but what in the world could they have talked about that would not be important?

In their grammar school, rumors were always circulating that Lunsbury was targeted for a first hit by the Soviet Union in the event of nuclear war. In fact, when all the children were gathered in the classrooms together, or crowding each other in the lunch lines, they took special relish in reminding each other of that very fact in loud voices. It was now and then passed among them as a trophy, a source of some excited civic pride. At night, in their own homes, each child sometimes brooded about the possibility of the vaporization of his or her own parents, siblings, and pets. Each year a few children experienced an early crisis of the awareness of mortality, but they received outpatient treatment at the university mental health facility, and they weathered it as well as anyone does.

There was no doubt about the fact that being blown to dust was not a good way to die. In the lunchroom over their tacos they weighed it against the desirability of perishing slowly from radiation poisoning or cancer, or even being hit by a car, as a student from their school had been two years ago—"Oh, my God!" they said. "He was just a vegetable for two months before he finally died." And it came down to the fact that it was only death they were considering, and one way or another it was a subject they were bound to consider eventually. The possibility of annihilation didn't ever, for more than an instant, lessen the immediate concerns of those sophisticated children.

And it was never the thought of death that bothered Jane. She spent her energies battling a peculiar hollowness that often rendered before her a setting devoid of depth. Today she finally caught refractions of herself from her friend, Diana, from the tensile grass, from the old oaks too thick to bend but rolling their heads like pinwheels in a crazy spinning of leaves and branches.

And under the old trees, so buffeted by a low turbulence that their tops seemed to be turning on a fixed stem—under the trees as Diana and Jane walked through the meadow in Lunsbury, Missouri, those two girls were as much a part of the destiny of the earth as the nuclear power plant that lay fifteen miles away in Fairhill, or the ICBM base seventy miles away in Sheldon. There they were, two girls who might have remarkable lives or might not, might be happy or might not. They were just two eleven-year-old girls walking across a meadow who might do anything at all.

At the Tunbridges' that afternoon Jane could not settle down to anything. She was giddy with the effort of trying to appease the odd sense of yearning that had come over her as soon as she had caught sight of the broad brick hull of the Tunbridge house when she and Diana had curved across the meadow. There it sat on the bluff with its wooden appendages of porches, garages, and gabled extra rooms that had been added over the years to meet the family's needs or to comply with various architectural upheavals. Maggie said that the main house was essentially a "center hall Georgian," but Vince had laughed and said that it was "just a basic dog run. The hounds run in the front door and out the back."

To Jane, the house bespoke continuity. The Missouri River could be seen from the upstairs windows, and across the river trains passed at intervals on tracks that had carried the first train from St. Louis to St. Joe, tracks which the house predated by fifty years. Vince's family had built this house, and he had filled Jane and Diana with tales of all its terrifying history and secret places when they were little girls, and Jane could never enter the building without wanting to reacquaint herself with every room, its every mystery. But finally the two girls settled down with Vince in his study, where he was watching a football game with Diana's brother, Mark, who was five years older than Diana.

The Tunbridge family was divided by appearance into two factions that didn't seem to be related. Mark, and Diana's nineteen-year-old sister, Celeste, were their mother's children, with her amiable lankiness, light hair, and wide-boned friendly face. Vince was shorter than his wife, but he was also perfectly proportioned so that he seemed better made, more carefully put together. His eyes were blue, like Maggie's, although otherwise he was dark and intense, and Diana, who was so much younger than her siblings and so resembled her father, was like an afterthought that only he had had. But while Diana's energy was precociously controlled and meted out with care, that same trait in Vince always made Jane anxious when she was in his company. His restraint, his discretion, was tense and palpable. In spite of herself, she was never comfortable with her friend's father, although he flirted with her and singled her out in any group. Now, when the girls settled in front of the television, he turned his attention to Jane immediately.

"The ladies are going to join us, Mark," he said. "Now what can I get for you two? Janie? A scotch? Join me with a beer? What'll it be?" He made a great pretense of surprise when she just smiled uncomfortably at him.

"Now, Janie! You're eighteen, aren't you? You're so glamorous these days. And you won't keep me company? You make me feel awfully ashamed of myself. Dissolute!" He spoke to her in the wheedling tones of a host whose hospitality has been spurned. Jane didn't know anything to do but just smile at him. He clapped his hand to his forehead in a pantomime of surprise.

"Oh, Lord! What am I thinking of? Virtue is visiting us. Now you certainly won't catch Virtue swilling the devil's own brew!"

Jane regarded him solemnly and didn't answer. Vince

was referring to the Halloween party she had come to in this house, and at which she had been so happy until she had caught on to the fact that her parents had somehow stepped out of the bounds that delineated appropriate behavior in society. But she had never understood what her parents had done.

The day of that party had been a day that Jane had put away in her mind in parentheses, bracketed by lesser moments, as a fleeting definition of her parents' marriage. Early that morning she had stopped and stood in the bathroom door while her father was shaving and her mother was sitting in her brilliant red robe on the edge of the bathtub, smoking a cigarette and gesturing as she spoke, so that her billowing sleeves followed her quick hands in a diaphanous accentuation.

Jane had known right away that they would have a good day. There was that current of animation and pleasure running between Claudia and Avery. They were filled with a glistening and elusive exuberance that puzzled Jane but was mesmerizing, also. She could only grasp the essence of their good humor now and then, and not with language; it was her instinct that informed her in this case and led her along into the same high spirits. When this temperament settled over her household for very long, Jane was relieved and agitated at once. She would have liked to know that pleasure. No couple could be as delighted with themselves as her parents sometimes were. No other two people she had ever seen were capable of enjoying each other so much, and oddly enough, when her father didn't have a single drink and her mother's affability overcame her melancholy disorientation, Jane sometimes fell into a brooding sense of dissatisfaction with everything around her. But on the morning of the Halloween party she was pleased to see her parents' enthusiasm because she was so excited herself.

"But I can't think of anything to go as," Claudia was saying when Jane stopped at the door. "Maybe someone out of Greek mythology. That would be easy enough to do with sheets. I think we have enough white sheets. And sandals.'' She settled back to consider this, bracing herself comfortably by putting both hands on the rim of the tub, and the puff of her sleeve slowly settled around her wrist perilously close to her burning cigarette.

Avery had stopped in the middle of shaving and was staring at himself in the mirror. He put his razor down on the counter by the sink. ''Now, wait,'' he said, still looking directly at his own reflection. ''I think I know what we can do. Now just wait a minute.'' He slipped his arms out of the sleeves of his T-shirt so that the body of the shirt hung around his neck. He studied himself carefully in the mirror, leaning forward to peer closely at his own face. He took hold of his T-shirt at the back of his neck and stretched it up to cover his hairline and ears and circle under his chin.

''A wimple! See! It's perfect.'' He turned around to face them, and he looked absolutely unlike himself. The shirt was taut across the top of his head and the upper part of his lean face, and then it draped in soft folds beneath his chin and onto his shoulders. It robbed his face of that sharp charm that he possessed, a quizzical look of irony, and he seemed unusually benign and sweet-natured in a dim-witted way. Both Claudia and Jane laughed.

''That's wonderful! That's just wonderful!'' Claudia said, and even Avery's smile, which always curved up a little more on one side of his face than on the other, was transformed into a simpleminded, beatific beaming. Claudia was entranced and immensely pleased. She got up and walked all around him to see how he looked from every angle. ''Okay, okay. That's great. I've got to see how it'll work for me,'' she said. ''I know what we can do. Now stay right here for a minute!'' And she left the room and came back with one of Avery's T-shirts for herself, a navy blue scarf, and Avery's academic robes, which the university had bought in his graduate school's colors for him to wear during processionals in the years he was teaching. Avery's robe was a dark blue almost the color of the scarf. The hood was scarlet and gold, but Claudia undid the buttons that attached it. "Some nuns dress in blue, don't they? I think so. They must. There's that ad on television with a nun riding a bicycle, and she's wearing blue, but it's brighter than this." She reached up to fix the scarf over Avery's head as a veil. "I wonder how they keep these things on. I'll pin it somehow. This blue will be all right, don't you think? I'll have to borrow an undergraduate robe and go in black. Avery, you'll have to call the custodian and see if he'll get one out of storage. I think this will be all right. I think this will be exactly right!"

They spent the day assembling these disguises. Jane went everywhere with Avery; he was such a pleasure to be with when he was benevolent with cheer. They picked up the black robe Claudia wanted and went to K mart to buy a black scarf to go with it, but they couldn't find one. All the scarves were printed in brilliant designs, but Avery was undaunted and on the alert in every direction. He was delighted when he spotted a revolving rack of sunglasses. He rotated the stand slowly and considered the glasses with great concentration, and he finally selected two pairs with plain octagonal wire rims. Standing right in the aisle, he twisted the frames gently until he could remove the plastic lenses. "Janie, nuns wear these sorts of glasses, don't they?" he asked her, although he was going to buy them anyway.

"I've never seen a real nun," Jane said. "I can't remember if the nuns in TV shows wear glasses or not. What should I go as? I don't think I can go as a nun, too. We have to go as a family. I mean we have to dress as a group. Something that all three of us could be."

Avery still worked with the wire frames of the glasses, holding the four abandoned lenses in his palm, but he looked startled. He was clearly taken aback, and he didn't say anything for a minute until he had adjusted the frames to his satisfaction, and he held them out to show Jane. He had bent the frame of each eyepiece into a shape that was pointed at its center but then curved outward on either side to the bottom edge, which went straight across.

"Gothic arches," he said, and he put on a pair so she could see how they would look. The points of the arches reached the middle of his eyebrows; it was a nice effect. He was abstracted, though, and forgot to take them off.

"The child of two nuns . . . let's see . . . what could two nuns possess? Not chastity. That wouldn't be any good, would it? That would be pretty predictable. What about virtue? That would be right, don't you think? You think that would work?" He looked very concerned as he studied her through the empty wire-rimmed glasses.

"Oh, yeah. That's good," said Jane, although she wasn't sure about this idea at all; she wasn't sure she understood it.

He took off the glasses and folded down the earpieces with care, leaving the price tag on for the checkout girl. "We could do that with a white sheet. We need a ribbon, though, and some paint. Gold." Her father was lost in his idea, and she followed along behind him while he bought three yards of stiff wide purple ribbon and two yards of plain black cotton fabric for Claudia's veil. He finally found some metallic gold paint in the craft section next to the macramé materials.

That evening after Avery had brought home dinner for them all from the drive-through at Burger Chef, he and Claudia fashioned a flowing white robe for Jane from a twin-sized sheet. From shoulder to waist, Miss America style, they pinned the purple ribbon on which Claudia had painted in the shiny gold paint "OUR OWN REWARD." At the party that night, when Jane and Diana were by themselves, Diana pressed her about this costume, but Jane was disdainful.

"I'm Virtue, Diana. If you don't understand it, you just don't have any sense of humor. Virtue is its own reward, you see!" She was so snappish that Diana didn't argue. She and her family had dressed as Mouseketeers, with Mickey Mouse hats from the dime store. Another family had come as Little Orphan Annie and Daddy

Warbucks, and they had dressed their four-year-old daughter as Sandy, the dog, but they had taken her home early to stay with a sitter. Some people had not dressed in costume at all. There was a man in a leopard-printed bathing suit with a woman in a sarong, and Jane finally figured out that they were Tarzan and Jane. All in all, though, she thought her own parents had come up with the most interesting costumes.

She and Diana sat in on the grown-ups' party for a little while, and Jane watched the couples dancing and thought that her parents looked wonderful and exotic, swaying across the room together with their robes flowing around their legs and their veils swinging behind them. When Avery had come to get Jane to dance with him, she had been thoroughly glad to be connected with her father and her mother. She listened to her father being clever and pleased with the things he said. When Maggie said to him that his costume was ingenious and asked whatever had made him think of it, he had grinned at her wholeheartedly.

"What could be more appropriate? I've taken the veil to save my family from disgrace. Now I can confess and go to heaven! It's your costume that is ingenious, Maggie," he said. "I wouldn't have thought of it. You look just right. You're the quintessential Mouseketeer!"

Across the room her mother had taken off her veil and wimple but was still wearing the glasses with her hair fluffing around her face as she laughed and gesticulated. Claudia was elated, too; she and Avery were alight with energy, and in any corner where they were not the party palled and went limp. That's how it looked to Jane.

Later in the evening, however, Maggie had come to find Jane and had leaned down to her in an attitude of worried affection. She was still wearing her mouse ears, and her short hair spiked out around the edge of the black felt cap in a way that exaggerated her look of concern. "Janie, why don't you sleep over with Diana tonight?" she had said, leaning forward in a sort of insistent entreaty. That particular night Jane didn't want to be away for even one second from her glowing parents, and she gazed at them across the room longingly; she didn't want to insult Maggie, either.

"I have to get up really early in the morning to practice my violin," she said. "I have a lesson at ten o'clock."

Maggie had shifted her position slightly, straightening up and then bending protectively over Jane again with her arm across Jane's shoulders. Her voice became more brusque, her intention more determined. "Look, Jane, you really should spend the night here. Sweetie, your father's had a lot to drink." She looked straight at Jane, and Jane held her face utterly still; she didn't let her expression change in any way, but she was shocked. Maggie had spoken to her so matter-of-factly, as though she could ever have the right to make such a comment. Maggie had spoken to her as if Jane were just anyone and as if her father were just anyone. Just people Maggie happened to know. Jane was learning early in her life that in order to like most people, she had to ignore most of what they said and did.

"It's really nice of you to ask me," she had said, "but I'm afraid I can't stay over tonight." Jane's intention had remained firm, although she had been as overwhelmed then as she was now, sitting in Vince's study and being cheerfully teased about her costume. Teased in a way that she suspected was somehow an indictment of her whole family. The emotion that began to creep over her as she listened to Vince's banter was almost like the disheartening pang of homesickness. She was touched suddenly by a loss of hopefulness; and since she counted on the Tunbridges to be her measure of all things normal, all things in their right proportion, it was essential to her that she evade this encroaching disillusionment. She was restless sitting there with Vince in his study, having to listen to anything he might say, and she suggested to Diana that they go upstairs.

They found Celeste sitting cross-legged on her bed, surrounded by books and loose papers and notebooks, talking on the phone and making notes. Jane and Diana stood in the hall idly eavesdropping on her until she spotted them out of the corner of her eye.

"Hey! You two!" She covered the mouth of the receiver with her hand. "Hey, in a minute how about playing just *one* hand of canasta? Or we could do a hand of bridge again if I can get Mark or Maggie to sit in." Celeste loved to play cards and was currently trying to interest Jane and Diana in learning bridge. Jane had once heard Maggie say to Vince that Celeste might ruin her grade point average if she didn't play less bridge. "Or we could play Michigan rummy. We could play that three-handed. One game. I promise." Celeste's bedroom was vast and was furnished like a living room, with her great-grandmother's desk, a reading chair, and a long couch. Jane had been there the afternoon Celeste and her friends had brought in the eight-sided game table and four wooden chairs that were set up at the foot of her bed. Maggie's whole expansive expression had drawn in with irritation, even though she hadn't said anything to Celeste; she had just gone on about her business.

When Celeste turned back to the telephone, Diana led Jane away. She knew that Jane would rather do anything Celeste wanted of them instead of whatever Diana could counter with, and she hated card games with her sister. Eventually Celeste did search out the two girls in Diana's room, and by then Diana had interested Jane in the idea of glamour. She was pinning Jane's hair up, unsuccessfully as it happened, but Jane was pleased enough with the new image of herself without hair falling straight down in neat panels on either side of her face. She didn't pay any attention to the clumps of hair pinned tenuously on top of her head with a bristling of hairpins. Celeste helped them devise disco outfits for themselves out of odds and ends from her own wardrobe, and Diana put a Pointer Sisters' album on her stereo.

When the music began, Celeste looked over at them. "I know that's a song you're not supposed to understand."

"Oh, we don't," Jane said. "We don't understand a word of it!"

They danced in front of Diana's long mirror for a while, believing that they looked like the best dancer, the black dancer, on Solid Gold.

When they were bored with that, they moved on to Maggie's room where she had set up her easel to catch the north light. She was working with her pastels, and Jane stood behind her and watched. Diana strayed around the room, trailing her hand across the dresser to touch the little bottles of perfume, Maggie's silver brush and comb, a pair of leather gloves left lying out; she lounged disconsolately against a windowsill, not especially interested in what her mother was doing. Jane would have liked to have the right to browse through Maggie's room like that, trifling with all of Maggie's possessions. It wasn't possible for Jane to retain any suspicion of, or disappointment in Maggie when she was in Maggie's company. From Jane's point of view Maggie, more than anyone else she had ever known, had the irresistible allure and completely charismatic quality of unalloyed competence. Competence under any circumstances. It was what Jane so admired; it was what she herself aspired to.

Maggie had organized the girls to pose for her, so for a little while Diana sat back on Maggie's chaise longue with her legs drawn up while Jane sat at its foot, leaning against Diana's knees for support. Maggie was working in quick strokes with charcoal, and before she handed the finished sketch over to them, she sprayed it with fixative and let it dry.

Jane took the sketch and laid it down on the coverlet of Maggie's bed to study it. She was entranced by her own earnest stare drawn in with firm lines next to a softer, more hesitant rendering of Diana's sweeter face.

"Look at this!" she said. "Just look at this! I look more like Maggie than you do." And it was true, because Jane had both height for her age and some grace, and she was fair, although not in the same pink and freckled way that Maggie was so blond. Both Maggie and Jane were tall and thin so that their joints—their knees and elbows—appeared to be marginally broader than their fragile arms and legs. Maggie was not especially pretty. She had a faintly simian look and a rather alarming smile that stretched her mouth too far into a grimace that bared her large, straight teeth. But Jane was pleased as she looked at the sketch. She had always thought that Maggie looked exactly the way Maggie ought to look, and she wasn't at all sorry to think that she might look that way, too. It delighted and hugely flattered her that Maggie had wanted to draw her picture.

When the girls finally drifted out of Maggie's room, just as Jane crossed the threshold into the wide upper hall, she experienced a momentary ecstasy of inclusion. She had a sudden piercing feeling of familiarity that made her want to open her arms and receive every nuance of that sensation, which she perceived as something of actual substance that radiated from the walls, the pictures, the dark wood floors, the people. At the very moment when she stepped out of Maggie's room, she had a sudden apprehension of the history of the house, its present, and its future. As she moved along the hall she did raise her arms a fraction before she remembered not to, and her aborted gesture was like the flap of wings. For the few seconds Jane was possessed by this phenomenon she was following Diana down the hallway, self-consciously aware of her own footsteps in her wooden-heeled clogs as they clattered across the floors of all the Tunbridge forebears and future generations.

By late day Jane and Diana sat in the dining room eating potato chips. They curled onto their chairs with their legs tucked under them and leaned their elbows on the table. They were delicate with the greasy chips, carefully lifting them to their mouths with the tips of their fingers and making two bites of the large ones while they looked out at the rain that had begun to fall.

It was an odd rain that didn't streak down out of running clouds sweeping over the region. This rain was pendulous and globular drop by drop, falling over the porch with a sound like cooked peas hitting the porch floor with a pulpy splash outside the shadowy room.

Maggie came in and joined them at the table without interrupting their silence. The rain fell, and Maggie ate a potato chip and also sat listlessly spellbound by the peculiar downpour. Each drop contained too much; it was an unpleasant sound all around them, a natural obscenity. Maggie took a handful of chips and moved to the French doors.

"Umm. This looks bad. It's turning to ice."

But Maggie went away to start dinner while the girls set the table, and the weather wasn't important when the whole family sat down to eat together. At the Tunbridges' house it seemed to Jane that everyone was the same age, and in her mind there was no sweeter equality. Tonight Vince was irritable, and Celeste was quiet and sulky with fatigue from having spent the day studying. But these were pale passions, nothing to conceal. Jane had never seen any member of this family really angry, and she thought that the knowledge of anger was her own secret shame. By age eleven she had already met in herself the height of any anger she would ever feel again. She hadn't revealed it, of course, because she still had only the status of a child, but occasionally she was relieved of it vicariously by one or the other of her parents if either one of them happened to say to the other exactly what Jane was thinking. What she suspected, though, was that her fury was a shabby emotion, because it could not be controlled, and everything about this household indicated that a modicum of restraint was the order of the day.

By the time Jane and Diana went to bed, Jane was sated with fellowship, and she wasn't sorry to be left alone in the small flower-papered bedroom that she had chosen as her own for when she slept over. It was known by all the Tunbridges as Jane's room. She didn't mind being separated from Diana, whose own room was down the hall. Maggie said it was barbarous to deny people privacy while they were sleeping. They had such a big house, she said, that it was ridiculous to crowd people together as though they were living in dormitories. Sleep was a solitary undertaking, a time to muse and dream alone, said Maggie. And after spending a day in communion with that family, Jane didn't think that Maggie's ideas were at all unusual or precious. She wouldn't have known how to think any thoughts like that about Maggie, and if the two girls had slept in the same room, they would have been far more likely to awaken each other and the entire family too early on the following Sunday morning.

At eleven o'clock Jane put on her pajamas and brushed her teeth and said good-night to Diana. She got into bed and under the covers that Maggie had turned down for her sometime during the evening and began to read one of the selection of books that were always left on the bedside table for her along with a glass of ice water. But she fell asleep within four pages of the first volume of *The Book of Three*. She had climbed into bed and settled back among her pillows without responsibility of any kind in this vast houseful of grown-ups, and that was a powerful soporific.

Jane woke up early, just before dawn, and she woke up alarmed. She lay still for a while, listening for the reason she had awakened. She was too young to care if she fell asleep again, but she did care to calm herself; she did want to lapse back into that same soothing state of mind in which she had gone to sleep the night before.

Finally she sat up and pulled the down comforter around her shoulders like a cape and crossed the floor barefooted to the window to open the curtains. She was just waking up, and her coordination was slumberous in spite of the shock of the cold floorboards and rarefied air. Overnight all the objects in the room had become just fractionally clearer to the eye, easier to discern in the crystalline atmosphere, but her attention was too lethargic to take this in. She struggled with the drapes, trying to fasten the tiebacks with one hand while holding the quilt around her with the other. At last she dropped the quilt on the floor so she could use both hands, and she settled the tiebacks around the drapes and hooked them in place with exasperation.

She looked out the window with only a drowsy interest, but when she took in the still dark panorama of the bluff and the river and the meadow to her right, she moved backward a scant step, and then she moved forward again to peer through the glass in earnest. She stood perfectly still, staring out for several minutes. She could not organize the scene before her into any landscape she could recognize.

The river roiled sluggishly wherever it had not crusted over, and the railroad tracks were furzed with ice. In the meadow nothing moved. The trees did not tremble, and their bright fall leaves hung glazed and heavy from the branches. The meadow itself, through whch she had made her way the day before, was smoothed over with ice, sleek and undulating and foreign. She made no sympathetic association to any bit of the earth she gazed out upon. What she saw exceeded anything she might have imagined. The landscape was icebound, desolate, and bruised where it mirrored the barely lightening sky. It slowly came into her thoughts that her parents would not possibly be able to weather such an extremity of climate, and Jane knew that she ought to do something, but she didn't know what would be expected of her.

She got dressed and made her bed and packed her backpack before anyone else in the house had awakened, and she sat on the edge of the bed, looking out at the mysterious accumulation of ice, and tried not to anticipate anything at all. She was puzzled the same way she had been the morning her mother had come in and curled up in Jane's bed with her after both of them had spent a sleepless night appeasing, avoiding, and enduring Avery's violent raging around the house. Her mother had put her head down on the pillow next to Jane so that her fluffy hair wisped across Jane's cheek and got into her mouth. On that morning her mother had chatted in whispers, as though anything at all could possibly awaken Avery, who was sprawled asleep in a living room chair.

"You know," her mother had said, "I think it's perfectly understandable that children do the things to their parents that they do. I was reading about a thirteen-year-old boy who climbed up on top of the refrigerator with one of those huge cast-iron skillets," she said. "He knew his father was going to come home drunk, and he waited for hours. Of course, when the man walked through the door, the boy hit him as hard as he could with that skillet and just killed him." Claudia had paused to think about it, and she had turned onto her back and pulled Jane's blanket up to her chin. "I don't really think that's murder, though, do you? They aren't even trying him for murder," she had added thoughtfully. "They're calling it self-defense. Don't you think that's probably fair?"

Jane hadn't responded at all to that. She had tried to sort it out and had never succeeded. She was fairly certain that her mother didn't want her to bash her father's brains out with a skillet, but she was just as certain that there was something that her mother did want her to do to make their lives easier. Yet, as far as Jane could see, she was without any power whatsoever.

This morning, however, as she stared at the ice, she did understand why, after all those nights when she and her mother had taken long drives out toward St. Louis on the interstate to be out of Avery's way, her mother always turned around and came home in the end. When Avery had thought of removing the distributor cap early in the day so that they couldn't forsake him, and when her mother had taken the precaution of going to an auto supply house to buy an extra one in case he should do that again—then Jane had finally asked her mother why they had to go back.

"I don't see why we have to go home," Jane had said. "I mean, why can't we just go to a hotel like Dad does when he really gets mad?'' She was curled up in the back seat of the car while her mother had stretched her legs out on the front seat. They had driven around town for a while that night and finally parked on a street near their house while they waited until they thought Avery had gone to sleep.

''Dad usually stays in a suite at the Oakwood, too, and it's really nice. We could go there.'' Jane adored being with her father when he was away from her mother and when she visited him in the nice rooms of a motel. Whenever he moved out, he and Claudia channeled information to each other through Jane, and they set up a pattern so that Avery would meet her twice a week at her music lesson at Miss Jessup's, and sometimes Miss Jessup would go back to his motel with him and Jane for dinner. Avery would order all sorts of things from room service because Jane loved to have her dinner arrive on a trolley underneath a silver dome that kept it hot. And even Miss Jessup would become lighthearted as they unveiled one surprising dish after another. They would settle down in the room to watch TV until it was time for Jane to go meet her mother in the lobby. Her parents didn't like to see each other during times like those. Avery had stayed away only two or three weeks at a time, but they had been the nicest times Jane could remember, and she didn't see why she and her mother couldn't try the same ploy.

But when she suggested it, Claudia had shaken her head forward and swung her face toward Jane in a pale orbit over the car seat, moving her hand in front of her to stave off any other question. Jane had been surprised to see that her mother was both angry and shocked.

''Don't be silly, Jane. What in God's name do you think would happen to your father? Where in the world would we even want to go? What do you think he would do?''

All Jane had been able to decide then was that her mother must love her father, but at last she understood that that wasn't all there was to it. She had never been sure, anyway, that being in love was the right idea to have about her parents. And this morning Jane knew all at once that she was looking out upon the world the way it was for her parents. It was a place in which there was no refuge for either one of them except the other. Now she needed to be home, although she thought that when she did get home, her father would have left them again. She didn't think he would stay until she could get there, and she didn't know how long he would be gone this time.

4

Avery left before the ice had completely thawed, and Jane came home the next morning, just a week before Thanksgiving. Maggie drove her home because the freeze and sudden thaw had turned the path through the meadow into a rivulet that flowed straight to the Tunbridges' side door, trickled between the earth and the old stone foundation, and came sluicing down the cellar wall in a narrow, steady stream of water that triggered the sump pump in the dirt floor. The Tunbridges' house reverberated ever so slightly even on the second floor to the whir and thud, whir and thud, of its emergency drainage system.

In the whole of Lunsbury water ran everywhere. The ditch from the golf course overflowed and churned beyond the banks of the Secret Feather River, dislodging and carrying with it debris and ragged sheets of ice that surfaced like tag ends of Ivory soap bars, opaque and dingy. All over town people struggled with water-logged carpets in their rec rooms, sodden woodwork and water-streaked walls and ceilings in their finished basements.

Claudia moved through the rooms of the house she and Avery had built, aware of the silky whisper of trickling water. When she put her ear against the wall, she could hear the water sliding down behind the foil-covered sheets of Styrofoam insulation, and she could see there were areas of pale gray carpet that had turned a wet slate color where moisture had seeped out along the baseboard. But Claudia did not struggle with it as her neighbors did. She made no effort to stanch the flow; it didn't seem to her that there was anything she ought to do about it. The slight stab of elation that had pierced her for a moment when she considered Avery's leaving had never returned now that he was really gone away from her. And he had planned it this time. She was afraid to let herself remember that it was not the usual passionate and frantic departure. He had considered it with some care. Her elation had been a sensation connected only to possibility, not to actuality. She was as deluged with apathy as her house and the town were deluged with the running water that poured through the gullies, down hills, and under the leaves that choked the square drains set into the city's streets. There the water paused and spun in tepid pools until it filtered through all the washed-up foliage and found its proper depth.

Claudia was astray in her own house. She didn't know about experience, about accumulating it, except on the most elementary level. Her very own history provided her with only a random illumination; she had never learned to cull from it a linear clarity. Because she had never mastered the technique of understanding how she got from her past to her present, she had no way of seeing how she could get from the present to the future. She had no manner of dealing with this loss of Avery, who had been hers one way or another for all the time she could remember. She wandered the rooms in a self-imposed stupor, because for all she knew of her life it was just the living of it with Avery that had required all her heat and cunning.

Jane occupied the same rooms in an entirely different frame of mind. She worried, and she badgered her mother for information about the state of their lives. She was as relentless as the water in her determination to find a stopping place. But she could not get past her mother's lack of animation, anger, or enthusiasm. Claudia's passivity had always been ameliorated by her passionate immediacy, but with Avery gone from the house so suddenly she only drifted, uninterested in the days. It made Claudia cross when Jane pressed her for answers.

"What will we do? If Dad's got an apartment, will we have to move, too? I thought he would just go to a hotel. Are we going to stay here? Won't Dad come back?"

"Oh, sweetie, he's just getting settled in his apartment. Of course he'll be back and forth. He's got lots of things to pick up." This was not said to give comfort; Claudia was prickly when Jane asked these questions. They set her in motion. As soon as Jane spoke, Claudia was up from the table or out of her chair and walking off down the hall, where she turned off into the bathroom and took a shower, or into the bedroom and took a nap. The answers she gave Jane were only shreds of sentences tossed over her shoulder as she scurried away from the unnerving insistence of her daughter.

Mostly Claudia slept and slept. She slept late into the day; she fell asleep curled at one end of the dark red couch, and she went back to sleep in the afternoon. When Jane came home from school, she didn't wake her mother; she just fed poor Nellie and made a sandwich for herself. She and the dog would eat in the kitchen, and Nellie would follow Jane wherever she went because she was so glad to find someone stirring about.

Claudia ate now and then during the day. Jane found her plates in the sink and jars left out on the counter, and she put them away before she made dinner for herself. So much sleep had made Claudia's face swollen, and her skin was blanched white under her eyes. She was irritated when Jane asked her anything that might require her to wake up, and for several days she didn't answer Jane sufficiently.

The day before the Thanksgiving holiday began, Jane herself was infected by her mother's fatigue. She woke up and couldn't imagine that it would be possible to spend a day surrounded by her friends and answerable to her teachers, so she didn't go to school, although Claudia didn't know it. In fact, Jane lay in bed awake while Claudia slept away the morning. When she heard her mother get up and go to the kitchen she followed her there, and Claudia didn't appear to think it was unusual that Jane was home. Jane settled at the table and began to hector her mother in a querulous tone that Claudia couldn't ignore.

"What are you going to *do*, Mom? Can we call Dad? I don't even know his number. And we're almost out of milk, too. We need to go to the store." Jane was so intent upon this that it made Claudia angry.

"He doesn't have his phone in yet, Janie. Maggie called last night to give me the message. It'll be hooked up day after tomorrow and he'll call you. Why don't you ride over to the Mini-Mart to get us some milk? You could take your backpack and just get one quart, couldn't you? I really don't feel good. I don't feel like getting dressed, Janie."

A tremor went through Jane from head to toe, a violent shudder. She could not make a dent on the events that were moving her life along one day to the next. No one asked her advice or even wanted her point of view. She only thought of one tiny way, that very instant, to regain a little control over her own fate. She sat at the table with her hands curled tightly as though she had slammed them against the surface with a thump. They were white and tensely clenched.

"Don't call me Janie! I hate being called Janie, and you don't have the right to call me that!" She jumped up out of her chair and stood in the center of the room, trembling and shaking her head as she spoke. "You don't *do* anything! You don't do anything at all! And I want you to call me Jane! And I mean it. Don't you ever call me Janie! Not ever again. Don't you dare!"

Jane's fury was so startling that it surprised Claudia out of her hazy lethargy. For one instant her senses registered the possibility that Avery might be gone for good. She had not heard from him except through Maggie, who taught her class in the same building that Avery taught his. She sat up straight in her chair and looked back at her daughter, who was shivering and shivering right before her eyes, and Claudia started to cry with a low moan in her throat. She only sat up straight and cried.

Jane stared back because she knew so little about this. She had seen her mother be sad, but she had never seen her mother cry from sadness. Now she observed her mother cautiously, and she remembered what Maggie had done when Celeste had come home crying because she had had an argument with the boy she was in love with. Jane did the same thing because it looked as if her mother might die of the loss of so many tears. Claudia made so little noise, and the tears flowed down her face like all the moving water in the world outside. Jane went over to her mother and put her arms around her, although she was afraid of doing this. The two of them had rarely taken the liberty of touching the other. With one hand she turned her mother's face against her shoulder while her mother cried, and she stood like that for a very long moment in her life. And at that instant Claudia thought that no one could ever be so kind to her again as long as she would live. She cried even more for this miraculous child who had somewhere learned compassion.

"Oh, Janie, I don't know. I don't know what to do. I don't know. I don't know. I didn't ever plan on doing things, you know. I don't know what to do about Avery."

That evening from the phone in her father's study Jane called Maggie to say that her mother had the flu and hadn't been able to shop or cook and could they have Thanksgiving dinner at the Tunbridges'. In the morning she woke her mother up fairly early and told her that Maggie had phoned to invite them over for the holiday dinner.

By Thanksgiving day there had been three days of mild but steady rain, the kind that in the spring is called a million-dollar rain by the farmers. In late November, however, when the ground had begun to freeze, it was disastrous, especially on top of the melting ice, and there were flash flood warnings for the low-lying areas. But as the rain droned on that afternoon, Claudia came fully back to attention. She took notice once again of exactly what she was doing, although she was groggy with the recollection of the past week that had moved by her while she wasn't counting the time.

She wasn't sure, as she stood there whisking lumps out of the gravy while Maggie drained the green beans, if the Tunbridges had invited her to dinner or if she and Jane had simply turned up in their kitchen. It never mattered in Maggie's household, and Claudia took care with the gravy and was simultaneously almost at the point of tears with gratitude at having friends so capable and generous. Maggie's house at Thanksgiving was always filled with interesting strays, whom Maggie had collected from one place or another. People to whom, at some time, she had offered solace. Claudia was dazzled, as she usually was by any Tunbridge event, and she beheld the scene with a liquid and blurred perception.

Maggie could orchestrate confusion; she had mastered the art of turning chaos into spontaneity—the shade of difference between the two was so very pale. Claudia admired her as she managed the kitchen. She was tall and lanky and lovely-looking in her straw doll kind of awkwardness, thought Claudia. Maggie would motion with her sharp hands and arms and scissor across the kitchen in long strides, never wasting a movement. She marshaled her forces with sweet efficiency. She nudged people gently this way or that. It had turned out that there were fourteen people gathered at her house for this meal, and they had grouped themselves either in the kitchen or in Vince's study, where the football game was turned on. Jane and Diana had been helping all morning, and now they were sitting at the kitchen table out of the way eating slivered, toasted almonds. Claudia was filled with a fragile, sentimental delight when she took into account her daughter sitting at the table seeming content while Maggie deftly directed all the movements in this sturdy household.

Claudia did notice with a twinge of sorrow that Jane's hair was hanging limply around her face and needed washing and that she was wearing a pair of old jeans and an orange sweat shirt that said "Missouri Tigers." Diana sat next to her at the table in the same attitude of clumsy repose, but Diana was as smooth and polished in the way she looked as a satin-textured stone taken from a stream. Claudia studied her briefly and tried to figure out how she had achieved it. It might be her shiny dark hair braided down her back. This was the sort of detail of other people's style that Claudia always tried to remember and get right, but that generally eluded her because she could never sustain her interest.

Maggie was talking to Alice Jessup, who also taught Mark violin and who had interested Claudia for some time. Claudia was always bemused by the intensity of this young woman's presence. She had come to Avery four years ago to enlist his aid in finding a publisher for a little book she had done on teaching techniques— modified Suzuki for older students. To everyone's surprise it was becoming a standard text, and Alice was invited all over the country to demonstrate and teach master classes. Avery had persuaded her to teach Jane privately, and she had taken on Mark, too. Since then she had become a sort of pet, a mascot, of their rather limited social circle.

Alice was dark and small and frail and serious. She had on heels today, so she didn't seem quite as tiny, but the shoes were an old, scuffed pair worn down at the outside, and her ankles bowed out ever so slightly like a child dressing up in her mother's clothes. Usually she wore flat-heeled, soft Chinese shoes that buckled across the instep. They were very fashionable these days, and both Jane and Diana had bought a pair in admiration of the violin teacher. But on Alice Jessup the little black strapped shoes looked like the shoes of a good little girl. Alice was so slight, in fact, that with her long, long hair she was often mistaken for a student, even at the grammar school where Maggie had persuaded the school board to apply for a grant that would allow the school to pay Alice to teach orchestra. Whenever she smiled, it was only a tiny break in her otherwise determined gentleness; it was only if she had made a *decision* to smile, or so it seemed to Claudia. She was a good instructor, though, coaxing the very best efforts from her students by the sheer force of her humorless devotion to the instrument. She and Maggie were at the forefront of the nuclear freeze movement at the university, where Alice taught a course in music theory, and the two of them were talking politics.

"I'll tell you what I really worry about, Maggie. Well . . . you know . . . *despondency* overwhelming the whole movement," she said. They were such a contrast. Alice was utterly motionless as if she had concentrated every ounce of her being into a single stream of thought. It was endearing to Claudia to watch this fragile, reedlike woman toss her thoughts into Maggie's wake. Maggie was in motion all over the room.

"I think people will stay more involved than you think," Maggie said. "Especially now that the people are the only ones who have the ability to define reality." She glanced at Alice, who remained stock-still with the effort of sorting out what Maggie meant. "What I mean," said Maggie, "is that *they* can define sanity, at least in this issue. The man in the street, don't you think? I mean, it's gone beyond being complicated. Well, it's so complicated that it's become simple. Are we *really* talking about deterrents with nuclear weapons? How complex does disarmament have to be? And is it even possible? We've reached a point where anyone's opinion on what's possible and what's rational is pretty valid, you see." Maggie was tossing the beans in butter and chopped parsley in a large skillet with one hand and with the other she reached for the serving bowl and put it in the oven to warm.

Alice stood staring at the floor in concentration, drawing her eyebrows together and biting her lower lip. She glanced up earnestly at Maggie's profile. "In the middle of an economic depression it seems to me that people aren't going to be able to concentrate on something that's basically abstract. A philosophy," she said.

"Oh, I think you're wrong," Maggie said. "In fact, if anything, the strain on the economy will fuel the freeze movement. It's something for people to pin their hopes on in an otherwise hopeless situation. And don't you think that the freeze movement gives the ordinary person a feeling of autonomy?" She emptied the beans into their dish and placed them on the counter. "But not to worry, anyway," she said. "I heard on the radio that this whole depression is only a *glitch*!" Maggie laughed, and Claudia smiled from her corner of the stove where she was still whisking, but Alice was solemn. "What in God's name is a glitch?" Maggie asked the company in general. "What do you think?" she went on. "I love it, don't you?"

Jane rose up on one knee that had been tucked under her on her chair. "I know, Maggie. I know! It's like a word game we have at school. Now, if a depression is a glitch, then it must be a gloomy bitch. A gloomy bitch! A *glitch*! Like in the cafeteria beef stew is barfew, and vegetable soup is vegoop!"

Maggie and Claudia both laughed, and Alice didn't seem to have heard, but Maggie was surprised as well as amused. Her wariness was apparent, and she looked to Claudia for a reaction, but Claudia was entirely pleased that her daughter was so clever.

Mark and Vince were in the room, too. Vince was leaning against the door, waiting to carry in the turkey, and he smiled, with his long blue eyes slightly squinted into the brightness and turmoil of the kitchen.

Jane had everyone's attention, and she became agitated with the pleasure of it. "And a gritch," she went on to say, "is a grinning bitch, right? And a snitch is a snobby bitch, and a litch is a lazy bitch . . ."

"I think a litch is more likely to be a female lech,"

said Vince in his lovely voice that had a hint of a nasal drawl. Whenever Vince spoke, he always had the effect of slowing down the pace of the conversation. His speech was lazy with what seemed to be suppressed amusement.

"A glitch is a computer term for a hang-up," Mark said.

Maggie gave them a blank glance and then smiled a little at Jane in the way of consolation. "That's enough," she said just to Jane, although it certainly wasn't a whisper, but then she enlarged her voice to include the room at large. "All right. Everyone has to fetch and carry! I want to get these things on the table before everything gets cold."

But Jane had got up and was moving around Maggie, trying to regain her attention in a ragged sort of dance of attendance. Maggie looked at her with a quick, preoccupied smile. She was handing various things to various people to take into the dining room.

Jane went on. "A fritch would be a French bitch, and a slitch would be a sloppy bitch, and a flitch would be a flirting bitch . . ."

Jane's voice was strung out high and thin with a groveling anxiety, like Nellie when she whined, and Maggie was very calm and deliberate. "Jane, don't say any more about it. All right? It's not appropriate." And Jane's mouth closed immediately into a straight, tight line.

Claudia was so surprised that it took her a moment to understand what Maggie had said to Jane, and then it rankled. She thought Jane was perfectly equipped to define what was or was not appropriate, just as Maggie thought that the man in the street was equipped to define what was sane.

The dining room of the Tunbridge house ran the whole length of the original building, and there were always shadows in the high corners of the room no matter what the time of day. When Celeste lit all the candles she had lined up down the center of the table, the shadows became a formidable presence, and the light flickering on the panes of the French doors and long windows showed up the streaming day outside. The table glinted with silver and crystal and candlelight, and the guests took on the aspect of refugees who had washed up at long last to the safest of harbors.

"You used the bone-handled silver, Celeste," Maggie said. "It can't go in the dishwasher, you know? We can't even leave it to soak." Most of the guests had seated themselves, but Maggie was still all around the room in a flash. The unexpected illusion created by Maggie's astringent, everyday practicality was that—with minor variations—Maggie's family was always thus: blessed with abundance and irradiated by this shimmering light while the rest of the world might weep with rain.

"We'll clear and wash up," Celeste said. "You cooked. Mark and the girls can help."

Celeste had set the table with the bone-handled silver and tiny salt dishes with miniature spoons from which the guests invariably poured too much salt all at once upon their food and had covertly to redistribute it with the blades of their knives. She had spread an aged damask runner the color of ivory down the center of the table and made an elaborate and sumptuous arrangement of apples and nectarines, pineapples, oranges, kumquats with their green leaves still on, and clusters of dark purple and pale green grapes. "Don't worry," she had said to her mother when Maggie had been distressed about all the bags of fruit she had brought home from the store. "It'll save you making dessert. I bought cheese, too." Celeste had spent the morning on this project, using toothpicks to anchor any piece of fruit that had rolled loose. The ten silver candlesticks stood in a row amid the apples and grapes, and Celeste had tied a bow of shiny gold ribbon around each white taper.

It was a jubilant gathering; each person felt so singularly celebrated. Mark moved around the table pouring wine while Vince carved the turkey. Only Jane, still anguished over Maggie's reprimand, gazed with pallid interest at the long table. When Diana reached into the centerpiece to take kumquats for them both to eat while they waited to be served, Jane shook her head that she didn't want one. Jane was sitting next to Miss Jessup, who was at the end of the table on Maggie's left. Maggie was sitting down, too. She had finally settled into her chair like a gaunt bird, with her hair feathering out around her head, but as the plates were passed to Vince for turkey, she leaped up again to preside over the sideboard. She removed the lid of a casserole and peered into the steaming dish of red cabbage and chestnuts in wine, and she stirred it a little with her serving spoon. It was the only experimental dish she had made for this meal; every other thing was exactly what she had cooked for this holiday year after year. She had even made the ginger pudding despite all Celeste's fruit. But this cabbage worried her.

"Now at least *try* this cabbage," she said, as if all the thirteen other people seated at the table were her favorite children. "It's Julia Child. It really isn't anything at all like real cabbage." Everyone was amused, and in this endearing way of hesitant apology she ensured that each guest would savor the pungent cabbage. Maggie had worried about it all morning, and Jane had been her ally in the face of Diana's scorn. It had been Jane who had arduously peeled the chestnuts and bobbed at Maggie's elbow with assurances of how good it smelled. Jane had hovered and helped and tasted while Maggie assembled this incredibly complicated peasant dish.

There were too many guests for the conversation to remain general. Maggie, at her end of the table, had enlisted Alice to help explain the music program in the public schools to William and Sally Fitzgerald, who were on Maggie's right. The Fitzgeralds had moved to Missouri from California and had arrived exactly two days ago. Will Fitzgerald was joining Vince's law firm, and he and his wife were listening to Maggie while also appeasing and diverting their disoriented and cranky eighteen-month-old daughter. The little girl made determined lunges at the gold-tied candlesticks each time her parents released her hands. Without seeming to notice their distress Maggie chatted on while she reached out and moved aside the three candles within the child's orbit. She plucked two lady apples from the arrangement in front of her and held them out to the little girl, who studied them with suspicion but then took them both. Now that each of her hands was engaged in the effort of holding on to those apples her parents began to eat their dinner with alacrity while Maggie carried on the conversation. That little girl knew she had been tricked in some way, but each time she put down one of the apples, Maggie made a mock grab at it so that the child snatched it back again with a shout of triumph.

As she listlessly moved a piece of turkey from one place on her plate to another, Jane was watching Maggie and that baby. She ate some beans and looked at Diana's plate to discover that Diana was waiting for a second helping. A new kind of exhaustion was overtaking her, as though she were a windup toy running down. She recognized the heavy pressure behind her eyes, and she didn't want to cry. Her lower lip began to tremble uncontrollably.

"I think I'm going to be sick, Maggie," she said all at once and with some belligerence. The prospect of someone throwing up quieted the whole gathering.

"I really think I'm going to be sick. It's this cabbage, I'm pretty sure. It's all that bacon in it. I think it must be all the fat in that cabbage that's making me sick." Jane said this to Maggie not loudly but with determination; her own mother was at the far end of the table next to Vince and Celeste.

Maggie looked at Jane, whose hair was dank and clinging to her head, and whose sweat shirt was spotted from her efforts in the kitchen. "Yes, you do look terrible," she said. "Why don't you go up and lie down, sweetie? Diana can bring a tray up to you later if you feel better."

Jane slid her chair back and stood up to leave. "I don't think I ought to have any more of that cabbage that has so much bacon grease in it. Just some turkey."

"No, you shouldn't. No, I think you shouldn't try anything but some plain soda crackers until you feel a little better," said Maggie. That was not the comfort that Jane desired, of course, but no eleven-year-old could have known how hard it might be for Maggie to appear relaxed and magnanimous while serving Thanksgiving dinner for fourteen.

Claudia excused herself and left the table a moment after Jane did. She followed her daughter and caught up with her in the upstairs hall. In the room designated as Jane's room Claudia pulled back the covers on the bed and slipped Jane's tennis shoes off while Jane lay down flat and stiff and tense and not crying.

Claudia sat down on the end of the bed and tentatively took her daughter's sock-clad feet into her lap and massaged them gently, running her long fingers along the muscles and tendons of the high arch of one foot and then the other. Jane was tall for her age. She had elegant, narrow bones like Avery's that Claudia could feel defined under her hand when she clasped Jane's slender foot. Claudia could discern the broad, round bone of the heel and the rigid sweep of the arch, and on the top of the foot she could feel the distinct delineation of the complex metatarsal bones beneath her probing fingers. The sensation of her own child's body beneath her hands brought upon her for a moment the most profound nostalgia. She held Jane's feet tightly to her in the all-encompassing memory of early motherhood. She perceived intensely and briefly a thorough helplessness of exactly the same quality she had experienced when she had paced the room weeping while Jane, at three months, had lain in her crib with a cold, struggling to breathe. Claudia had wept then at her inability to be of any help, and now she sat stunned with the same idea of futility in the face of being anyone's parent.

She got up and tucked the covers snugly around her

daughter, then stood away from the bed, wanting to do something more for Jane but completely at a loss as to what it should be. Jane turned her face away and lay perfectly still, looking out the window into the rain.

"I'll come up later, Janie, and see if you want something to eat. I can bring you a turkey sandwich. I know how you like them. I'll put cranberry sauce on one side, okay?"

But the gray light that filtered into the room fell across the tense jaw and the angry, pouting, turned-away mouth of her daughter, and Claudia was afraid of her. She took two awkward, hesitant steps backward before she turned and left the room, as if she were moving away from Jane because Jane had accused her of something.

While the Thanksgiving dinner progressed downstairs through the second helpings, more wine, various turns of conversation, Jane glided like a sylph through all the upper story. She was triumphant slipping along the corridor so secretly, like a wraith, like a spirit. She wasn't fearful of all the wisping shadows as she sometimes had been in this house on other days, after Vince had told them all the stories she and Diana asked to hear once again. She had, in fact, the peculiar sensation of moving with the house, of being one little bit of all that was mysterious about the Tunbridges. She was finally permeating their history, that great stretch of events that belonged to them alone and was their frame of reference. Jane lost the consciousness of the weight of her body; she floated as if she were the embodiment of all the mottled shades of gray that fled along the walls and around the corners with even the smallest shift of light through the windows.

She went to Celeste's room first and traveled around its edges, as though she might be discovered if she stepped into its central space. She paused at the night table and leafed through Celeste's journal, which had intrigued her ever since the first time she had seen Celeste writing in it. It was a large black leather-bound volume that Celeste had special-ordered from the stationery store. But it was disappointing. It was full of Celeste's notes to herself about classwork and meetings, with scarcely anything personal and nothing at all about Jane.

She circuited Vince's room briefly, although she didn't linger among his things; they didn't interest her. In the huge bath and dressing room that connected Vince's room to Maggie's she opened all the closets and cupboards and studied with great satisfaction the many folded towels arranged by color, the shelf of pretty soaps, bath powders, lotions, and creams, and in one corner closet she found a toilet bowl plunger, exactly like the one in her own house, tucked away with a mop and bucket and sponges. She closed each door behind her before she opened another. She stood for a long time looking in at Maggie's shoes and dresses and suits and blouses and slacks, which were hung on a clever, multiple hanger.

She opened the old wooden cupboard where Vince's shaving kit was, and cough syrups, aspirin, Pepto-Bismol, Alka-Seltzer, Paropectolin. She picked up a beige box to scrutinize its prescription label:

Celeste Tunbridge: Motrin: One or two tablets at onset of cramps then one tablet every four hours as needed.

She rummaged through all the plastic bottles of prescripton medicines and read them carefully:

Celeste Tunbridge: Lasix: One tablet each morning with orange juice as needed for fluid.

Margaret Tunbridge: Percodan: One tablet every four hours as needed for pain.

Margaret Tunbridge: Valium: 1/2 to one tablet before each meal and one/two before bed.

Diana Tunbridge: Ampicillin: One tsp. every four hours.

Diana Tunbridge: Novahistine DH: One tsp. every four hours as needed for cough.

The Novahistine DH had crystallized into green sugar all around the channeled childproof cap. Jane opened the bottle, sniffed it, and took a taste of the liquid onto her tongue, but it had a vile sweetness. She capped it again and put it back right where it had been on its sticky circle. She lined up all the bottles carefully just as she had found them, but before she closed the cabinet, she took down the bottle of Percodan tablets and put them on the counter while she used both hands to shut the heavy hinged doors so that the clasp would catch properly. She took one tablet from the bottle and swallowed it with water she sucked up from her cupped hands beneath the faucet. There was no water glass beside the sink. She put the bottle in the pocket of her jeans and pulled her sweat shirt over it.

Before she left the room, she turned to be sure that nothing looked disturbed, and she wandered into Maggie's room, which was the place of most solace to her in all the world. At Maggie's long window next to the chaise longue Jane peered out toward the river, but it was obscured by the steady rain. She moved over to the dresser, where Maggie's comb and brush lay intertwined with short strands of white-blond hair that were almost incandescent in the gloom. Jane had always wanted to know the feel of that brush in her own hair, and she stroked her head gently and was surprised to find that the bristles were not very effective. They were soft and short in the elaborate chased silver base, and she tended to bang herself on the head with each sweep of her hand. She replaced the brush just as it had been and stood regarding herself quietly in the mirror. She took up a handful of change from a silver dish next to Maggie's purse and put it in her pocket along with the bottle of pills.

Except for the nickels and quarters she had pocketed nothing was changed in Maggie's room, nothing was askew, and she left the room and shut the door softly behind her. She went back to her corner room under the eaves and resettled herself peacefully under the covers, enclosed as though she were in an envelope by the sweetly flowered wallpaper and the rain outside. As she lay there, a feeling of absolute contentment began to come over her in degrees in the same way warmth suffused her body when she came in from the cold. She was removed from any careful consideration of her life. The knowledge of the events that had moved along in the past few weeks coursed through her, but it only rushed along like a dark river as seen from a high, safe, grassy place along the bank. All that knowledge was at a far remove from any emotion she felt at the moment. She was snug in her warm bed with the muted sound of a party at a comforting distance. She was so pleased that she was mildly surprised by her own condition. Her silent investigation of the Tunbridge rooms seemed to have been perpetrated by another self, some restless other child who did not feel the hum of tender self-satisfaction unnumbing all the far reaches of herself. She fell asleep with pleasure, not with any wariness at the idea of being unconscious.

In the dining room the long meal had reached that tattered stage at which point the hosts and guests alike had begun to suffer from an undefined regret. Any successful celebration has some momentum of its own, and Maggie had carried the day along for a while with her own idea of how the time should go. Finally, however, the whole party began to sense that they had stayed with each other past the peak of interest. Curiosity abated, and the energy of the gathering was rapidly dissipating.

Sally and Will Fitzgerald were taking turns walking their daughter around and around the table because she was fussy from sitting so long, but they were not quite yet ready to take themselves away. Trays of cheese had been put out after the dinner and dessert dishes had been cleared away, and people had switched places or got up to move around a bit.

Claudia had come back to her same seat next to Vince and across from Celeste, and her energy had flagged so early that when she had run out of conversation to have with them, she did not even have the impetus to move on to another group. She sat quietly over her coffee. Claudia knew all the other guests in the room with the exception of the Fitzgeralds and their daughter. She had met them at Maggie's at one time or another. However, she didn't know any of them very well, and one glance around the room convinced her, in the middle of the color and sound, that all these people had clear plans ahead of them for after this meal. In a little while they would be off. They would hurry through the rain toward whatever they did, and this notion intensified that sense of loss she had felt as she had tried to give comfort to Jane.

Claudia had inclined her head forward a fraction and raised her hand to push her hair back off her brow. She was not aware that this was her habitual gesture of avoidance, a private gesture to distract herself from unpleasant thoughts. Vince had been leaning back in his chair at the end of the table and watching her for some time. He made a sweeping motion with one arm, inclusive of the room, the day, the idea of Thanksgiving.

"These traditional celebrations," he said, and paused with the irony in his voice curling over even the notion that very much was worth such a ceremony. "These kinds of days are a strain on the best of us." He didn't smile at her, but he leaned back even farther in his chair, stretching his legs out so that the chair tilted backward, and regarded her with interest.

Claudia was not guileful. She tipped her extraordinary face back and looked at him in surprise. She was startled at being caught out in what she was thinking. Her hand still held back the cloud of her hair, and she released it, and it settled gently in place again over her forehead. The candles had burned so low that they cast an uplight over Claudia's pointed face, but even with the light trapped beneath the high arch of her brows in a way that threw her eyes into shadow, she had no expression of concealment about her. She only looked as though she were struck with wonder. This was the face she turned to Vince.

"The main thing," she said, "is that I don't have any idea of what to do now."

Vince looked on at her without changing expression, and after a moment he clicked the front legs of his chair back to the floor as he gathered himself forward to stand up. Just as his head was nearest hers in that one movement he spoke without looking at her. "Well, we'll think of something. I've got a couple of ideas." But his tone was vexed, and he didn't elaborate; he moved off to chat with the Fitzgeralds, who had their daughter bundled up and were ready to leave.

Claudia stayed where she was, and in a few moments Maggie took the place Vince had left vacant. She settled into the chair with a great flurry of garments coming to rest, of herself being collected. Whenever Maggie stopped, it was as if some other part of her had to catch up—a stray hand that was busy finishing some other task; her attention, which sometimes seemed to be several paces behind her. However, when she was absolutely there and assembled, there was no concentration as powerful as that which she could bring to bear on whatever had caused her to relocate in the first place.

She put her elbows on the table and hunched forward toward Claudia, holding her cup of coffee firmly with both hands. She was soft-voiced with the power of a secret to impart.

"When I talked to Avery this morning, I told him that you and Jane would be here for dinner. He was going to come along with Alice, but he thought it would be better for everybody if he didn't come, too. You know, he's been absolutely sober this past week." Maggie pursed her lips over her coffee, sensing that it was too hot to sip. "He'll be coming by about seven-thirty. I thought you might rather not run into him. Of course, Jane's welcome to stay and have a chance to visit with him, but I knew it might be hard for you to see him."

Claudia stared at Maggie without comprehension, except that she knew from Maggie's tone that Maggie was doing her some favor. That much was clear, but grateful as Claudia knew she ought to be, she suddenly felt claustrophobic, trapped as she was under Maggie's wing. "Maggie, I'm only *angry* at him." She wanted to see Avery very much, and when she noticed Maggie's face cast over in disapproval, she wondered if Avery had requested not to see *her*.

"That's a lot to expect of Jane, isn't it?" Maggie said.

"I don't know what you mean. Jane misses Avery, too."

"I know she does, but, still, having to see you together again and then apart. Shouldn't you see Avery when she's at school? There's not much you could get settled tonight, anyway, in the middle of all of us."

Every one of those considerations went out of Claudia's mind, though, when the idea Maggie put forth came into focus as a picture of what would happen. She would see Avery and stand near him—his long body— and not touch him. He would not touch her, and before she would ever touch him again or be touched by him, there would be all the conversations, anguish, endless talking. That condition had never been so between them. Their other separations had been only brief and private; they had not been such public property. The two of them had always had access to the other since they were children. Claudia was defeated, and she looked down at the table to avoid looking at Maggie, who had imposed this condition upon her. That was not a rational conclusion, but it was what Claudia thought, and she was very angry.

"I'll go check on Jane," Claudia said, and left the

table. But when she was in Jane's room, she didn't wake her because Jane looked warm and safe and comfortable, and Claudia could not deprive her of a condition she yearned for so desperately for herself right now. She went down the back stairs and found Celeste in the kitchen.

"Jane's sound asleep. Phone me when she wants to come home, and I'll come pick her up." Celeste said she was sure that Jane was welcome to stay over and that she would look in and check on her later to be sure she was all right. Claudia left the house through the kitchen door and trudged all the way around the enormous building in the rain to get to where she had left her car. She did not want to have to thank Maggie for a lovely day, although she didn't like herself for her own stingy nature.

5

Claudia thought that as Christmas ap-
proached, the days passed with remarkable
singularity. They did not oblige her and slip away into
weeks. Instead each day rolled out long and inflexible
from morning to night; there was no snap to any one of
them that marked it off succinctly so that she could have
the satisfaction of reaching a particular moment and
going on from there. And the weather was sullen, too.
The rain had stopped at the end of November, and a
deep freeze had settled in with no precipitation. The
meadow spread away from Claudia's house pocked with
muddy patches of ice. The long grass was flattened and
yellow and was brittle underfoot, and the sky, day after
day, stretched out low and dull and unshifting. When
Claudia went out, which was seldom, or when she looked
through her windows, she thought the landscape looked
mean.

She watched passively and without curiosity as the
world tightened down unsympathetically into hard winter. She put off making plans of any kind. She avoided
thinking about the future to such a degree that she had
not even settled into a state of waiting since Avery left;
she was only being there until the time went by.

Maggie often dropped by without warning, and that made Claudia mildly uneasy all the time. Maggie had expectations of her, and just now Claudia didn't want to expend the energy even to figure out what the expectations were, much less fulfill them. When she thought about it, the most Claudia wished from her friends was that her own life not be a topic of their consideration.

One afternoon Maggie arrived on foot, having come up the hill through the frozen meadow, and Claudia was caught unawares, without even the sound of Maggie's car as a warning. Maggie gave a perfunctory knock and stepped straight into the house. She always entered that way; she stepped straight into one's life all prepared to help out and set things right. She walked in that afternoon and startled Claudia, who was sitting at the kitchen table drinking coffee and idly bending over the pieces on the chessboard. She was wearing her long red robe, over which she had put on an oversized mustard-colored cardigan sweater that Avery had left behind. She sat back in surprise when Maggie put her head around the kitchen door, and she pulled the cardigan more closely around her and hugged her elbows.

"I can only stay a minute," Maggie said, "but I wanted to talk to you about two things." She was, as always, very deliberate about this: *two* things. It was her habit to warn people, to insist upon their endurance. But Claudia was thrown back in time into the sort of dread with which a child hears a parent announce in midafternoon that after dinner the two of them must have a serious talk. In Claudia's experience this had never amounted to a conversation; it had always turned out that Claudia sat and listened while someone else gave her unwanted instruction or advice. Now and then Maggie had said to Claudia that she and Vince had met at Belden's restaurant or the Faculty Club to discuss this or that problem in their marriage or with their children. She had tried to admire Maggie's rational determination, but she had always cringed for Vince, who probably approached that meeting place with his usual air of detachment, but with his stomach clenched. Now Claudia looked back down at the little chess pieces and tried to indicate by her passivity that two might be just a little too many things to discuss.

"Um-huh. Okay," she said mildly, making it as clear as she could that although she was right there in the room, her attention was not all it might be.

"Well, first," said Maggie, settling in across the table from Claudia, "we've got to decide what you're going to do about Christmas." Claudia gazed up at her after a moment without any inflection of expression. "Celeste has offered to take Diana in to Kansas City in March for the Men at Work concert if I'll buy the tickets. They're playing at the Kemper Arena. It would be a much better present for Diana if Jane could go along. I thought you might like to give Jane a ticket, too. I don't think they really know if they like the music or not. It's the idea of going that they'll like. They can stay overnight with one of Celeste's friends who lives right outside Kansas City. Diana will be ecstatic." Maggie said this with a wry smile, to encompass the eccentricities of eleven-year-old girls. But when she saw Claudia smile back at her automatically without having paid attention to what she was saying, she became more abrupt. She leaned forward on her elbows to be sure that Claudia listened to her. "Diana says that Jane won't *do* anything with their group anymore. And, I have to tell you, when she's at our house, she's only barely civil to Diana. Of course, Diana will put up with anything from Jane. As far as she's concerned, Jane hung the moon. But Jane's hostile to every overture Diana makes, even though she seems to need Diana's company. Jane's always around." She stopped for a moment and opened her hands in a gesture of helplessness. "I don't like to be the one to tell you this. I feel as if I'm betraying Jane, because she seems to count on us somehow. But she's right on the edge, Claudia. She's right on the edge of losing it." Maggie was absolutely sincere, but Claudia could not hear these things said without also hearing the undercurrent of satisfaction that Maggie felt because her own child was not in such a state. Maggie continued, "I can't keep insisting that Diana's friends try to include Jane in everything when Jane's so antagonistic to all those little girls!"

Claudia turned her head away and looked out the window so that nothing in her face would show how much she was hurt for Jane. Claudia knew that Jane was the best of all. The best of all the people she knew, the best of all the people she had ever known. Claudia was injured for her daughter, and she was very angry. It was the clearest thing she had felt for days.

"Maggie, compared to Jane . . ." she began, but she stopped. She was not sure how she meant to finish. She wanted to explain that compared to Jane, who had known exactly when to embrace her own mother . . . compared to Jane with her lovely long bones and serious face, there was not a child in the world who was more than a piece of blank paper. Compared to Jane, Maggie's own daughter, Diana, was . . . and she thought of a phrase of Avery's. "Listen, Maggie," she said, "Jane's no small potatoes!"

Maggie just looked at her. She didn't ask what that could mean. "Jane needs some help, Claudia," she said. "She could get some good counseling at the university. In fact, I brought over a copy of the form. It's covered on Avery's insurance. You know, any of you could go. It's a good program. There's only a hundred-dollar deductible."

But Claudia had drifted off into her own thoughts while Maggie chatted on. Claudia was imagining herself advising Jane on any matter whatsoever, and she was thinking that they had long ago passed that point. It would be an unthinkable presumption. They had passed that point as soon as Jane had understood, at about age two and a half, that she had her own separate will. It was lucky, Claudia thought, it was one of the nicest things in the world, that Jane had been born with a natural magnanimity.

"Anyway, here are all the information sheets on the

health plan," Maggie was saying, "but the second thing I wanted to tell you about is something that could turn out to be a wonderful job for you. I think we have it all arranged."

Claudia got up from the table and put the kettle on. "You want some coffee?" she asked, and without turning back to Maggie, she began running water in the sink to rinse the leftover breakfast dishes before she stacked them in the dishwasher. "I don't really want to think about a job right now."

Maggie was as close a friend as Claudia had, and Maggie's friendship was not entirely conditional, but on this point Maggie would not give way. She was a respected scholar; she wrote long, erudite articles for major literary journals. She was becoming an important critic, and in fact, last year a student at Columbia had done his thesis on her. She believed in achievement; she believed that there must be something Claudia wanted to do in her life, and since she could never discover what it was, Claudia's apathy had become a burr under her saddle. She seemed to resent it and view it as a threat to the way she lived her own life. Claudia didn't know this; she only knew that Maggie's prodding wearied her, and she didn't have the inclination, this afternoon, to try to explain herself to Maggie.

"When Avery and I get this settled, I'll think about a job. I've got plenty of money, you know, Maggie. Enough money, anyway." Maggie didn't reply, and Claudia eyed her apprehensively.

Maggie had pushed her short hair behind her ears and was looking straight ahead. She had tucked in the corners of her mouth so that her lips puckered slightly, and Claudia knew that look well. Maggie was like a terrier, and she wasn't going to let go so easily; she wanted everything settled for her friend. So Claudia dredged up from the very center of herself the energy she needed to answer Maggie's silent indictment and disapproval. Because she could not bear the weight of Maggie's disapprobation, her words stretched out with a soft, lilting note of persuasion. "Listen, don't worry about me. Lots of things interest me, but there never has been anything I've felt I need to do. Frankly, Maggie, I've always thought that the whole idea of doing something out of some sort of belief . . . I know it's one of the things that you and Avery feel the same way about. I mean, you both have ambitions. I don't know why it bothers anybody that I don't! I'll tell you the truth, it seems to me that ambition is sort of a naïve optimism. Well, maybe it's more like hope. Or religion. Either you really are convinced or it's too late to jump on board."

Claudia had spoken lightly and not in a manner of great conviction. This was a subject, in fact, that bored her. She glanced at Maggie and saw that there was an even grimmer quality to her silence. Maggie had settled down into herself in such a way that Claudia bent over the dishes in great concentration. She did not want to face the relentless power of her friend's sense of purpose.

"I invest pretty heavily in my friends," Maggie finally said, softly, as though she were ruminating. "You aren't especially frivolous, Claudia. And you've got such a good mind . . ."

Claudia was more careful than ever not to turn around and look at Maggie. She didn't want to acknowledge or debate her responsibilities as Maggie's friend. In fact, she felt an embarrassing, tearful constriction in the back of her throat because she was suddenly panicky in her need not to hear whatever Maggie was going to say.

"But, my God, Claudia! I'll tell you, I hope more than anything that Avery doesn't come back! You . . . I don't think you have the right to impose the two of you on the rest of us. Jane. And me and Vince. And, of course, for Alice . . . well. You two can't be together. It's horrible for everyone. It's like watching two people in a state of combustion."

Maggie ran her hand nervously through her hair, disarranging it more than ever, before she went on, and Claudia remained frozen at the sink with her back to her. "Do you know that he's been absolutely sober since he left? He's meeting his office hours. He's even made it to committee meetings. I mean, Claudia, I know he doesn't need to teach. Don't you think he needs the discipline of it though? He has tenure, but it was getting to the point that something was going to happen.''

Claudia put her hands up to cover her face because all at once her chin began quivering and her features became elastic and uncontrolled around a sudden flood of tears. "Oh, Christ, Maggie!" She had to pause until her throat untensed. "Oh, Christ! Please leave me alone!" She had never said anything as strong as that to Maggie. In all their long acquaintance she had never bothered to make any demands, but at the moment she had no control at all over anything she might say.

"Sober! Avery's been sober! What does that *mean* to you? He's teaching well? Going to meetings, for Christ's sake! That's not his *life*, Maggie. For Avery . . . Don't you know that for Avery sober is . . . is just like being drunk? It's a *luxury* for Avery. It's a choice! Sober is just one of his fucking vanities!" Claudia was not sobbing, but she had to pause, phrase by phrase, with each fresh onslaught of tears.

"What do you think? Shit, Maggie, what do you think about how people lead their lives?" Her voice caught roughly on the phlegm in her throat, and finally she subsided into a wet coughing, and she leaned against the sink, still resting her hot face in the palms of her hands. She was exhausted and aghast at having told the truth in front of Maggie. What Claudia usually allowed herself to say was, in fact, the best possible camouflage for the things she really thought. But evidently Maggie hadn't even taken into account the words she *had* said. Or maybe what Claudia had suspected all along was true: If she said the things she really thought, her meaning wouldn't be clear to anyone at all. Claudia knew that she might be so out of kilter that what she said when she told people the truth would be as incomprehensible as if she had spoken to them in an alien language. There were very few people who were important to Claudia. In fact, there was almost no one to whom she felt the need to make herself clear.

Maggie was quiet while Claudia pulled herself together, and she went on in a less insistent and more soothing voice. "We won't talk about that, now, Claudia. Let's not talk about Avery. It's always been hard, anyway. We always seem to be talking about two different people. And I like him less and less. I can't help it."

This both stung Claudia and comforted her. Maggie saw things so distinctly that she would be bound to take sides, and since that was going to be the case, Claudia wanted her on her own side. Besides, Avery had never liked Maggie much, either, not without enormous reservations. He didn't even like the way she looked. "I don't mean I can't see that she's attractive," he had argued to Claudia because Claudia had wanted them, in this case, to share the same enthusiasms, "but I just don't like the way she looks." They had never agreed about it.

"But, Claudia," Maggie said, "you'd really like this job. It's just a *job*. It'll keep you busy and get you out of the house. I'm hardly offering you your purpose in life. And it would help Vince out. He thought of it, as a matter of fact. Well, he can explain it all to you. Why don't the two of you have lunch or something someday and discuss it?"

Claudia was concentrating on drying her eyes and regaining some composure, and she was turned away from Maggie, but she nodded her head in assent just to be done with it. She was only thinking how much she wished her friend were not here.

"And listen, Claudia, if you want me to get a concert ticket for Jane, I really think she'd like it. I'm going to call Ticketron tomorrow, and I'll get the best seats they have left." Maggie's voice had become gentle with sincerity, with a real desire to be of help. "I know Jane would love it," she said. "She and Diana would have a wonderful time. I didn't have to twist Celeste's arm. She likes being with the girls, and she wants to take them out

93

to dinner at some place she loves. For barbecue ribs. I'll put the tickets on Visa, and you can pay me back if you want one for Jane.''

Claudia listened to the concern in Maggie's offer, and she also suddenly realized that she hadn't given a thought to Jane's Christmas present. She hadn't even glanced through all the shiny catalogues that were stacked beside her bed, and she hadn't been out shopping at all. Besides, that was what Avery usually did. He usually had the best ideas about these things. She felt a little calmer and a little grateful to Maggie, who meant so well. She turned around and gave Maggie a slight smile and a small shake of her head to apologize for her outburst. ''That would be great if you would do that, Maggie.''

The two of them were in the kitchen at the table drinking coffee when Jane came in from school, and Claudia was still guiltily eager to be delivered from Maggie. So when her daughter entered the house in the dim afternoon, Claudia was ripe with entreaty, ready to discuss anything.

''Janie! Listen, I have an idea. We haven't really made any plans for Christmas. I mean, we haven't done anything yet. Maybe we could fly down to Natchez and open the house there.'' She got up and went to the sink again to rinse her cup and finish clearing up, with the hope that Maggie would take it as a signal to leave.

''It would be so much warmer. It wouldn't be the prettiest time of year, but it would be warmer than it is here.'' Jane was still in her coat and boots, although she had taken off her gloves and was peeling an orange while she listened to her mother.

Claudia hadn't thought about Christmas at all this year. She had made only the odd gesture toward it. For families with children Christmas roughly divides the academic year. It becomes the day at which all things are either before or after, and it looms with a certain amount of gravity. However, this year it only wavered in Claudia's thoughts like a mirage. She had spent the preceding Sunday making flat sheets of gingerbread for what had been, in their family, a traditional gingerbread house. But she had left the cakes sitting uncut in their pans. The gingerbread became rock-hard, and now and then she or Jane had prized off a chunk and fed it to Nellie, who preferred it to the generic dog biscuits that Claudia bought for her at Kroger's. Finally Claudia had thrown it all away and washed up the pans. Now that she thought of it, it seemed to her a very good idea to go south for Christmas.

"It wouldn't be much trouble to open the house. I even know where the decorations for the tree are." She was all ruffled up with enthusiasm now that this idea had come into her head, and she didn't even take into account Maggie's stern presence at the table. Jane was eating her orange and watching her mother. "We'd probably have to get new lights," Claudia said, "but we could get the other kind. You know, the sort of bulb-shaped ones that come in different colors. We wouldn't have to get those little Italian ones that your father likes." She turned around to look at Jane, standing in the center of the room. "There are so many things going on in Natchez around Christmas. All kinds of parties. And everyone goes to the parties, Jane. I mean all ages. Even Christmas Day I'm sure we'd be invited out to Rosedown for brunch. Oh, and then everyone goes over to the Adamses' for champagne, and Santa Claus comes and gives out quarters to the children."

Jane stood with her orange half-eaten, considering this. "When would we go?" she said.

"Oh . . ." Claudia waved that away. "Well, I'd have to see when we could get reservations, and I'll have to check with Annie to see what's going on. I'll have to make some calls."

"The thing is," said Jane, "I'm concertmaster of the orchestra for the concert on the twenty-third. I can't miss that. I've got a solo. The Bach piece. I've been working on it for three months."

"Oh, that's right," said Claudia, and she began to

subside a little, not in disappointment—not at all—but she began slipping back into a sort of permanently absentminded state. "We might go down for New Year's," she said, although it was not a question or even a declaration. Claudia was feeling a familiar and welcome lassitude creep over her again, and Jane left the room and was out of the way of her mother's undependable optimism before she even removed her coat and boots.

Maggie got up and began assembling the clothes she had shed over the whole time of her visit, as though she had been molting. She put on a sweater and then a vest, a scarf, her jacket; she dropped her gloves, and it made Claudia so impatient to watch her that she sat down at the table while Maggie put herself together. Claudia sat tracing designs in the light dusting of crumbs and spilled salt that powdered the area around Jane's place mat. They could hear Jane practicing her scales and then doing a warm-up with a fiddler's tune. Claudia knew that Jane would be closed away in her own room for well over two hours until she had run through all her music and had played her concert piece over and over, with and without the tock, tock of her metronome. The prospect of the melancholy notes reverberating through their odd little shell of a house made Claudia very sad.

"You ought to think about getting away for New Year's," Maggie said as she was in the process of wrapping herself up in all her garments. "You know, that's a wretched instrument," she declared, startling Claudia, who looked up at her.

"The violin? You don't like it?"

"No, no. *That* violin. Can't you hear how bad it is? Alice says Jane is the best pupil she's ever taught. She thinks Jane is very talented. Maybe you should talk to her about getting a better instrument for Jane. It would be a good investment."

Claudia couldn't quite catch up with what Maggie was talking about. "Oh, well. We're only renting this one, you know. Until we're sure she's going to stay interested."

"You ought to be pretty sure of that by now," Maggie said. She was finally settled into her scarves and her hat and her quilted jacket, and she was brisk and in a hurry all at once. Claudia had never got used to the fact that in this weather people dressed up to look like upholstered furniture. "I'll talk to you soon," Maggie said. "Take care!"

Claudia sat on at the table after Maggie left, thinking a little bit about going to Natchez for New Year's, and then she abandoned that subject and began considering what she should do about dinner. Claudia could not pin anything down; she couldn't make any decisions. To be in the house that Avery had built without Avery was to suffer a wound.

Avery had designed the house. It was a partially solar, geodesic dome that looked to Claudia now and then, as she approached it up the steep drive, like the outcropping of a mud puddle during this bleak brown winter. It was darkly shingled in green, but in the gray days it looked almost black. Claudia didn't care about it, really; she wasn't interested in where she lived. When it was being built, though, she had caught on to Avery's passion, and for a while it had been their mutual obsession and their mutual adversary. They had had an awfully good time being united in an endeavor.

Avery had planned the ingeniously spaced and shaped windows that caught the right light at exactly the right moment, and the superstructure had gone up in the summer five years ago, during a long sunny spell. Every time they had visited the house to be sure everything was going all right it had been like stepping into a prism. Light poured in some windows and was refracted off others. Avery had expounded to their builder, Harry Oliver, about how the flat planes of the building—the wood floors, the ceilings, the pale walls—would give the illusion of motion as the light changed with the seasons and even during the length of one day.

"It will be different with each change of the *weather*, really, Harry," Avery had said. And that particular day

Claudia remembered noticing for the first time how attractive Avery could be to all sorts of people in all sorts of ways. Avery was nicer than she was, she had thought at that moment. His interest and generosity were enormous as he engaged his builder's enthusiasm—coaxed Harry into imagining the building—while she stood impassively by like a mannequin, peering up out of the unglazed windows and drawing lines with her foot in the sawdust on the floor. She cared only that Harry did the work; she hadn't cared if he enjoyed doing it. She wasn't going to share with him her sparse allotment of warmth. But Avery was insistent, leaning over Harry with fervent enthusiasm. "Don't you see? The space we'll be enclosed in in the summer will be cool and shady because of the trees, but in the winter the walls will seem to fan out with the light. I think it'll counteract that feeling of being closed in in winter." He had never quite induced Harry to be interested in the theory that propelled the construction, though. Harry was concerned only with getting the job done, and he worked well because he was very fond of Avery, but he had never cared about Avery's idea of a house so flexible that one would not feel defined by or trapped within it. Harry had been much more interested in getting the oddly shaped windows to fit and storm windows to fit over them.

One day Avery and Claudia had arrived at the house and stepped inside, and it had been nothing at all like stepping into a prism. In fact, they had been so surprised that both Avery and Claudia had reached out to brace themselves against the sensation of falling down into their own hall. The floors, as far as they could see until a wall cut off their line of vision, had been turned a dark blackish brown instead of the lovely pale unstained oak. Avery had been in despair. Every pinpoint of light that fell in through the glass panes seemed to be absorbed by that dark surface. He guided Harry through all the rooms, showing him how it was wrong, explaining how major a disaster this was. Harry followed him along, and he was sorry about it, although he also seemed to be baffled by the scope of Avery's distress, which was so broad that it had not been translated into anger.

Finally the three of them had stood clustered around the beautiful hand-hewn beam that ran the entire height of the house, and Harry shifted back on his heels to make an apology.

"I'll tell you," he said, "I'm afraid it's that Jacob Bean."

"Harry, what do you mean?" Avery said. "Did you contract this out? I thought your own crew was going to finish the floors for me. I could have gotten Len Maroni even though it would have cost more. It's going to cost more, anyway, to redo this."

Harry had stooped down and run his hand along one of the dark floorboards. He traced the grain that showed up in black ripples across each plank. "I don't think we can ever get this as light as it was. We'll have to take it down at least a quarter of an inch. No, I used that Jacob Bean. A lot of people use that on oak these days. It gives it this real rich look. We might be able to bleach it after I take it down, but you'll lose a lot of the grain. The floor will be real pale, though." While he was assessing the floor, he handed a can over to Avery, who looked at it and then passed it over to Claudia. It was a can of Gordon's Jacobean wood stain.

Avery had straightened up, and he and she had looked at each other. They were too dumfounded to be amused or outraged; they had only exchanged a mute acknowledgment of the ironies of life. And they had never had the floors redone. They had run out of time and energy and money and had carpeted the living room and left the other areas as they were. But often, when Avery had been drinking, he would expound upon a theme he had developed that turned upon the incident of their dark, shiny floors.

"It happened because we managed to attract our own ghost," he would say. "By the sheer force of our personalities. We're haunted. We're haunted even though we're right here in the middle of the country without a history and without a place. We're the new Americans. Transient! Right here in the middle of the country you'd think we'd be without consequence, wouldn't you? Not like Maggie and Vince and their house. Secret passages and so forth. Tales of the Underground Railroad. There never was an Underground Railroad, you know, but it makes a good story. It never existed. But that's not the point. We're contemporary. We have a brand-new house and a brand-new ghost. The only thing is . . . the trick about spirits . . . is that you don't get to choose the kind you get. Jacob Bean is an American ghost, but I'm not sure he's an amiable ghost. He does give us stability, Claudia. He gives us resonance! Still, I'm not sure of him. He's certainly a dark character. The dark side of things. He could be the incarnation of all the dreadful possibilities.''

Not all the consequences had been dreadful, however. Avery had written a very successful book called *American Ghosts*, and the story of Jacob Bean had been a jumping-off place for a long investigation of transience and melancholy. He had worked very hard on that book, and Claudia had thought it was fine, although she had noticed that to fit its tone he had turned her into a petite and ethereal sort of woman with long, drifting hair. ''I wish you had at least left me with a little sex appeal,'' she had said. ''And I'm five-nine.'' She had meant this lightly, although Avery had been insulted. She never remembered not to tease him about his books.

But the whole thing had never been a joke to share, even though on many occasions they had entertained Maggie and Vince and various other friends with charming and artful stories in which the progenitor of Jacob Bean, Harry Oliver, was portrayed as a caricature of a stubborn Missourian, a wily and obstinate native of the Show Me state. Those were other stories, though, of unmatched doorknobs at a bargain price, or ''Colonial windows'' Harry had bought on sale with the hope that they could be made to fit the unique spaces that called for a clear glass pane, unbroken by *mutton bars*, which was Harry's term for mullions. Early-on and innocently Claudia had theorized that "mutton bars" were used by early settlers in their glassless windows to keep out any curious sheep that might be in the vicinity. These were the stories they told to their friends. Claudia never even thought about Jacob Bean if she could help it. He was not a spirit with whom she wanted to do battle.

Avery had moved out, but he did not stay away. He was back and forth, meddling in their lives, muddling their days. Privately, and on some unadmitted level, Claudia was always glad to see him, relieved to know that he was right there. He arrived often in the late afternoons with a sack of onions or a bunch of parsley to chop in the food processor, or he would have a block of cheese to shred and meat to chop because he was going to make tacos. Sometimes he would come by to pick up a book or a blanket or a pan he needed or wanted to borrow. These appearances made the quality of his absence like that of a festering sore. Claudia fretted over his presence or his absence with a kind of morbid interest and doleful satisfaction. She edged around and around the issue in her mind and picked and prodded at it from all different angles. Her state of mind was pocked like the landscape with its own frozen pools of hostility, hopefulness, passion, and anger.

Avery came in just after lunch one day, when Claudia was making soup. She was feeling a little pleased with herself for having worked up the energy to make herself so useful and busy. She hadn't heard him knock and didn't know he was in the house until he leaned around the door of the kitchen. He had taken to knocking, and so she had learned to expect it. It irritated her today when his sudden materialization took her so much by surprise that she gave out a little yelp.

"I knocked," he said, "but no one answered. What's the matter? I didn't mean to surprise you. Aren't you decent?"

She didn't say anything to him while she turned back to her soup. The fact that he had taken to knocking at his own door discomfited Claudia; it filled her with a strange, cringing irritation, and a little fear. She didn't like to contemplate this new and mysterious otherness from her that Avery had assumed.

"What do you think?" she said. "Did someone kiss you and you've been transmogrified into my dear old uncle? I wish you wouldn't be such an ass!" She loved Avery, and she knew that as much as he was charming he was also foolish. But he had something on his mind, and he wasn't a bit insulted. In fact, she turned away again when she noticed that he was filled with some sort of charitable goodwill this afternoon. She didn't watch him cross the room. His whole body, lately, was inclined toward her differently, in a puppyish, awkward apology. She couldn't bear it that he was in her kitchen; she couldn't bear to turn and see him in this new attitude toward her because it would arouse in her once again that powerful sense of defeat and utter helplessness. It would put her into that hopeless state that accompanies grief. She wanted to believe that, like all she believed about Avery, this new manner was simply one more pose.

He leaned on a counter in the kitchen, out of the way of her cooking, although he didn't come to rest, exactly. He stood there in the manner of someone who has only stopped off for a moment.

"I was talking to Maggie today at the Faculty Club," he said. "She said you hadn't done anything yet about Christmas, and you know, I was thinking about it. It's already the ninth. I've got an idea." He seemed to be pleased that she hadn't done anything about Christmas. "Why don't you let me and Janie do it? Remember how she loves it? God, remember how she's so particular about picking out the trees? It doesn't matter to her that not all the sides are going to show. They've got to be perfect, anyway, all the way around."

Claudia hated the fondness in his voice, the revolting

nostalgia. He hadn't been gone long enough to have earned this new attitude. She loathed his animation and cheerfulness. She took great care lining up sticks of celery in the Cuisinart so they would slice evenly. Avery was watching her with good-natured attention.

"What are you making? Are you making that chicken soup? The kind without the corn? And no tomatoes? You were always right about that. I mean the tomatoes. It's a much better soup without them. The broth is so good by itself."

Claudia looked at the vegetables spread out on the counter before her and was immediately discouraged about the project—carrots to peel, and onions. She wiped her damp hands on a paper towel and sat down at the table, crossing her legs and turning at an angle to Avery. She thought she might die of the fury that overtook her because he was in her kitchen and saying these simple things to her just now. She could not endure it unless she only allowed him into her peripheral vision. She only granted him a sidelong presence, a corner-of-the-eye sort of being there. She held her hair back with one hand absentmindedly and did not let her thoughts come together. She didn't try to think of anything to say to Avery.

"Why don't I wait and see if Janie wants to go with me and get the trees and the greens? We could do it this afternoon. She should be home pretty soon since this is her short day at school, and Alice doesn't want her at her lesson today. She wants to reschedule for tomorrow at four-thirty. And Janie'll be disappointed if we don't put up the decorations. The house is pretty dreary in December without them. So gray."

Avery constructed the celebrations of his life like houses of cards, with deliberation and the utmost care so they balanced all alone but were the result of his creation. He had always directed the goings-on of holidays and birthdays, and that had been fine with Claudia. Those things didn't interest her much; those occasions might have drifted by without her remembering them. However, this year, in her kitchen, unremittingly sober and with a slight aura of earnest melancholy, Avery exuded a greedy enthusiasm that was for himself alone. Claudia knew that Avery was relishing his new sobriety, and he was very pleased with his expansive benevolence toward her—she, who might fail to pull the holiday together. And most of all, Claudia thought he was pleased to find out how well intentioned he was, and she begrudged him every one of these pleasures. It irritated her even more to know that lurking beneath his self-satisfaction was the real thing—a childish and simple delight in festivities. She sat at the table for a moment and contemplated him with a cold eye.

"Okay. I think that's not a bad idea," she said. "Maggie says that she thinks that Janie's having a hard time." And she cocked her head at him to indicate that this was his fault. She tilted her chin at a self-righteous angle that suggested that he owed his daughter this much after all. "But let's make a party of it like we always have. That would probably please Janie more than anything. I'll invite anyone I can get for this evening, and we'll let everyone help with the decorating. You and Janie go get the greens and trees, and I'll get food and wine and call everyone."

She was so lonely all of a sudden, only for Avery, and he had somehow put himself beyond her, but it was with celebrations that Avery marked off the days of his life so that this was all that was left to her by way of seduction.

Avery and Jane had picked out three handsome spruces in graduated sizes. The tallest tree, which stood over ten feet, was anchored against the honey-colored central beam of the house, and the other two were cleverly placed to simulate a small grove of trees. All over the living room stood laundry baskets that Avery and Jane had filled with white pine boughs they had cut from the stumps at the Christmas tree farm. Avery was on the spiral staircase, where he could drape the top of the tall tree with string after string of tiny white lights. They were the only decoration he would allow to adorn the elegant spruces, and he was directing people here and there who were busily arranging the same sort of little white lights among the branches of the other two trees.

"You see how it'll be?" Avery asked at large. "Magic, Janie!" he called to her. "It'll be magic." He was drinking a cup of the wine punch that Claudia had made, and he was relaxed and delighted.

Vince was working with the Petries, who lived farther up the hill, on one of the other trees, and Alice Jessup and Maggie were finishing up the smallest tree. When Claudia had phoned to invite the Tunbridges, she had said to Maggie, "Janie will be so pleased. I'm sure it'll cheer her up. Don't you think so?" But Maggie had made it clear that she was dubious about the whole enterprise.

Diana and Jane were cutting greens with garden shears and arranging the shorter stems behind the pictures and along the mantel. The Fitzgeralds were there without their daughter, but they were a bit at sea, never having been a part of this frenzied activity before. Sally Fitzgerald was in the kitchen, helping Claudia make quiche, and Will took over the makeshift bar on the sideboard and kept the punch bowl full. Even Jane and Diana were drinking punch, and Jane had swallowed one of her last five capsules from the Percodan bottle she had taken from Maggie's medicine cabinet. She was quiet and dreamy but extremely amiable and friendly. She was watching the party as though she were the stable center of a turning merry-go-round.

It was a Wednesday night, and by ten o'clock people had eaten and drifted off to leave Claudia and Avery to finish the last of the decorating. Jane had gone up to her room where she slipped fully dressed under her covers to lie stretched out, gazing at the ceiling in a sort of rapturous contentment.

Claudia cleared the living room of plates and glasses and left them in the kitchen. She sat down on the couch and sipped a scotch and soda while she watched Avery go from picture to picture, improving on the arrangement of greens that Diana and Jane had made behind each one. He was not so jovial anymore, though. He was growing tired and cross.

"You could fix me another one of those, too," he said. "No soda." He had come to the final task, and he sat on the bottom step of the staircase and unwound the sixteen-foot garland of white pine while he drank his scotch.

"This isn't so easy, you know. Getting everything right. It's not as easy as you probably think. You've never done it." He was petulant and sorry for himself because of all the work he was doing. He laboriously wound the unwieldy garland in and out of the balustrades and over the banister so that it swagged magnificently up the central curve of the house. Then he carefully entwined the garland with more strands of little white lights, taking care to conceal the wires among the spiky tufts. When he picked up his glass to take a sip, he left a handprint of sap on its slick surface. He plugged the final string of lights into the plug at the top of the stairs that he had had Harry install for just this purpose. But, by now, no part of this activity afforded him any satisfaction.

"How come you don't *care* about this?" he said to Claudia. "How come you didn't do this for Janie? You never pay any attention to what people need!" He was speaking very loud to be sure Claudia would hear him at the foot of the stairs and all the way across the room.

"You haven't even found the Christmas stockings! Have you? Have you even *looked* for the stockings? Poor Janie! At least you could have found her stocking so she could hang it up!"

Claudia began to protest. She was as astounded as usual to see Avery so frantically distressed. So loud and angry. And she didn't like to be accused in this way. But before she could say so, he flung himself down the stairs in three bounds and crossed the room to stand menacingly in front of her. She was so dismayed that she raised her forearm instinctively in front of her face, because his expression was bleak with anger. He grabbed her arm and pulled her up so abruptly that she was not quite balanced, and she sagged against his hold on her.

"You didn't look for those stockings! You didn't *look* for those stockings. So let's find them. We're going to find them now!" He pulled her out from behind the coffee table that separated them and moved her along, and she staggered in front of him stocking-footed until they stood in front of the storage closet that was under the stairs. He pulled the door open and shoved her in the direction of the shelves. For a moment he dropped his hands to his sides and watched the back of her head as though he had forgotten what he was doing. He said to her again, "See if you can find them! If you really look for them!" And he moved away to get his drink.

"You could do that much! You could do that much for your own daughter!" And when he turned and saw that Claudia had put her arm against one of the closet shelves and was only standing there with her face buried in the crook of her elbow, he was back behind her in a flash. He yanked her other arm and pulled her around to face him.

"You're a bitch! A bitch! A bitch!" he said in a loud voice barely under control. "You really think this is all a waste of time, don't you? You really think it's all shit!"

"That's not true . . ." she began to protest, as she always forgot she had protested countless times before.

"Don't *say* anything!" He exploded at her, and he turned her forcibly around toward the three sparkling Christmas trees. "They're just shit, aren't they? They're nothing at all to you! You think it's nothing. You don't care, do you? How much do you care about this? You wouldn't *do* it yourself, because you don't think it matters. You wouldn't make time for any of this shit! And poor Janie! You don't care about *her* Christmas!"

He suddenly let Claudia go and wheeled around to face the three trees himself. He stood rocking slightly from one side to another, studying them for a moment. Then with one huge exertion and sweep of his arm he toppled the two smaller trees, which burst upon the floor with sparks and breaking glass. He stepped over them and began to pull at the larger tree, which was wired tightly to the central beam. For a few moments he pulled at it with both his hands, but then he subsided slowly against the tree as if he desired it. He folded his arms into it and fell against its springy branches. He lay full out against its resilient boughs, and his voice was harsh with despair.

"Oh, Christ!" he said. "I wish I didn't know you. I wish that I could *unknow* you somehow. I just wish . . . I just wish that you thought that there was one thing in the whole world that was important."

When Avery had swung around at the trees, Claudia had stepped backward up three of the steps to get out of his way, and now she stood looking down at him, so hurt by what he said that she was crying. "Please, Avery. Please. Please. Come up to bed with me. Please, Avery. Come up and sleep."

Avery lay against the tree for a fraction of a second longer, and then he pushed himself away from it and turned without saying anything more and slammed out of the front door. Claudia sat down where she was and put her head down on her knees. She stayed like that for a long time before she got up and went to bed.

Upstairs in her room Jane had not moved. She lay still stretched out straight and dry-eyed, but all the contentment and delight had sunk in upon itself with the effect of a collapsing star, a black hole. She became emptier and emptier of any sensation until finally she fell asleep.

In the morning before school, while Claudia was still asleep, Jane made lunch for herself and packed her books and got her violin, which she would need for rehearsal. She left them by the back door, and she dragged the two small trees out to the edge of the driveway to be taken off by the garbage man. She swept up the fallen evergreen needles and the broken glass bulbs, and she put the ruined light strands and bits of glass into a trash sack, which she placed outside with the discarded trees before she gathered her things together and went out the back way to her school bus stop.

6

Claudia ran steaming water from the
shower head. She was standing outside the
bathtub in her robe, leaning into the steam at the far end
of the tub and fluffing her hair, pushing it away from her
neck while the moisture collected heavily around her
head and penetrated the waves and puffs of her hair so
that they coiled a little more tightly. She left the shower
running and moved to the mirror, which she had repeat-
edly to wipe clear with one hand while she used the
other to make up her eyes. She peered closely into the
mirror through the steam to apply shadow just a shade
darker than her skin and to outline her upper lids with a
soft brown pencil.

Three days after the disastrous decorating party she
had called Alice Jessup, who had agreed to have Claudia
drop by, and the prospect of that meeting made Claudia
feel nervous and oddly intimidated. It was true that
Claudia was not often impressed; however, she was
quite easily intimidated by people who believed they
led reasonable lives. She had not taken a step so conclu-
sive in a very long time, but when the baffling idea that
Avery was not going to stay with her had settled in,
Claudia had roamed the house he had designed with an

urgent restlessness. The past two mornings she had got up early with Jane and got dressed and put on makeup and then wandered fitfully through the rooms that curved and angled in diverting and charming ways. She experimented in the house, trying out different rooms to get a reading on their atmosphere. She wandered into Avery's study with its long windows set into the wall at an odd curve, and Jane's room, in which Claudia could only stand upright at its very center because of the arc of the ceiling. She lay down on Jane's slender Scandinavian bed and gazed up through the round window directly overhead and watched the snow slowly obscure the sky as it gathered on the flat glass pane. Had Avery anticipated this effect? The white light that filtered through the snow illuminated the little room with almost the same eerie glow produced by neon. Claudia lay on the bed and thought that she was like a figure in one of the glass domes that children get in their Christmas stockings. She knew that she was as endangered right now as if she were enclosed in just that way; she was as vulnerable to any hand that might pluck up her habitat and shake it to make the snow fly. Until now she had not realized that she had assumptions about how her life would go; the things that had been certainties to her were suddenly loose in the world; now they were a part of her history.

She had thought a good deal about what Avery had said to her. In retrospect she was very often enraged with answers and thoughts that hadn't occurred to her then. But it did seem to her that thinking about what people needed might be some sort of option for her now. Perhaps he had been right when he had said that she didn't anticipate other people's needs. She was willing to consider the possibility that she was sometimes insensitive. At the very least, thinking about what other people needed was something to do. It was a little nugget of activity around which she could begin to organize herself.

All she was certain of for the time being was that she was miserably at loose ends when she was alone in the house, with only Nellie as company. Nellie was such an obsequious animal that her presence didn't have much value. Claudia was unhappy when Jane was at school, and she was making an effort to rally and cheer herself up. She had called Alice Jessup in order to make arrangements to buy a good violin for her daughter, because she was swept up in tender gratitude toward Jane, who was so loyal to her and was such a sturdy soul. She was pleased with herself for having thought of this gesture.

And she was also pleased to discover that when she got up in the morning and got dressed and went out to the bank and the grocery store and to fill her car with gas, the time went by. The day did pass in spite of the fact that Avery had always said that she would never be able to manage without him. Sometimes he had said it with a sort of melancholy fondness, and sometimes he had said that to her in such a rage that it had signified danger, and she had taken Jane with her and the two of them had driven out along the highway or around and around the town until he was asleep. But she was all right. She didn't need money, because she had a little from her parents' estate, and she didn't need courage, because she had Jane.

Nevertheless, it wasn't particularly gratifying to Claudia to be seizing these new responsibilities. Initiating this surprise hadn't done as much for her as she had hoped it would. She found that she had taken on a rather frightening burden. Surprises so often alter people's lives.

When she had finished shading and outlining her eyes and had smoothed on a pale blusher beneath her cheekbones, she went to the closet and forlornly considered all the various garments hanging on the rack or folded on the shelves. She was without vitality in the face of this single decision of what to wear. Her wardrobe let her down, and even the tweed skirt and nice gray blouse she chose didn't lessen her apprehension. In fact, she lost interest in her outfit even as she was buttoning herself into it. Before she was all finished, she had forgotten the effect she was after and had put on the boots that were nearest to her in the closet. They were very high-heeled shiny black boots that were a little bit wrong with the muted country woolen skirt.

She was shy about her meeting with Alice Jessup, because Alice knew some things about which Claudia was mystified. When she had talked with Alice over the phone about buying a good violin for Jane, Claudia had become increasingly uncomfortable while she listened to Alice talk about the three violins she had brought back from St. Louis for another interested parent to choose among. There were two fine Tyrolean instruments to be had, although Alice thought it would be wiser to buy the reconditioned Hungarian violin that wasn't so expensive. It had a one-piece back, and it had been cracked, but Alice trusted the man who had repaired it, and the violin was now in excellent condition. Alice was absolutely sure of all these facts. She cautioned Claudia against buying a French or German violin which, in all probability, would not appreciate in value. Claudia was immensely uneasy as she listened to Alice's soft voice because she was entirely at the mercy of Alice's knowledge.

"Oh, Alice," she had said very lightly over the phone, "I'll leave it to you to decide which one's best for Jane. I can't even read music!" But Alice didn't react with polite amusement; she was silent over the wire. She was often the same in person. Alice had the disconcerting habit of listening with great attention to the things people said to her and considering carefully before she replied. It unnerved Claudia. It pained her in a mild way not to be able to draw Alice out.

When Jane had first begun taking violin from Alice, Claudia had sometimes been irritated by those early, discordant notes and especially by the shifts in tempo. "Jane," she had said, "can't you sense the rhythm? Why don't you tap your foot? That would help." Alice had telephoned her after the lesson that had followed that advice.

"Mrs. Parks," she had said very politely but definitely, "violinists *never* tap their feet. If you allow a child to tap his foot in the early stages of learning any instrument, it might be easier to teach—especially the percussion instruments—but you'll have to stop him later. You have to teach that child later that what you let him do for so long is completely wrong. And you see, I don't use those techniques. The *violin* is what Jane should be concentrating on, not her foot. Her foot is the farthest thing from her brain.''

Claudia had thought that Alice had meant this last as a little joke to moderate her sternness, and she had laughed, but then, too, she had been met with silence from Alice at the other end.

Alice lived near the university close to the apartment Avery had rented. There were a large number of handsome turn-of-the-century houses that had been converted into apartments. They lined the narrow streets that crisscrossed College Avenue in odd juxtaposition to the large and unremarkable yellow-brick university buildings that ranged away row after row over the gentle roll of the campus. Claudia climbed the stairs at the back of the house to reach Alice's apartment, and when Alice opened the door, Claudia was relieved. She was comforted at first glance to see that Alice's rooms were in a state of disarray, and Alice was so slight and solemn—an earnest little candle of a person—that Claudia felt that she herself was immensely tall and loose and easy-limbed and lovely. It relaxed her for a bit.

''I've still got the three violins here,'' Alice said, ''but one of them may be taken. It isn't the instrument I had in mind for Jane anyway. Jane's ready for an intermediate instrument. I wouldn't want to see you spend more than . . . oh, between fifteen hundred and three thousand. She may want to move on to a better instrument when she's older. You shouldn't spend any more than three thousand at the most.'' Claudia had followed her along through the little entry into the living room where three violins were displayed on a table that stood against one wall and seemed to double as a desk. Stacks of papers and folders and books had been pushed out of the way to make room for the instruments.

"I'd like you to hear all three. I can give you an idea of how they sound even though I'm not very familiar with them. And really, Jane will have to be sure herself. She ought to use whichever one you take today for several months before she decides. And it will feel awful to her for the first few days. But at least it will be a surprise for her at Christmas, even if she doesn't keep it. Give her some time with it. I'm still trying to adjust to a new bow I invested in at the first of the school year."

Claudia wasn't paying close attention. She knew that she wouldn't have any idea which violin had the best sound. "It's nice of you to go to so much trouble, Alice. Jane's always working on her music these days. I think she'll be delighted."

Claudia sat down on a couch that was covered with a patchwork quilt, and Alice didn't reply. She had moved over to her music stand and was fitting an unusually light-colored violin against her shoulder, adjusting her small head until she was comfortable at the angle required by the cradle of the chin rest. She lifted her head for a moment and turned to Claudia. "You'll hear the difference with this bow, too. Jane needs a good bow, and I brought back several from St. Louis."

She settled her head once more, and Claudia felt a vicarious twinge as she watched because Alice's waist-length hair was so out of proportion to her small, oval face and slight frame that Claudia thought it must hurt for her to bend her head forward. It looked to Claudia as if Alice's heavy brown hair would pull against its own roots. But Alice began to play a familiar Handel piece with an ease that alerted Claudia all at once to reconsider where she was.

The confusion and disorder in Alice's apartment were revealed to her in that moment as the odds and ends that collect around people who are otherwise devoted. This was not disorder that sprang from malaise or lethargy or absentmindedness. The pile of mail on the end of the couch, the newspapers and books stacked here and there were not casual messiness. They were the natural dross that gathers around a person who proceeds along a chosen course as straight as an arrow. These things were scattered around because Alice was busy; her attention was concentrated on her music. Claudia was at a loss once more, uncertain about how to behave around this odd young woman who clearly had deep convictions about the things she did.

As Alice played for her, Claudia got up and went over to look at the other two glossy dark instruments, and she thought that they were so beautiful to look at that they would be a pleasure to own beyond the fact that they were good instruments.

"Avery liked the dark wood, too," Alice said, "but I really think this is a better violin for Jane. At least this is the one that I think she should try first. You have to remember that it will take her about a month to get used to it and see if it's right for her. It's a terrible mistake to select an instrument because of the way it looks. I did that myself when I bought my first violin, and I sold it before the year was over."

But what Alice had said had stopped Claudia entirely from trying to sort out the merits of the violins. "How does Avery know about it, Alice? This is supposed to be a surprise."

"Oh." Alice's features went straight and blank with alarmed solemnity in the middle of her sentence. "He was helping me bring these in from the car. I was afraid to carry them up the steps because of the ice." She looked worried now, and like a child in her fragility and unease. "He thought it was a wonderful idea. And it's a surprise for *Jane,* isn't it? I mean, I know Avery would never tell her and ruin Christmas for her." No one could ever be less guileful than this small, intense woman, Claudia thought, but she still didn't like to hear what people did or did not know about Avery.

"Oh, it is Jane's surprise," she said, "but I really meant for it to be the big surprise for everyone this

Christmas. I meant for this to be a sort of family surprise. I mean, we don't usually spend this much money . . . Well, it's a lot of money to spend.'' Claudia heard her own voice thin out into querulousness, while Alice gazed at her somberly and with what Claudia perceived to be gentle indulgence. ''Avery will be over Christmas morning to give Jane her presents. I'm sure he plans to. That was really when I wanted them both to know about this. To see the violin for the first time. But it's fine, Alice. It'll be fine.'' She could hardly stand to hear herself speak; her voice was still quavery and filled with a defensive tone that she couldn't control.

At last she had gone away as quickly as she could, clasping the pale violin in its case like an infant as she descended the precarious wooden staircase without giving the other two instruments another thought, she was so glad to leave. She didn't ask Alice how long Avery had known about the surprise because she didn't want to know how long he had *not* felt impelled to put in his own two cents' worth about this whole idea. She knew that it was the sort of surprise and situation that Avery loved and could scarcely ever be kept out of.

When Jane was at home, she spent most of the hours practicing with a kind of intensity that even Claudia, who knew so little about it, could hear in the music she made. The notes were drawn-out with a new definition. And she was glad when Jane was in the house. Knowing that Jane was so diligently present upstairs invigorated Claudia and gave a shape to the long domestic days. It helped pull her out of her languor, and she straightened the rooms and vacuumed. One day she and Jane tried a recipe on the back of a Bisquick box for ''Impossible Tuna Pie.'' Another day Claudia found the waffle iron at the back of the storage closet and took it out to make waffles for dinner, but there was no syrup in the house, and they weren't very good with butter and jam.

Most of the time Jane was practicing, Claudia was lingering in the vicinity. She stood in Jane's doorway or came into her room or sat on her bed. She began to think that the garishly orange-stained rented violin had a thin, whiny sound compared to the full tones of the Hungarian violin that Alice had played for her. She watched Jane work and work at a single phrase of music and could scarcely keep her mind off that other violin in its buttery-colored worn leather case that she had hidden away in her closet. She became more and more pleased with herself for thinking of making this gift to Jane, and she became increasingly anxious to see the pleasure it would be to her daughter to discover the surprise.

Jane had stopped going to school altogether on the fourteenth, which was the Monday following that Christmas decorating party. As soon as she had stepped aboard the school bus the day immediately after the night of the party and her friends greeted her, she had begun to feel peculiar. Her muscles became heavy and inert, and mild cramps and nausea set in. And, also, on that Thursday and then again on Friday Jane found that sometimes she had nothing to say. Friday, in language arts, when Mrs. Hollis had asked her a question, she had not been able to answer. She had not intended to refuse to answer, but her face had suddenly gone numb and tingly. When she had begun to speak, her lips would not work; she could only mumble. It was a strange sound she made, and her classmates were kind. They had laughed tentatively, thinking that she meant to make a joke, that she was mocking someone, but Mrs. Hollis had looked at her carefully and gone on to ask the same question of another student. She spoke to Jane after class, as the other students were leaving, but Jane still had not been able to reply. She stood next to Mrs. Hollis completely in the power of that peculiar paralysis. Finally Mrs. Hollis had said to Jane not to worry about anything. "I know it must be hard for you with your parents separated. I'm sure it will all work out."

But what Jane was finding so wearisome was the effort of clarifying the images that drifted in and out of her own memory. Every night she lay in bed remembering how her father had planned the round window over her bed just for her, and with irrepressible enthusiasm, because he and she shared an interest in astronomy.

These December nights she could lie in bed and look straight up into the winter sky and name the constellations within her view. It would come into her mind over and over again how pleased her father had been, the year before last, on the day his new Celestron telescope had arrived. He had unpacked it in the living room and examined each piece with a deep delight that was not like his usual restless excitement; his enjoyment had been almost reverential. "Claudia, I don't see why we don't make an occasion out of this," he had said. "Listen, I'll take the barbecue pit down the hill, and we can cook out after I set up the telescope. It won't be too cold with the charcoal going." He had called this out to Claudia, who was somewhere else in the house, but she wasn't much interested in any of it. In fact, it was Jane who had sat on in the living room, watching her father, although Claudia did pass through. She had come into the room to say this or that to Avery, although she was strangely jumpy and irritated, and she never stayed in the room long enough to inspect the new telescope.

When Jane and her father had gathered everything together and were ready to set out for the meadow, Claudia had followed them as far as the back door. "Avery, do you really think it's such a good idea to do this now? Janie has school in the morning." And she had that expression on her face that indicated faint irritation, faint disdain.

But when Jane and Avery had found the best place in the lower part of the open meadow, Avery had been engrossed in the process of aligning the tripod and telescope exactly right, so that they headed precisely due north. Whenever Jane pictured him there, in the long grass, so angular and intense and lonely-looking, she was filled with puzzling remorse, as if there had been something she had not done for him. She always tried to replace that picture with any other picture at all, but she never could, and she grieved for her tall, handsome, lanky father working so hopefully with his telescope.

He had adjusted the scope so Jane could look through it. He helped her find the Orion Nebula, which Jane thought was such a beautiful, hazy shape as opposed to the sharp definition of the stars. She found the giant stars, Betelgeuse and Rigel, and identified them by herself, which had pleased her father as much as she thought she had ever pleased him. While she was still following his directions and gazing at the rings of Saturn, Claudia had drifted down the hill, following the path, and waded through the tall grass toward them, carrying a tray of drinks and a plate of tomato sandwiches. It was cold, and she had put on her long black woolen cape with the hood drawn up so her pale face cut through the dark like some ghostly, celestial phenomenon, itself, in the surrounding night.

What Jane could not forget as she lay in bed at night was the odd twist of regret that had shaped her father's mouth just for one moment, as though he were a child caught out in something shameful, when he first saw Claudia come toward him from the house. But the three of them had sat down to eat the sandwiches, and finally her mother had urged them inside. "It's past nine, Janie, and you can play with this again tomorrow night." She had got to her feet and waved away Avery's suggestion that she look through the telescope, too. "It's really awfully cold out here. It's much colder than I thought."

These were the things Jane thought about at night, but in the morning she had to train all her senses on her peers: who to sit with at lunch, what couples had broken up, and who was now going together. It was work; it was hard work, and Jane found, all at once, that she had simply run dry of energy.

That Thursday and Friday at school, if her friends spoke to her, she turned away because she could not make her mouth work, and oddly enough, this made her angry at them. She began to hold them in contempt. She sat in class feeling like some foreign creature, completely dissimilar to the students around her. She quietly began to regard those other children and thought that they were grotesque. In social studies on Friday she found herself studying the hand of the student who sat in front of her, which was splayed out over his desk, and she could not make sense of it. She could not name it, but she gazed on in fascination at the pale, cylindrical, sausage-shaped digits attached to the fleshy, hairless palm. She became so dizzy as she stared ahead of her that she put her head down on her desk since she thought that otherwise she would fall out of her chair. Mr. Alberti had noticed that she seemed ill, and he excused her from the room.

So Jane stopped going to school, although she continued to get up in the morning and get dressed and go down to the kitchen to have breakfast before returning to her room to read for a while. Her mother had only been curious that first morning, and Jane simply said she didn't feel good. But even that first Monday Claudia was only vaguely inquisitive; after that she seemed to accept Jane's presence as a given.

Jane spent a great deal of the time working on her music, on the Mozart Miss Jessup had just given her and on the two Bach pieces for the Christmas concert. She knew she was making unusual progress, and she knew that Miss Jessup would be very surprised when she played her solo at the concert because she was also skipping her music lessons. She called her father, who always took her to music, and told him she was sick. When he stopped by the house for one thing or another, Jane took care to stay in her room and stay in bed. Lately she had developed a great reluctance to be away from her mother; she didn't want to leave the house if Claudia was in it. She knew that Claudia wouldn't think of the lessons unless she was reminded of them.

The nights were a trouble to Jane, but these were lovely, lovely days, these days at home. Her mother was her only companion, and she was the most enchanting person Jane could imagine. Not competent, like Maggie, but quick and magical and young. Jane could bask in her mother's risky enthusiasms that previously she had only observed; she hadn't dared take part. Now that Avery wasn't home it was mostly a pleasure to Jane that her mother lacked caution, and the two of them talked about all sorts of things: the adventures of her mother's life; the foibles of her mother's friends.

One afternoon when Jane was practicing, Claudia wandered into her room and sat cross-legged on the bed with her head cushioned against the wall by the pillow of her frothy hair. Claudia listened idly and was looking up out of the window in the ceiling when all at once some private thought amused her and she came away from the wall, leaning toward Jane with her elbows on her knees.

"What?" asked Jane, continuing to hold the violin beneath her chin but dropping her bow hand.

Her mother's face was pleased and relaxed in a lazy smile. "I was thinking about the Tunbridges. Maggie called, you know. She's very anxious that you come to Diana's birthday party on the nineteenth. She says even if you don't feel great, she thinks it would be good for you." The two of them looked at each other; in the past few days they had become conspirators without ever admitting it or carefully thinking it out. "You're over there a lot," Claudia went on. "Don't you think that Maggie is a strange person? I mean, for all her good qualities . . . sometimes she's so rigid, I think. Of course, that's why she and Celeste are at loggerheads all the time." Her voice dwindled off with this thought, and Jane sat absolutely still in case her mother might notice her and not continue. Jane could scarcely believe that in Maggie's life there had ever been a bit of trouble. Jane knew that Maggie would not allow it. And Claudia did go on, gently talking and plucking at the bright printed flowers on the Marimekko spread with her fingers.

"Maggie's so definite about everything. It's kind of endearing. Well, I always think it's touching. It drives your father crazy, of course." And whether she knew it or not, she glanced over at Jane with the exact expression that came over Avery's face when he was exasperated. Then, just as quickly, her face became her own again, pleasantly reminiscent. "Do you know what I mean? Things are *this* way"—and she moved one hand in a chopping motion and held it stiffly suspended—"or they are *that* way." She made the same motion with her other hand, and she sat like that for a second to illustrate Maggie's nature before she turned her hands palms up and let them fall to her sides, smiling at Jane blandly as though the two of them had agreed upon something. But then she tilted her chin down and glanced at Jane as if she were doubtful and were having second thoughts. She was musing as she spoke. "Maggie said something so odd to me once after she had been out to Seattle to see her mother when her mother was dying. It was a horrible situation, of course. Her mother had cancer, and she had been misdiagnosed at first. Oh, well, it was sad and horrible . . . but Maggie was over here one afternoon, and she was just incensed." Claudia paused to think if that was right. "No, she was indignant! She said, 'You'd think that if they can make a missile that can hit a target halfway around the world, they could cure this disease!' " Claudia lifted her full face to Jane with her eyebrows stretched into an arc of amused wonder. "That's how she sees things," she said with a shade of amazement in her voice. "She believes everything is *related* somehow. And she really does believe that anything can be solved if people will *apply* themselves."

Claudia shook her head just a fraction to indicate her resignation in the face of other people's peculiar notions. Jane was watching her carefully, though. She had put her violin down so she could study her mother, because she herself would have thought along the same lines that Maggie did. When she saw her mother's remarkable, mobile face indicate the folly of that restricted point of view, Jane's own mind flew wide-open to all sorts of possibilities, and she fell in love, entirely, with her own mother. She had been caught between her two parents for such a long time that this retarded sensation was all the stronger for coming over her so late in her life. She didn't even have a frame of reference for this fit of joy that had overtaken her; she just sat in the room, watching her mother and feeling weightless and without any responsibility. She was in the throes of devotion, and she sat in the sunlight, elated.

"But that's not the thing you were thinking of that made you laugh, was it?" she asked her mother, who seemed surprised and took a moment to backtrack in her thoughts.

"Oh, no. No." And she laughed again. "Well, after Celeste and Mark were born, you know, Maggie went back to teaching, and she did a lot more writing. Reviewing and articles. Anyway, they really didn't want any more children, and, my God! Maggie checked out every possible birth control device." She looked at Jane and smiled. "You know how absolutely thorough Maggie is. At every dinner party we would end up talking about the pill versus IUDs. What she *wanted* was for Vince to get a vasectomy, but then she would go on and on about how Vince was sure that if he had a vasectomy, he would get fat. Poor Vince. Vince would look so detached when she launched into all this that your father said he was afraid that some night Vince would come loose from his moorings and just float away out the window. You know, though"—and her face closed down for a moment in a hooded expression of contemplation—"Maggie just doesn't have that sort of radar . . . it's not a question of bad taste, really. I mean, no one was offended. Mostly we were just bored with the whole subject. But Maggie's so odd sometimes. Don't you think it has something to do with a lack of charm?" She glanced at Jane to confirm that notion. She wanted to be sure that Jane shared that idea, and she subsided against the wall again to think about it herself.

"Is that the story?" Jane asked because she didn't

understand it. The point wasn't clear to her, but she was delighted to be entrusted with information that no one but her mother would ever have given her.

"Oh, no," Claudia said, and gathered herself back into the moment. "Maggie was horrified when she got pregnant! She wouldn't even believe it for the first four months. She went to two doctors, in fact. She really didn't want that baby, and she was *outraged* when it finally sank in. She was so mad that she and Vince filed suit against the company that made the condoms!" And Claudia laughed with no malice at all, only a kind of helpless delight. "After all that research they were using condoms! And they sued for the amount they calculated it would take to raise the child and educate it. Oh, God . . . we spent hours . . . your father, well, you can see that it's exactly the sort of thing he can't possibly leave alone. Maggie and Vince figured in the cost of the university. Oh, you know, your father just can't ever resist baiting Maggie. Avery threw himself into it totally. He rushed around phoning all over the place. 'Why not Harvard?' he would say. 'Have you thought about Reed or Oberlin?' " This still surprised Claudia and amused her whenever she thought of it, and she was almost giggling. "Do you know that when they were first married, Maggie sued a frozen food company because she'd found a fly in one of her TV dinners?" Claudia laughed indulgently again, although she had never laughed when faced with Maggie's fury on these matters. It astounded Claudia that anyone as intelligent as Maggie would expect perfection in the world.

Jane looked on at her mother, pleased but dumfounded. She was trying to grasp whatever it was her mother meant to signify by all this. "Did they win?" Jane asked.

Claudia looked up at her and waved her hand to dismiss the whole topic. "Oh, they got a case of frozen dinners, or something. I'm not sure what finally happened."

"No, I mean about Diana. Did they get money for Diana?"

Claudia was quite still and silent for a moment. Jane could see that her mother was wary and somehow taken aback. "Well, it wasn't really *Diana*. I mean, it was an abstract thing, then. Maggie didn't want another *child*! But Vince and Maggie dote on Diana. They just panicked at the time. They love Diana."

Jane didn't say anything at all. She would have to think this over in her own time. It was an unexpected weak spot in her best friend's enviable life.

In the evenings Jane and her mother cooked exotic meals together as an adventure, and Claudia came in to watch *Magnum* and *Matt Houston* and Jane's favorite, *Remington Steele*, on TV and then persuaded Jane to stay up and watch the reruns of *Hawaii Five-O*, which, she argued, was much more professionally produced than any of her daughter's favorites.

"And, Jane, you can tell when you're watching that show that Jack Lord really does believe that he's the head of a police force! Oh, it's great! I hope they show the one where he's running around in a rain forest wearing a sort of safari outfit and a planter's hat. He can do it. I mean, he can carry it off with a straight face. I bet his camera crew hated him. Well, just wait! Wait till you see what I mean!"

They sat up late at night in front of the color set, and Claudia played a game that was much more entertaining to Jane than watching the show. More often than not, Claudia could anticipate the lines and say them with the characters on *Hawaii Five-O*. Jane and her mother would sit on the couch with their feet tucked up under them and a bowl of popcorn between them, and Claudia would follow the show and stiffen her torso and cock her head precisely at the moment Jack Lord did the same thing on the screen. She would say with him, "Okay, what've we got, Chin?" A few moments later she would swivel straight-backed toward Jane and synchronize her lines with the TV once more. "Patch me through to the governor's office, Danno!" And her face would take on the same ludicrous expression of absolute conviction with which Jack Lord played Steve McGarrett. At the end of the show she would watch very carefully and turn her head in perfect imitation of the hero's resigned disdain. "Book 'em, Danno!" she would say as justice inevitably prevailed.

Claudia was a quick study. She could walk with a swivel, like C.J. on *Matt Houston,* or feign Sue Ellen's bewilderment on *Dallas.* "Oh, J.R., I'm so confused!" Claudia could become anyone she wanted to, and she utterly charmed her daughter as they sat together watching television in the empty house.

For the moment her mother had collected all the diverse and free-floating aspects of her personality into one bright stream of energy, and it flowed around Jane and assured and cosseted her. It was the most gratifying thing in the world to be the object toward which her mother directed every element of her piqued and newly delighted regard. Jane thought that she and her mother were having a wonderful time.

And these days, too, her violin finally did begin to feel like an extension of herself, as Miss Jessup had predicted it would. Jane did not have to collect words and speak them; she only had to balance the bow on a slight angle and with delicacy, and the music came as it should. The sound she made satisfied her, and she learned all the tricks of this particular instrument. She avoided the friction of the poorly glued fingerboard, she used a little more pressure from her bow than she ever had before, and she coaxed forth a very pleasing sound from the mass-produced and peculiarly boxy instrument. The use of vibrato was all at once a perfectly natural thing; it came to her with a miraculous and easy control. She was beginning to know that she had made more than progress. She realized that something extraordinary was happening to her to allow her to play this music.

Jane stayed at home, and most of the time she was serene and pleased with the smooth days. She didn't spend any time with her friends until the afternoon she

had to go to Diana's birthday party. She had no choice
but to go because Maggie would not accept her excuses.
Diana had invited Jane and three other girls over to
spend the night, and Jane was comfortable among them
for a while and even smugly proprietary as she always
was in the Tunbridges' house. In the late afternoon
Maggie asked them to help her ice the cookies she
always used to decorate the huge tree in the kitchen.

"Now listen," Maggie said, coming a little way into
Diana's room, where the girls had stacked their sleeping
bags and were lounging and gossiping a bit disconsolately
and with the edges of ill temper beginning to come
through. They were ranged around the room, leaning
against the furniture or sitting on the bed. "Listen, I'm
afraid you girls are going to have to help me. I'm
frantic. I've got to get this tree done before tomorrow night. I'm
sorry to interrupt you, but I just can't get everything
finished myself." Maggie was brisk and confident. She
waited for a moment to see that all five girls were
gathering themselves together to get to their feet, and
then she turned away and went back to the kitchen. She
knew they would follow her. It was at that very moment
that a final, hard wedge of doubt began to come between
what Jane thought and what Jane did. It was not Maggie
with whom Jane was suddenly disenchanted; it was the
state of childhood itself, the terrible dependency of it,
the awful hypocrisy one suffered because of it.

Jane realized, after spending such a sweet time with
her own mother, that all this was condescension on
Maggie's part. Maggie pretended to these girls that they
had a choice and were doing her a favor. But when Jane
came into the large, crowded kitchen, she saw how
carefully Maggie had planned this activity. There were
sheets and sheets of cookies laid out on the counters,
and on the table were separate bowls of colored icing at
each place, and sprinkles and cinnamon hearts were
ranged around the table within everyone's reach. Jane
knew, anyway, that Maggie had never needed them for
this task. Maggie was only pretending this urgency to

avoid any scorn that might attach itself to this diversion, which had always been a ritual part of Diana's birthday, since it was in December. In case any of the girls might think they were too old for this, now, Maggie had fore-stalled their complaints, and this cookie decorating would keep them busy until dinner.

"I'm sorry, girls. I'm sorry," Maggie said as she moved among them, distributing butter knives with which they could ice the cookies, "but I've got to get this done. Mark will be here later to put the lights on the tree, so you don't have to hang these till after dinner. You can go on and put the hobby wire through them, though. I've cut it in lengths for you. I've got two dishes to finish. The broccoli and a dessert. I haven't even de-cided what I'm going to serve for dessert, and I've got twenty-three people coming, so I'm counting on you girls and Mark to get all this finished."

Mark's imminent arrival made an impression on Di-ana's friends because he was good-looking and intrigu-ingly older than they were. They gathered around the table and sat in their chairs with an air of detachment. Even their various postures implied their disassociation from the whole thing, as if they weren't connected with what they were doing. All but Jane, who was disoriented by this easy trick Maggie had played on them. When she took her place, she jostled Linda Barber's elbow so that Linda's knife skewed across the cookie she was working on and spread red frosting over the sleeve of her shet-land sweater. But Jane just looked at her. She didn't even think to apologize.

"God, Jane! Be careful! Leave me a little room, okay?" And Diana and Stephanie and Linda and Heather con-tinued the conversation they had begun upstairs. Jane sat there with a cookie in her hand and felt thoroughly removed from herself and these four friends.

"I've got a terrible headache," Linda said. "I'm doing the Scarsdale, and I think I've got low blood sugar."

Diana and Heather both told Linda that she didn't need to diet.

"Just three pounds. I'm not anorexic! Don't get excited."

"I think your headache is completely psychosomatic," Jane said loudly and grudgingly, surprising herself. "It's just neurotic!" She had no idea why she was so angry at Linda. "Your headache's all in your imagination." Jane was there in her chair saying that, and at the same time she was watching the whole world from another angle, and she saw Linda and Stephanie exchange a look. She saw Diana bend over her work to avoid everybody's eyes, and she saw Maggie stiffen and turn and approach the table. Jane knew as well as anyone that it didn't matter whether what she said was true or not. It was not the kind of thing these girls said to each other. At the very least it was unkind to Linda, who always lacked the attention she wanted, and it was rude, in any case. Jane knew also just then that she had somehow got so far past her friends' experience that they could never be of any help or comfort to her again. She didn't think there was anything about herself that she could ever explain to them.

"Oh, Jane . . ." Maggie said. "Diana, why don't you . . . No, you have icing all over your hands. Jane, would you run upstairs and get some aspirin for Linda? It's in the medicine cabinet in my bathroom."

Jane moved off through the house, carrying with her a sensation so deep and cold that she didn't experience it as much as she was possessed by it. She moved by rote; she didn't think, but when she looked through the cabinet for the aspirin, she also pocketed Maggie's newly refilled prescription for Percodan. She did this without consideration, also. She didn't even bother to worry about if anyone would notice that it was gone or whether she would be suspected of taking it.

Jane stayed to spend the night, but early the next morning she decided to leave before breakfast. From her new and expanded point of view she could see that her departure was a relief to everyone. And now that her mother had come out of some sort of haze of her own,

Jane was at least at ease in her company. Claudia never treated her daughter with condescension; she didn't treat Jane at all as if she were a child, and so Jane came back into herself a little and for the most part was free of that horrifying, omnipotent perspective. Even when Jane was in her own room and Claudia was somewhere else in the house, Jane was not overtaken by that alarming separation from her own actions. She played her music and she was at home.

In the mornings, when the sun melted the frost off of the little porthole over her bed and the straight beam of swirling light fell across her room, she was sure it boded well and was significant. She had tucked the little vial of Percodan tablets into her bottom drawer, but she didn't take one very often because she was in no real need of the expansive oblivion it brought on. She began edging herself into sleep each night by thinking of the triumph she would have when she played in the school concert. Maggie would be there, and Mark, and her father, and of course, Miss Jessup would be conducting. Day by day her anticipation of this event grew into a conviction of what lay ahead of her, and as long as she was involved with her music, she was in a state of satisfaction.

7

Claudia would not acknowledge to her-
self that she was waiting, but in fact, if there
had not been some sort of expectancy at the core of her,
if she had believed that her life had come to the point at
which it settled, it would have been intolerable to her
sensibilities. Suddenly, instead of having to fight off
lethargy, she was having trouble sleeping. It wasn't that
her dreams were disturbing—her unconscious seemed to
have reached a state of exhaustion beyond dreams—but
in sleep she was washed through with a sense of such
awful isolation that in order to bear coming back to
wakefulness, she forced herself through the process of
placing herself in the world. She would envision the
house, the town, the state, the country. Then at least
she would be located, but so lonely that the sensation of
it truly weighed upon her as she lay helpless in her bed,
heavy in every part of herself.

She was beyond dreams, but she was possessed in her
sleep by memory, and she awoke without animation.
She awoke in a state of grief, as if a death had happened. So she strolled through the nights, smoking and
drinking wine. She circuited the house and sorted through
the drawers. She cleaned the refrigerator. Nevertheless,

she couldn't entirely escape sleep. She awoke one morning on the couch in the living room, where she had only sat down in the early hours before it was light. She woke up struggling away from an image of herself and Annie Dobbs fifteen years ago sunbathing on her porch roof in Natchez and looking down through the crepe myrtle and across the drive where Avery was mowing the yard in front of his house.

He was concentrated and methodical, pushing the mower down one long side and then across the front at a right angle, then up and down again while the fine, moist grass flew up and clung to his long calves. When Claudia had seen his face, dispassionately plotting the elaborate checkerboard he was making with the pattern of his mowing, she had felt a terrible, sad lurch of longing even then, at seventeen. She would have liked to capture his attention and lie down with him and lick the little flecks of green from his bare chest and back and down the long muscles of his legs. She had been so filled with yearning that it must have been quivering toward him in the air. She knew in remembering that it must have been a tangible thing, piercing the hot, sunny day. And yet he had gone on tracing the intricate crosshatching upon the ground with indifference, ambitious and determined even in that project. She awoke filled with the sensation of the lush heat of that summer day, and to find herself stiff and cramped in her living room in the dead winter of the Midwest was threatening to her hopefulness. Memories are much worse than any dream. Memory was the worst thing for Claudia.

She tried to walk through her need to sleep. She tried to keep busy. She made extensive shopping lists and spent one day making chicken Kiev, and she and Jane set the table with the Dansk candlesticks and had a celebration. Jane was earnest and quiet and accommodating, and Claudia had a great need for her company. When they had been sitting across the dining room table from each other eating the buttery little rolls of chicken, Claudia had looked at Jane's straight glance directed her way and been immensely reassured. She was filled with the deepest affection for her daughter. It seemed to her that the generosity of that embrace Jane had once extended to her reverberated between them. Jane was safe as houses; she was what Claudia counted on most.

Now and then in the warm little house, when Claudia was taken with a fit of organization, she would call to Jane to bring a trash sack, and she would light a cigarette and begin to sort out another closet or some odd drawer. If the ashes from the cigarette drifted onto the floor, she would tell Jane not to worry; she would vacuum later. If she were standing on a rug, she would simply grind the ash in with her heel.

"It keeps the moths out," she would say.

It was a great help to her to have Janie with her. At times Claudia's nerves were drawn so taut that she was rendered listless, and she would stop right in the middle of reordering the minutiae that had accumulated in some kitchen drawer. She would stop and consider whatever she had come upon—packing tape, freezer labels—and she would wander off with it, vaguely wondering when she had ever had such optimism that she had planned to date and label the food she put in her freezer. But the next time she looked at the same drawer she would find that Jane had finished the job and left everything aligned and tidy. She thought her daughter was a remarkable person to be so industrious in her every endeavor. A dozen times a day Claudia would pass through the room where Jane was practicing or reading or luxuriously watching soap operas, and she would feel a little better each time. She could even sleep for an hour or two when Jane was up and about and Claudia could hear her moving around somewhere in the house.

And to Jane those days before Christmas, those cozy days at home, were the longest days of lazy serenity she had ever known. She was right in the house assured that her mother was safe, that things weren't changing, and that she had no order imposed on her time. All the hours were there for her to shape, and to Jane that was an unusually pleasant condition in the world.

But Maggie could not leave Claudia alone about Jane's staying home from school. When the phone rang and it was Maggie, Claudia would hold it to her ear and listen with reluctance. She could not understand why Maggie continued to badger them. Why did it matter to her in what ways the two of them found a small bit of comfort, a little bit of satisfaction in their dome in the icy meadow?

"Diana is so worried about her, Claudia. Especially since her birthday party. And all her friends are asking about her, too. Do you think this is really a good thing to let her do?"

Of course, Claudia couldn't answer her on the phone since Jane was in the vicinity; besides, it seemed to her a very strange question. Maggie ought to know them well enough to see that it wasn't a question of letting Jane do one thing or another. It went through Claudia's thoughts occasionally that Maggie was intrusive in their lives in the same way the sluggish, freakishly hatched winter flies were distressing as they lived their short lives trapped between the storm and windowpanes, clicking and whirring against the glass.

Finally she agreed to meet Maggie for lunch and talk with her because she knew that otherwise Maggie might come to the house and worry Jane herself. She had given in when Maggie had said, "Look, meet me for lunch and we'll talk it over. I can take it as a business lunch. It comes off my taxes, you know." And Claudia had agreed, but she had wondered, also, if all those little problem-solving luncheons with Vince had been tax-deductible, too.

She went out into the cold and snow to meet Maggie at Belden's, and just the effort of getting there was unpleasantly adventurous. She and Jane, for several days, had made only the most selective forays into the world. They stayed out of the way of people; they had gone to a grocery store across town where they wouldn't meet anyone they knew who might ask them how they were, and they agreed to this obliquely.

"Let's go to the Safeway downtown," Claudia said; "maybe the produce is better." And Jane would slouch down in her corner of the front seat with only the back of her head visible through the window.

When Claudia walked into Belden's in the middle of the noon crowd, she felt horribly exposed, as if all the little nooks and crannies of her sorrowing were illuminated and revealed. To be abroad in the world while harboring these little secrets of loss was oddly shameful.

Claudia was so taken aback, in fact, as she stood at the entrance behind two other waiting couples, that she refused to give up her coat to the attendant; she simply clasped it around her and shook her head. And the attendant was surprised by her face. He glanced back at her as she moved away. There is a certain masked, waxy, impermeable expression that he was accustomed to seeing on the faces of the crowd that moved in and out of the restaurant when he was on duty. It is a protective expression, a bit arch, carefully nonanticipatory. That was not at all how Claudia looked; her face was so rigid with dread that she was alarming to see. But when she caught sight of Maggie already seated across the restaurant, so bright in a red sweater, so amiable and good-intentioned with her long frame canted sideways in the little chair and everything about her bespeaking kindness, Claudia relented. She smiled, and as she walked across the room, she relaxed and was even pleased at the prospect of the meal ahead.

They were seated in the modish restaurant at a fragile and tiny table for two under the latticed ceiling hung with a jungle of plants in large clay pots. And throughout the room were partitions made up of small forests of ficus trees in thick leaf and tall, feathery palms. Claudia knew that the plants were supposed to counteract the bleak landscape rolling away beyond the huge windows, but so much greenery in the wrong season made her uncomfortable. Belden's was relatively new and very popular with a clientele Claudia never saw anywhere else. The rooms were filled with well-dressed men and women in their late twenties and early thirties who seemed to exist only at lunch. Claudia always wondered where these people came from. She never saw them around campus or at PTA meetings or at Kroger's. She sat there with Maggie while they waited for their Bloody Marys and decided that these people came straight down the interstate from somewhere and then were right back on the highway after lunch in a ritual and bright migration of all the snappy little cars that filled the parking lot.

After greeting Maggie, though, Claudia was not talkative. She was pleased to be there, and she settled her coat on the back of her chair and around herself like a little nest, but there wasn't anything she wanted to say to anyone, really.

Maggie seemed unusually placid. Most of the time she was filled with conviction and enthusiasm about one thing or another, but when she leaned toward Claudia, her voice was soothing. She lightly touched Claudia's arm, but then she drew her hand back as if Claudia might easily bruise. "You look so good. Are you all right? How are you?"

Claudia looked back at her a moment; she watched as Maggie leaned inclusively toward her. There was a note in Maggie's voice that suggested that Claudia was even more damaged than Claudia might know herself.

"I'm fine, Maggie." But she felt slightly apologetic when she said so, because she had the clear impression that it was not what Maggie wanted to hear, and of course, Maggie knew it wasn't true.

"No, I mean it, Claudia. I know how hard it is. And you do just the opposite thing than I do when you're upset. I turn into a stick. Just a string bean. But as a matter of fact, I like your face fuller like that. Not so sharp. I turn into a stalk when anything bothers me, but you look wonderful. Really voluptuous. Vince always says you're like a ripe peach, anyway."

Claudia looked beyond Maggie out the window. Her

eyes stung slightly with fatigue. She thought of her own disgusting habits, pacing the house in the middle of the night with a glass of wine in one hand and eating, eating as fast as she could. A peanut butter sandwich, an old and crusty piece of Brie, a leftover roll of chicken Kiev, cold, with the herbed butter congealed at the center. She felt nasty now, reminded of it. She felt sullied.

"Well, Maggie, sensual pleasures are my best thing! Ripe peaches are just the ticket. Vince has the right idea." She surprised herself with her unquavering snappishness; it was so rare that she bothered to be cross at anyone she didn't care about inordinately. She surprised Maggie, too, who looked abashed and didn't say anything for a moment. She fluttered her hand and shook her head to suggest that Claudia had taken this all wrong.

"Listen, Claudia, I've really been awfully worried about you and about Jane. Avery's worried, too, you know. He didn't have any idea that Jane was staying away from school. He thought she was only missing her music lessons. I talked to him, and he said he was going to call you. You know how he feels about me, though. He'll go to any lengths to avoid advice from me, and I'm not sure he sees what a problem Jane's having." She smiled across at Claudia, acknowledging disarmingly that she *was* intruding, that she even sympathized with Avery's reluctance to listen to her. But there was also a look of conspiracy in her gently self-deprecatory expression, as though she and Claudia were in this together in opposition to Avery. "I'm not going to betray Jane to him," she went on, "but what does he think you ought to do about her? Is there anything he can do to help?"

Maggie's whole person indicated genuine concern, and Claudia could hardly stand it. She had not talked to Avery about Jane at all. She looked around the restaurant at the stained glass windows in the bar and the old oak atmosphere there that changed into a gardenlike setting upstairs where they were eating. Claudia wondered if someone had thought this out, had perhaps done a market survey and concluded that exactly what was needed in Lunsbury, Missouri, was a restaurant that combined an English pub and a gazebo. Avery hated this restaurant, but Claudia sat back and regarded it with interest. And people turned to look at her, too. Even in her plain brown wool dress that was now a little snug through the bust and hips she was striking with her huge, hooded eyes and the corners of her mouth drawn down tight. Maggie reached over again and touched Claudia's arm to elicit her response, to catch her attention.

"I understand what she's doing," Maggie said, "but I'm really worried about her. She doesn't want to admit that Avery's gone for good this time. That he's moved out. That's perfectly natural. It really wouldn't even mean a thing to her to explain that he's staying sober and working on his book. He's her father. And I think it's hard for a girl especially. If she faces her friends at school, she'll have to deal with it. But you know, she'll have to deal with it eventually, and it isn't ever going to get easier. Sometimes I think that those children are so sophisticated that they already take comfort in each other's disasters." Maggie was trying to keep her intention light; Claudia saw that, but she was astounded that Maggie would sit there and say these things to her. She just stared at Maggie, and Maggie tried again. "Well, it's classic denial, I guess. But it's gone on over a week. I'm worried about her."

By this time the waiter had brought them their drinks, and Maggie stopped talking to consider the menu. Claudia was watching her with excruciating attention. The flat winter light was filtered over their table through the fronds of a large palm, and shadows shifted slightly over all the surfaces so that Claudia couldn't fix Maggie's face; she couldn't decide if it was because of the shadows or if Maggie's expression really was so elusive. But she did see a tiny muscle twitch beneath Maggie's eye as Maggie turned a concern equal to that she professed for Jane upon the decision of what to have for lunch. And Claudia abhorred every single thing about her all at once. Suddenly Maggie was enlarged in Claudia's perception, and monstrous. Every small line and crevice of Maggie's freckled skin, the white blond hair on her forearms, the pale lashes and eyebrows—these things disgusted Claudia, and when Maggie looked up, she was met with an expression of unquestionable loathing. It was so forceful a look that Maggie instinctively leaned back in her chair, and after a moment her whole manner changed. The sweetness of her sympathy and concern left her, and she was matter-of-fact.

"You know," she said, "I didn't know anything about how to be . . . kind. I didn't really know about empathy or compassion until Celeste was born. I was only ambitious. I don't mean I thought it through like that. I didn't even have enough information about myself to think it through. But what I mean is . . . Well, don't you think that the only way to get out of absolute self-absorption is by having children? It's such an incredible connection. God! I became completely absorbed in Celeste! You *become* your child. Well, I mean, for a while there your two egos are the same! And then it gets harder. Then you have to separate yourself from your children. You can't define yourself by your children's reaction to you. Don't you think that's true? I mean, don't you think that's the hardest thing to learn?"

Maggie put this question so tentatively, and with a slightly embarrassed laugh, that it seemed entirely reflective. And Claudia didn't have an opinion because she wasn't sure she grasped exactly what it was Maggie was getting at, but she was appeased a bit by Maggie's concession to their mutual humanity.

"Listen, Maggie, Jane's just sad," Claudia said. "She's as sad as I am." She hated to admit her own sorrow to Maggie, but she had to throw up some barrier to protect Jane from Maggie's ferocious scrutiny. "When Avery and I get this settled, she'll be fine. It's not as though she's missing anything academically. Jane can judge that for herself. My God, Maggie! You know Jane! She's not childish. She's just sad and tired, and so am I."

Maggie sat back and didn't say anything while the waiter served them. She looked around the room and reached up to smooth her short, spiky hair into place. She studied her chef's salad thoughtfully when it was put in front of her, as though someone had asked her opinion of it. "Oh, Claudia . . ." And she seemed tired, too. "Well . . . you're thirty-two years old, and Jane's only eleven. She *is* brilliant." And she gestured with her fork to hold Claudia at bay for a moment. "There's no question about that, and there are things she can do. I think that probably she has things she wants to do. But she's so self-destructive right now. She's hostile to all her friends if they phone her, and those little girls aren't completely without sympathy. If nothing else, they like the sheer drama of the situation. And Diana is really devoted to Jane. Jane's a powerful little girl in her own circle. But she *is* childish, Claudia. She can't decide what's best for herself." She looked down at her plate and carefully speared a bit of everything—a little ham, some turkey, a shred of cheese, an olive—but then she stopped short as she brought the fork toward her mouth. "Look, Claudia, I don't want to betray Jane in any way at all. I'll be absolutely honest, sometimes I'm furiously jealous of her for Diana's sake." She looked at Claudia beseechingly, to see if this admission would mitigate the rest of what she planned to say, but Claudia didn't react one way or another. In Claudia's opinion it was perfectly reasonable that Maggie would want her own daughter to be more like Jane. Maggie lowered her eyes again to study her salad.

"It's a sign of real trouble, though, you know. I think you ought to know about it, Claudia. I'm pretty sure Jane's stolen some things from our house. I've missed loose change from my dresser, and what worries me most is that twice, now, a prescription has disappeared. The first time I didn't worry about it. I just thought I'd lost it, but now I'm really upset. It's a prescription for Percodan. It's a narcotic. I don't really think that Jane would use it, but it's missing. The second bottle. And

Jane was definitely around. I've talked to my three kids, Claudia"—and she glanced up apologetically across the table—"and I really do think that it must have been Jane who took them."

Claudia had never understood how to parry back and forth, how to cajole or purposely be charming in order to defend herself, but she did think that she was being attacked, and in this case Jane was being attacked, too. Claudia just looked at Maggie, and she was absolutely at a loss, because she was filled with fury, but all she was able to do with it was to assess the immediate moment and tell the truth. It often rendered her childlike, so much younger than her own daughter. "Oh, Christ, Maggie!" And she didn't pretend that she wasn't angry. "She did not either!"

Maggie had said what she had come here to say; she had got it over with and was relatively unperturbed. She was eating her salad. "You might keep an eye on her, though. You might want to look around and see if my prescription turns up. It's a small bottle. It really does worry me."

And then Claudia frightened herself as much as she ever had because overhead there was a faint quiver in the air and a sudden downshifting draft, and a twenty-inch pot of English ivy crashed directly onto their table, shattering the clay pot and the two salads, and spraying both of them with shards of terra-cotta, lettuce, ham, blue cheese dressing, coiled roots and vines, and potting soil. Maggie leaped out of her chair, tumbling it backward and she was shaking and enraged while Claudia was still just sitting there amazed.

"God damn it!" Maggie said. "God damn it! That could have killed one of us! That could have killed us!" And there was a hurried rush of people around them, waiters and a man from the next table, but all Claudia did was watch them in a daze and in mounting horror as she grew more and more certain of what had happened. The table had been whisked away, but Claudia had not moved at all. She sat with her legs neatly crossed and one hand resting on the napkin in her lap while with the other she still held her fork poised in midair. Maggie had gone from tender solicitation to a state of utter terror at having an event occur that was not at all within her control—and Claudia sat there positive that she had wished that pot down on Maggie's head. Claudia believed that for a single powerful and concentrated moment she had hated Maggie to death.

The maître d' hovered over them and helped Claudia to her feet, gently taking the fork from her hand and passing it to someone behind him. After a moment he turned to Maggie, leaving Claudia to drip soil and lettuce onto the little straw rug on the red-tiled floor. In fact, a small cluster of people had gathered around Maggie, whose voice had dropped into intense anger. "No, no! I won't stay in this place for a second longer than I have to. My God! I wouldn't sit at another one of those tables for a million dollars!" Claudia saw that the tip of Maggie's nose had grown red, and a flush was spreading across her white, white face. Even her eyelids were rimmed around with pink, and she looked rabbity and hysterical.

"But I'll call my husband who's a lawyer. I will do that! I'll stay here until my husband gets here with a photographer, and if you clean away one bit of this mess before I get pictures, I swear I'll call every guest in this room as a witness!" There was distress everywhere in the restaurant, and Claudia had become just another bystander. She edged up to Maggie and got her attention for a moment.

"I'm going on, Maggie. I want to go home. I'm covered with food." Maggie only noticed her enough to nod in her direction. When Claudia got into her old blue Volvo and glanced around at all the little Mazdas and Toyotas, she began to tremble as violently as Maggie had. She had to lean her head down on the steering wheel for a while until she was calm enough to drive. She was sure that Jane was far too cautious and too honest ever to steal anything from Maggie. Jane adored Maggie. She knew that Jane would surely never take things from the Tunbridges' house. Claudia didn't think that Jane would do that to her.

She drove along the roads banked with snow on either side, and suddenly she was so exhausted by her increasing perception of the barrenness of the world that tears slipped down her face. She arrived home with her cheeks shiny and wet and every bit of color drained away. Immediately she saw that she had alarmed Jane, and it made her cross.

"Oh, there was this stupid, stupid accident," she said. "At the restaurant. It's nothing. I'm just really tired." Jane didn't say anything, but she looked on at Claudia with her grave glance, and Claudia became infuriated all at once. All the safe days she had spent with her daughter fell away from her, and she was unsure about things and angry and shaken.

"Jane, for God's sake! You don't have to watch me every single minute! You make me feel like I live in a fish tank. You ought to call some of your friends, or something, and not just mope around after me!"

And this time Claudia went to bed and pulled the quilt up around her ears and hugged her pillow to herself and didn't care if Jane was in the house or not. She slept without any inner or outer disturbance.

8

It was Jane, in fact, who felt as though she lived underwater. In these past quiet and gentle days the time had been without tension, muted and silky and languid. Suddenly the current had shifted and she was losing her bearings. Even the day after her lunch with Maggie, her mother was still cross and uncommunicative and brittle. It was worrying, and it made Jane restless. She couldn't concentrate on her music or even on a book with her mother's nervously grim disposition afoot in the house. To counteract this, Jane took one of Maggie's pills in the afternoon so that the delicate sensation of safety and optimism would come upon her, and if her mother became mysteriously angry or critical or irritated, Jane could be in the same room with her and yet be away from it. Then she would look on beatifically at her mother, who was either a whirling dynamo of bristling energy or limp with absolute but equally irascible languor. In either case, when Jane was in that state in which she felt she embodied contentment, her mother was satisfying to observe. It made Jane happy and calm to have her mother nearby, and in that becalmed state she practiced her music and watched television and didn't dwell on anything else.

A few days after the luncheon at which there had been that mysterious accident that had so altered her mother's mood Jane was left on her own in the house. Her mother had been so glum that she had retreated to her bedroom, again, to lie down, and when Jane looked in on her, she saw that Claudia had fallen soundly asleep and was completely still under the quilt. Jane felt so separate from her that it made her quite desolate and lonely.

Jane went to her own room and sat cross-legged on the bed just staring up through the skylight for some time. She was sad and restless. Finally she got up and swallowed two of Maggie's pills and sat on the bed again, leaning against the wall and waiting for them to work. She became dreamier and dreamier, sitting there, settling into a feeling of euphoric idleness. Her thoughts wandered and turned and drowsed. Eventually she was slightly bored by her own contentment, and from the table beside her bed she took up her school notebook, in which she had laboriously diagrammed sentences. She read them over with some attention. She studied the little lines of verbs and nouns and adjectives branching off at right angles and slants, and finally she reached for a pen and began to write on a fresh page. She watched the letters as she formed them and was pleased with each new shape; they opened up into large, looping swoops and curls instead of the tight, small script that crawled across the pages of her writing assignments. She wrote:

I am falling down the hole like Alice.

She wrote that because she felt a little the way she had felt when she had been anesthetized to have her tonsils out and had experienced the strange sensation of tumbling slowly and helplessly through the ocean. And now she began writing the things that she had thought then to stop herself; she wrote down the thoughts she had used to fight the anesthesia:

My mother will catch me.

She wrote that in such a large hand that it filled a whole line, and she sat back against the wall to study it with satisfaction. She skipped down two lines and wrote:

My father will catch me.

Somehow this upset her. Those lines bothered her in conjunction with the words sprawling luxuriantly above them.

Who will catch me

She wrote, and then thought for a long moment about whether to put a period or a question mark, but in her large, dopey script those four words just exactly crossed the page from the dark red line on the left to the pale reminder of a line at the right-hand margin, so she put a period. There was no room for a question mark, and when she studied the effect, she was amused because she saw what that did to the words and to the intention of them, and she went on writing, carefully skipping one line between each sentence. Now her page looked like this:

> *Who will catch me.*
> *I don't know who.*
> *Who could be Maggie.*
> *Who could be Dad.*
> *Who could be Mom.*
> *Who could be Alice.*
> *Who. Who. Who. Who.*

She had had to call Miss Jessup Alice so the message would have exactly four words; that was very important to her. She read over the page several times and then carried her notebook to her desk and took her scissors from the drawer and cut all the little messages into separate slips like papers from fortune cookies. She was vastly pleased when she spread them all before her, and a grand idea came into her mind. She folded each slip in half and in half again so that she could not see the words, and she hid them in secret places all around her room. She put one in her pillowcase and one in each dresser drawer. When she noticed the little vial of Maggie's pills that she had put back in her bottom drawer, she paused a moment and replaced it with one of the notes. She slipped the bottle into her pocket and distributed the rest of the folded papers in other parts of her room. She decided that when she was her other self, whichever of the notes she came upon first would be an important clue to know about her life. She stood still in the center of the room for a while, savoring the mystery she had created, glad that the sun was beaming into her little cavern, illuminating everything but not uncovering any of her secrets.

She wandered off after a while to her father's study, where she had set up her music stand, and she practiced for about a half an hour, but she had discovered that when she took any of the pills, the sound of the music she played was, to her own ear, muffled and distant, and she put her violin away and curled up in the Eames chair that faced the window and the long stretch of snow-covered meadow that rose up beyond her line of vision. Her thoughts became muddled in a comforting and pleasant way, and she finally let herself go into sleep.

When she woke up, it was dark; the afternoon was long gone, and high in the black sky was a perfect crescent moon and the North Star. She was aware of a heavy, unpleasant, muzzy feeling behind her eyes, and she was very careful when she got up. Although she could see fairly well in the light reflected off the snow and through the windows, she still extended her arms on either side to help her navigate. She made her way through the dark house to the light that was on in the kitchen. Her mother was there in her long red robe in a flurry of activity at the sink, rinsing dishes and stacking them in the dishwasher with a great deal of clattering and in sudden, jerky movements. But Jane wasn't sure about this; she often saw the world in rapid motion just after the pills wore off.

"Do you want me to fix some soup, or something, for dinner?" she asked her mother. Claudia scarcely turned and did not answer; she went on working through the pile of dishes.

Jane went to the refrigerator and opened it. She stood before it, assessing its contents and feeling slightly queasy but hungry at the same time. Behind her there was a sudden crash, and she turned around to see her mother holding two edges of a china plate that seemed to have exploded in her hands. She dropped the two pieces on the floor and took up another plate, which she brought down with terrific force on the porcelain edge of the sink.

Jane was horribly startled, and she stood back against the open door of the refrigerator and stared at her mother. Claudia's face was contorted into the most frightening expression Jane had ever seen. She was truly filled with a sickening fear because at eleven years old Jane was mostly a child, and she looked at Claudia and thought that her mother was irrevocably large and wild in the compact kitchen.

"God damn you!" Claudia said, and her voice began to rise. "God damn you! You could have told me the truth!" She kicked the mess around her feet and sent little pieces of glass flying all over the room. "I just want you to tell me what you're doing!" Claudia was shrieking, and Jane was very conscious of her mother's height and fury. She could only stare back with her glance aimed directly at her mother in terror. Her body felt as if it were sinking into itself.

"Look! Look! What are these? What do these mean?" And Claudia pulled from her pocket a handful of Jane's little notes she had written to herself, unfolded, but bent in angles where they had been so carefully creased.

"God damn it! What *are* these? What are you doing

all by yourself in your room? What do these mean?" But Jane stood there paralyzed, seeing that her mother was crying and flushed.

"Answer me, for God's sake! Is there something wrong with you? Can't you *hear* me?" Claudia's voice had become strained and frantic, and Jane's mind was blank. Suddenly her mother leaped toward her and slapped her across the face with a smack of her hand that Jane heard before she felt it. It was Claudia, though, who then doubled over as if she were in pain and began crying in earnest. Sobbing and gulping for air.

"Oh, God, Jane. Oh, God. Aren't you happy at all? Am I so terrible? What can I do? What can I do?" Her voice had trailed off into a helpless quavering. "Why won't you help me? Oh, God. I really am the foulest person to walk the earth. That's the truth, isn't it?" She backed up and sat down in a kitchen chair, and laid her head down on her arms, which she spread across the table, and she was still sobbing. Jane just stood gazing at her for a little while, stunned. At last she went a little way toward Claudia but stopped again in the middle of the room. Her face stung, and she was terrified to approach her mother. She did move closer, though, close enough to reach out and stroke her mother's back down the line of her shoulder. She stood shyly tracing her fingers along her mother's shoulder, and she left Claudia when Claudia was no longer shaking. She left her mother there with tears still streaming over her cheeks and soaking one of the billowing sleeves of her robe.

Jane went to her room, walking through the house in the dark, and lay down on her own bed and did not cry at all. She just lay there feeling light-headed and nauseated and knowing that she had done something terribly harmful when she had addressed this self from her other self. She was filled with pity and anger and humiliation, and those powerful and contradictory emotions sapped her of wakefulness. She finally fell again into a deep sleep.

* * *

Claudia fell asleep, too, at the table, but she didn't sleep long. She slipped in and out of being awake just long enough to stop crying, and then she opened her eyes in the bright kitchen, where the water was still running in the sink and the refrigerator door stood wide open. The machine whined and hummed behind her. For one instant she didn't remember where she was, but only for a few seconds; then she got up to turn off the water and close the refrigerator door, and she was engulfed with self-loathing.

She could not bear what she had done, the way she had behaved. She could not stand to be only with herself, and she moved out of the bright kitchen and through the house without flipping on any of the light switches. She moved without thinking and looked in on Jane, who was deeply asleep with a pale light falling across her bed from the round window above it.

Claudia left her and paced the upper hall, despising herself, sick with her own nature, but trapped in only these several rooms with everything she was or had become. She was trapped with the consideration of consequences. She had infringed on her daughter's dignity, and the picture of Jane's guarded but horrified gaze as she stood immobile in the kitchen was so painful to Claudia that she put her hand up over her eyes briefly—like a flinch—and she tried to divert herself. She went from room to room in search of her cigarettes.

That afternoon she had been appalled at finding the strange little slips of paper tucked away around her daughter's room, just as she was also appalled that she was searching the room at all. But she read each note as she came upon it and tried to put it together in her mind with Jane's long and serious face, her sweet, straight eyebrows, her total lack of guile. As she turned up yet another note, dismay and anger spread through her with a rush of blood to her face and fingertips. Even the backs of her hands turned rosy red. And she thought of girls and women and their smug secrets. Maggie at lunch and all the things she had only implied. Herself and the things she never said. She thought of female bodies and their recesses and mysteries and hidden places. And finding Jane asleep in the study had heightened this sudden ire. Whatever could be more exclusive than the body of a sleeping woman? It was a repudiation. She was baffled and enraged, and she hadn't awakened her daughter. She had known that she was beyond reason at that moment and untrustworthy. She had known that she was terrified of all the things she might not know and might or might not find out.

Claudia found her cigarettes in the kitchen, and now she smoked and walked and despaired of herself. Jane hadn't stolen anything. She hadn't hidden money; she hadn't hidden pills. The only things she had hidden away in her room were the peculiar and melancholy little notes. But it had been unbearable to Claudia that her daughter had hidden away her thoughts. She felt more bereft and alone than she had ever felt before in her life because even though Jane might have her secrets, it was also true that there was no one else Claudia had ever trusted so much. Whatever Jane might know about her mother—all the private things that Jane did know—she could be counted on to encompass that knowledge and still extend to her mother far more mercy than any other person ever would or could, male or female.

Claudia was desperate, as she walked the house, to find some way to make amends, and she had a sudden burst of enthusiasm when she thought of Jane's new violin tucked away in her closet. She went straight up to her room and brought it out from hiding and opened the case on her bed to look at it, to see if it would be sufficient. She turned on all the lights in the bedroom, even the overhead fixture, and walked around the bed, considering it from every angle. She didn't know if it would impress Jane; it was such a plain brown instrument. It would have to be properly presented, and Claudia took the violin down to the living room to prepare a surprise for her daughter, to try to construct an apology.

She plugged in the lights of the Christmas roping that swagged up the stairs, and she turned on the lights on the tall tree that was still wired upright against the towering center beam of the house. She took her black cape from the downstairs closet and spread it over the Danish teak coffee table, taking care to drape it in elaborate folds, and she put the open case on one end of the table, exhibiting its plush red interior. She placed the violin at the other end, turned at an angle with the bow canted across its strings.

As always with Claudia, one passion was quick to follow another without any sensational carryover. No immediate nostalgia or shadows colored one mood to the next, and she had moved in the space of a few hours from a state of bereavement to anticipatory euphoria.

She went back to the top of the stairs to see how it would look to Jane as she came down the steps, and she decided it lacked drama. She went to the dining room for the Dansk candlesticks and searched through the storage closet for the elaborate candelabrum she had brought with her from the house in Natchez. She even unpacked the set of twenty-four little votive candles that released insect repellent as they burned, and that weren't brought out until summer, when Avery placed them at intervals along the broad top railing of the deck. She put the eight-armed candelabrum on the parson's table behind the couch and then had to go back to the closet to see if she could find eight candles. It took her some time to insert them properly because the eight she had come up with were different sizes and colors, and she had to take the cellophane from some of them and wrap it around the stem ends of several candles so they would fit tightly. She worked in a great hurry, though, fervent as she was with this new enthusiasm.

She dispersed the small votive candles around the room and the two Dansk candlesticks on either side of the violin. At last she went to the kitchen for wooden matches and lit them all. Then she sat down on the couch to enjoy the full effect of the flickering light and even the sweetly pungent odor of insecticide enclosed in the winter-tight house. She was deeply satisfied with the arrangement, and she had everything prepared, but it was only five-thirty in the morning.

Claudia tried to wait until six o'clock, but after fifteen minutes of moving around the room to see how it looked from every corner she lost patience and went quietly up the stairs to Jane's room. When she stopped in the doorway this time, Jane opened her eyes immediately and saw her there and sat straight up in bed. Her mother was lit from behind by a strange, quavering light in her gauzy robe, and it alarmed Jane. She didn't say anything; she couldn't see her mother's expression, and she was wary. Claudia felt the reverberations of her own yearning fan out into all the angles of Jane's small room. What Claudia wanted at that moment above anything else was to extend comfort to Jane as Jane had once extended it to her, and she crossed the room and awkwardly put her arms around Jane's shoulders and stooped slightly to lay her cheek against the top of Jane's head. But it was a fleeting embrace, a reluctant and mortifying welling up of so much emotion that she only risked a soft encompassment of her daughter for a moment. And Jane felt as though she had been briefly enfolded in wings. Claudia moved off to circle the room.

"I'm so sorry, Jane." Her voice was very solemn, and she had her back to Jane. It wasn't enough to say, and she knew it. She knew that nothing could be forgiven in this instance, and it seemed to her that, after all, there was a sort of justice there. There would be an indelible picture, for as long as Jane was in the world, of Claudia galvanized with rage and holding out a streaming handful of the fragile little papers toward her daughter. For all the rest of her life there would be in Jane's head this little tableau of her mother's betrayal.

Claudia moved again to the doorway, where her robe glowed transparently around her. "Janie, isn't tonight the night of the concert? Do you feel like getting up now? Could you just come downstairs for a minute and

help me with something? And I can fix us some breakfast. I don't think either one of us had anything to eat
last night." Even when she mentioned the night before,
Claudia's voice dwindled away bleakly, and Jane was
still thrilled from her mother's touch. Her entire sympathy was awakened by now and was directed toward her
mother, who was so encumbered and overflowing with
sentiment; she was so awfully vulnerable in a new way.

Jane got out of bed at once and followed her mother
to the top of the stairs, where she only watched her
mother's back preceding her down the steps, and then
she became aware of the peculiar scent of insecticide, a
smell from midsummer, and of all the little candles everywhere. But it was not until her mother had moved
away from the bottom step that Jane caught sight of the
violin, and she froze in place with one foot still slightly
raised above the next step. She did not move or speak
for a moment. Across the room, standing against the
light, Claudia expelled a slow sigh of gratification, although she was uneasy, too, because she didn't want
Jane to thank her. Claudia had always anguished over
giving gifts; it had always seemed to her an awful thing,
embarrassing to everyone and even unfairly burdensome
to the recipient in various ways. She thought people
preferred to be prepared. She was not in the least stingy,
but she lacked the courage of the natural-born gift giver;
she had no idea of any graceful way to accept thanks.

In fact, before Jane said anything at all, Claudia pre-
empted her and began to speak very rapidly. "It's just
that I couldn't stand not to give it to you now." And she
held up her hand as if Jane were having some thought
that she shouldn't have. "And I know . . . Well, I don't
think for a minute that this is to make up for anything. I
wish it could, but I don't really think that one thing can
make up for another. I mean, both things have still
happened." She paused at this point, because she heard
herself nervously chattering away, getting caught up in
one of her pet philosophies. And she wondered if she
even meant what she was saying. Certainly when the

idea had occurred to her, she had intended this to be a
gesture that would wipe away the night before. She
talked on, though, because one way or another it didn't
really matter if she meant it or not.

"It's really your early Christmas present, Janie, but
you have your concert tonight. Actually I liked the dark
wood better, but Alice said that this was a better instrument. And don't worry. Alice selected it. You know that
I don't know anything about choosing a violin. I mean,
don't worry that it's the wrong one. Anyway, Alice said
that you could try it for a few months." She had finally
become so nervous that she had to stop. There was
something more that she meant to convey to Jane, but
she didn't know exactly what it was or how to do it, and
Jane was still standing on the stairs stiff with surprise.

"But why don't you try it, Jane? I think you ought to
try it by yourself, and I want to go fix some breakfast
for us anyway. I'll fix French toast. And later today I'm
going shopping for a dress for you to wear tonight. Something really special. A beautiful dress for tonight. They'll
be so surprised at the concert! Everyone will!" And the
triumph in her voice was solely on behalf of Jane.

When Jane was left alone in the room with the violin,
she stood still for quite some time, looking at it from
across the room before she moved over the rug to see it
more closely. She was afraid even to touch it. She was
horrified by it because she knew that she had trained
herself to a state of mastery of the rented instrument she
had learned on and played for the past five years. She
had been coached by Miss Jessup and had learned for
herself all the ways to compensate for the irregularities
and deficiencies of the other violin, and she had planned
to amaze everyone—and anyone, too, anyone who might
ever have taken her lightly, even her father. She had
been sure she would surprise them all when she stood
alone on the stage and played the Bach. Every energy
she had had for the past weeks had been directed toward
that one idea. The only other thing in her life for that
time had been her newfound and unconsidered adoration

of her mother. Until these past few days she had basked in and absorbed the remarkable, shimmering quality of her mother's undivided attention, and she had pinned any thoughts of the future on her music. But she had seen such pleasure on her mother's face as she stood in the room raptly happy and irradiated by the candlelight that she could not possibly have explained to her that she ought to refuse this gift. She was unable to think of any way to postpone accepting it. Jane had understood, when she saw the tension in every line of her mother's body as Claudia stood over the violin and among all those candles, that she was completely responsible just now for her mother's happiness. All hope for herself and her own triumph began to fade as she contemplated the light golden and beautifully made instrument lying before her on the table.

She finally lifted the violin with great care and fitted it beneath her chin, but she did not pick up the bow yet. She stood with her bow arm hanging lax as she adjusted her head and looked down the strings. At last she raised her hand just to pluck the strings to see if they were in tune, and in spite of herself, the real tension of them— not the reluctant elastic feeling of her rented instrument— the pleasant resistance of those strings as she plucked across the bridge filled her with excitement. And then she did pick up the bow and began tentatively to play the "Air for the G String." As soon as she first drew the bow across the strings, she was aware that she had left herself and was speculatively observing her own playing. She was aware that no conscious part of her was controlling her own actions, that she was floating away from herself as she played the lovely, light, graceful violin and produced a sound of real brilliance. It was to be one of the rare moments in her life, as she stood there in the middle of the lightening room among the many little pinpoints of candlelight, when all the lines of coincidence and fate and circumstance intersect and a small miracle of luck occurs.

9

    Toward the evening of the twenty-third
of December there was a general stirring in
all the houses where there lived a student in the Lunsbury
Central Schools who played an instrument, orchestral or
band, or who sang in the chorus. Some children did all
three, and in those houses there was a buttoned-down
tension more concentrated than in other houses. Even
so, each music student basked in the attention of his or
her family members, enjoyed the meal served early on
his or her account, and dealt one way or another with
the combined excitement of the music concert and the
upcoming holidays. They were pleasantly burdened with
the heavy and titillating anticipation that hangs over
children as festivities mount toward what is always a
disappointingly benign celebration.
  Jane arrived in the auditorium faintly dazed from the
long day and also from her sudden reimmersion into her
particular society and the bedlam of backstage activity
after the sweet, quiet time of seclusion she had taken for
herself. In fact, she was intimidated and alarmed by all
the stirring about, by the jargon of the day being thrown
from child to child to impress whoever might be listening.
  "Oh, my God, Jane! You look really good! I saw that

dress at Halls in the designer collection, but my mother won't let me shop there. You look really fantastic!'' Linda had been dashing by but had stopped still to give Jane that quick compliment. Jane was out of practice, though, and just looked back mutely and moved out of the way.

Jane was the object of a good bit of ostentatious solicitude. All the girls in the group—genuinely kind-hearted girls for the most part—took care to adopt a somber attitude of sympathetic inquiry when they approached Jane. They surreptitiously vied with one another to be the one most thoroughly concerned about her. And their concern was not at all feigned, but it became more and more intense. Their scrutiny of each other was so close that each consoling gesture any one of them made in Jane's direction affected in the others real emotion and an almost frenzied need to prove their magnanimity toward Jane and her plight. Jane's friends were flying around, doing errands for the chorus director or instructing the younger children in this or that— they were gleefully self-important as sixth graders. But they would spot Jane and come to a halt, and Heather or Stephanie or Linda would move gravely toward her, touch her arm, and speak to her softly. Then they would dash off to be seen at some other important job. Only Diana stood apart from her and was quiet and withdrawn. Jane had hurt her feelings very much over the past few weeks, which was a fairly long time in the social lives of those girls. Diana stood at the far end of the corridor from Jane, dispiritedly holding her flute and waiting for the orchestra to take its seats.

Jane didn't notice that Diana was ignoring her, and even the benevolent attention aimed her way roused in her a longing to be away from all the people and the noise, but at the same time she was in the grip of a keenness for a certain kind of power. She was eager to perform and test herself with the new violin, while she was also terrified that she had tricked herself into believing she sounded better than she did.

She stood backstage against a wall to be out of the way and leave the passage behind the curtain free while her friends passed back and forth. The other girls all had a self-conscious look of sly pleasure, and they drifted here and there, in everyone's way, much taken with themselves in the long-skirted Laura Ashley dresses they had bought at the Honeybee. They were eager to be observed, but they pretended a kind of cavalier boredom with it all. And the boys were equally and less subtly impressed with themselves in their gray flannel slacks and brass-buttoned blazers.

Jane was fairly oblivious to everything going on around her and especially to the clothes she had on. She was so tired from the short night and long day preceding this evening that she was queasy with a surge of adrenaline through all her body. Her hands trembled slightly, and her legs felt wooden and locked at the knees. She was also concentrating to some degree on keeping her violin out of sight so Miss Jessup wouldn't notice it and insist she play the other one for this performance. She did not want her mother and her teacher to be at odds with each other. She stood where she was, worrying about the pieces she would play and staying out of the way.

But any of the adults who came backstage for some reason or another and even some of the other performers—when their attention momentarily slewed away from themselves—could not help noticing Jane. She was not dressed in one of the sweet Laura Ashley dresses. It would never have occurred to Claudia to check with any other parent and find out what might be the order of the day. She had not even thought to shop in the Girls' Department of Halls; she had selected Jane's dress from the same collection from which she chose her own clothes, whenever she remembered to do that. Clothes weren't important to Claudia, and she always bought what appealed to her at the moment. Jane stood against the wall dressed in a plain knee-length white wool dress and matching waist-length jacket that had no ornamentation whatsoever except that the squared neckline of the jacket was gently scalloped and framed Jane's collarbone and long, arched neck. It was a dress of very restrained femininity, and Claudia had bought it that afternoon as soon as she saw it; it was a dress she would have liked to wear herself, although she had the wrong figure for it. She didn't think about the fact that Jane was only eleven years old, even if she was tall, and that this dress was sophisticated for a child to wear successfully. The dress had fitted Jane perfectly.

Claudia hadn't known what to do with Jane's hair, and Jane hadn't cared one way or another. But just before they left the house, Claudia had brushed Jane's dark blond hair straight back and wound it as best she could into a French twist. This left Jane's smooth, wide brow clear, and her eyes were large and serious in her oval face. Without her hair hanging down on either side, the planes of her face were apparent, and the firmly rounded chin and the strong, distinct line of her jaw.

The dress Claudia had chosen was exactly right for Jane, as it turned out, because she didn't have the face of a child, and people turned to look at her. She had the heart-stopping look of wisdom that one observes in the faces of young ballet dancers. She had such an expression of assured devotion that Mr. Walters, the band director, noticed her, and it went fleetingly through his mind that she looked like a young nun. But then he moved on in his thoughts to worry about whether to reposition the drums so they wouldn't be too dominant. There was a plethora of drummers this year.

Claudia had dropped Jane at school early and gone to Burger Chef to get some dinner for herself. When she returned, the parking lot was full, and she had to leave the car two streets away and make her way toward the school on foot. All around them, as the parents of Lunsbury negotiated a path along the shoveled, icy sidewalks beneath the streetlights, was a fine, black, misty night. A vaporous condensation rose from the ground, and the air seemed rich and loamy in contrast with the white, crusted yards and brittle banks of snow along the

161

plowed roads. Only long feathers of clouds moved through the upper distance to break the dark, and snowflakes fell sparely and in such cold that they landed on a dark coat sleeve or shoulder in tiny but perfectly delineated crystalline formations, and then they were gone again in an instant.

Claudia moved with the throng in her long wool cape and was pleased to listen to various parents greeting each other. She was in a state of such optimism and excitement that the communal calling back and forth and laughing and polite joke-making seemed to her an almost unbearably poignant reminder of the possibilities of civilization and goodwill. Her perceptions were on a hair trigger this evening, and she was so convinced, in this crowd, of the occasional benevolence of humankind that she was near tears.

When she entered the auditorium, she had no idea that her face took on an expression of gratitude that cast a vulnerability over her features. She attracted attention in the same way her daughter had backstage. The two of them looked, tonight, like people around whom something is bound to happen. Everything about them bespoke an intrinsic drama. Claudia was startling to see with all her hopes upon her delicate triangular face, and she was tall in the crowd in her black cloak. And although she was somberly dressed among all the bright goose down jackets, she was also jarringly glittery with refracted regard, because Claudia was indifferent to the opinion of strangers. She did not absorb their consideration, and it bounced back at the observers, any one of whom felt oddly slighted.

It was not until she caught sight of Avery smiling at her from the third row that she became self-reflective and put a hand up to brush back her hood and settle her hair. She made her way down an aisle and smiled at him and then sat down beside him, and he leaned over and gave her a polite little kiss in greeting. She was sitting forward a bit, and she stayed perfectly still for a mo-

ment. Such a clear-cut friendliness from her own husband unnerved her, but she settled back in her seat and
shrugged off her cape and crossed her legs.

"Wait till you see Janie tonight," she said to him.
"She looks so . . . grown-up, I guess. I'm not sure how
to describe her. She looks very elegant, and, oh, 'serene' is as close as I can come. 'Grown-up' isn't quite
what I mean. It's very surprising when you first notice
the difference. Avery, it almost broke my heart." Claudia had turned to hold his gaze directly. To Avery she
generally said exactly what she meant, which caused
her, quite often, to sound overwrought, even though her
voice was perfectly calm.

"That's probably what was bound to happen," Avery
said. "Even when she was little, she never really looked
young. She'll go from being an ordinary little girl to
someone you have to take seriously."

Claudia looked at him more closely. That terrible note
of self-indulgent nostalgia was infusing his voice again,
although he was absolutely sober. Claudia didn't think
he had had even one drink. She knew him so well that
she could gauge his sobriety just by the small degree of
muscular tension in his face.

Avery was pondering and sorting his ideas as he spoke,
and he went on. "She could end up being one of those
women who are frightening. Admirable but alarming. Do
you know what I mean? She's always had that quality
around the eyes. . . . Well, I know what it is." And he
sketched vaguely with his hands to try to describe his
daughter. "She's watchful. It's judgment. She'll always
have a slightly secretive look. Remember, even when
she was a baby, she always looked as though she were
weighing everything in the balance. You used to pick
her up to feed her and say, 'Oh, come on, give me a
break!' Remember?" And he laughed. "She's always
been able to make up her mind and look out for herself." And he meant this. He thought he loved his daughter. He and Claudia had no idea; they had no idea at all
how mysterious parents are to their children. Claudia

and Avery both thought privately that Jane was a rather strange child who didn't altogether approve of them.

Claudia glanced away. She looked around the room, where people were still greeting each other and chatting in the aisles, and she looked at the stage, where the chorus was falling raggedly into place. She thought Avery spoke as if he were no longer related to his daughter, as if he were relegating her to memory.

"My God, Avery," she said, "she's your own daughter." But she said it so softly; she spoke out toward the stage without any particular inflection or urgency, and Avery only picked it up with the corner of his attention and didn't comment one way or another.

The room was filling rapidly, and Claudia turned in her seat to look for Maggie and Vince. Beyond the wide double doors of the auditorium the heavy, cold air and the dark clung so closely to the earth that as the people entered, it was as though the icy gloom had adhered to them and then evaporated upward in the warmth to chill and shadow the remote corners at the rear of the large room. The colors of the sweaters and blouses and shirts were vibrant, and the company took on an extra degree of animation. The scent of the snow and the night were exciting in this safe enclosure. The frigid dark was something substantial to have come in from. It was an evening that enhanced humanity and made all the people glad to be with their acquaintances.

The seats were filled now, although parents and grandparents and aunts and siblings continued to stream into the lighted room, and so the men in the audience began to get up, many of them, and move out of the rows of seats to stand against the walls, vacating their places for their wives and mothers and children, or for the wives and mothers and children of other men. Avery made his way to the aisle and joined Vince and Mark, and Maggie and Celeste came to take places next to Claudia. Maggie and Claudia exchanged a customary light embrace and a pleasant greeting, and Maggie turned to chat with a woman she knew who was sitting in the row behind them.

Avery and Vince leaned their shoulders against the long black-paned windows, and Avery stretched his arm out loosely across the high sill while he leaned toward Vince to tell him something. Claudia was watching them, and she absently raised her hand to her lips and passed her fingertips softly across her mouth as though she were stopping some words she might say. She looked at the two men and all the other fathers in their crew-necked sweaters and tweed jackets and then, in the audience, at all the women leaning together to speak to each other, or bending forward to rein in a small child who was heading off on some adventure. Claudia had a sudden inclination to double over and bury her head in her lap, to hide away from the evidence of such kindly sexuality. One father caught an escaped child and lifted him to sit high on the windowsill; another raised his daughter up over his head so she could straddle his shoulders and hold on around his neck. Their wives, sitting down at last, were weary from the effort of organizing the children, rushing them through the early dinner, worrying over and reassuring that child who would be performing.

Claudia looked around and knew that later a husband in his nice blue sweater would collect his family after the concert, would move them along toward the car, would, perhaps, put his hand at his wife's waist to guide her through the crowd and through the snow while she glanced back to be sure the children were coming after them. And she would not take special notice of that hand at her waist; that wife would be accustomed to that touch, and her husband would be accustomed to the touching. Claudia looked once more at Avery and Vince, who appeared to be unmoved by the implication all around them of such intimate involvement. It seemed to her all good, those intricacies of domestic life. It seemed to her to be a condition full of ease and grace, and she even imagined that the orderly sensuality she attributed to these people was something she had once had. Then she did have to look down at the floor, and she put her hands up to her face, because she was wounded by what was lacking in her life, she was overcome by lust and longing.

The houselights came down, and the audience began to grow quiet as the musicians took their places. The string section was seated, and Jane was the last to take her seat in her position of first violin. Alice Jessup stood calmly waiting for her students to settle into their chairs, and Claudia watched her and was moved by a wave of sympathy and goodwill as she studied that serious little figure at the front of the brilliantly lit stage. In fact, as Alice raised her arms and the strings began to play their first piece, a selection from the *Messiah,* Claudia could not turn her eyes away from Alice Jessup to look at Jane. Her attention was riveted to Alice's slightly undulating figure as she coaxed forth the right notes at the right moments. She was so very small and straight with her long, long hair to her waist, and she was wearing her black-strapped Chinese shoes and, strangely enough for December, a mid-calf gauzy beige skirt with an India-inspired design around its hem. Against the light the skirt was completely transparent, and Claudia could not look away from Alice's thin, slightly bowed legs beneath the skirt and her bright turquoise blue bikini underpants with elastic that was sprung so that they slipped fractionally with each upreach of her arms.

Claudia didn't dare glance around to see if anyone else had noticed this; instead she directed toward the stage the intense wish, on Alice's behalf, that the wispy little pair of underpants would not fall down around her ankles with her next exhortation to her students. And she forgave Alice everything. She forgave her for her superior knowledge of music; she forgave her for the absolute possession of her own life; she even forgave her for the slight and mysterious disdain with which she suspected Alice viewed her. Alice had endeared herself utterly to Claudia by such an amazing lack of vanity and foresight.

When the two Handel selections were over, Alice did not turn to the audience while they applauded her and her string students. She had caught sight of Jane's violin and was watching Jane intently during the brief applause before she moved to adjust Jane's music stand at center stage for Jane's solo. She met Jane's eyes for a moment, but she was stopped by something in Jane's expression from indicating anything with that glance, not even a question. When Jane stood up and came to the front of the stage, she had to wait while Alice tried to get the stand to slide to the right height. Jane stood still, holding her bow across her waist and her new violin straight down the line of her right thigh, and she looked out for a moment with a clear, half-lidded gaze at the goodhearted and generous-spirited audience. She was full of alarm and awfully conscious of fatigue and fear that weighed down her arms with a peculiar numbness. But the audience became still, too, frozen there in their kindly tolerance. All their benevolent intentions were caught up and stopped dead as they were held so briefly in Jane's regard. She was tired to such a degree that she was not associating the performance she would give with the audience who would hear it. It was only Miss Jessup who worried her. She stood beside Alice and waited, and she looked out over the audience with curiosity and an air of pure assessment that was disconcerting to them. It was only for a moment that she stood and plied her gaze over the rows of people, but a faint stir broke out where her eye had passed.

"Hasn't she grown up?"

"She's gotten so tall this past year, hasn't she?"

"Isn't she going to be an attractive girl?"

They turned to each other uneasily because they saw something about her that made them want to alleviate the peculiar trepidation they felt as she stared so intently ahead. She was forfeiting their charity. And when Alice moved away and Jane poised her violin beneath her chin, they felt that just by the assurance of her motions she was indicating that it might be a grudging concession to them that she was performing at all. She drew out the first note of Bach's "Air for the G String," and it was a clean, pure sound that the audience listened to with attention. She had called forth their judgment with her level gaze. She had alerted them not to listen with a sympathetic ear and its corresponding condescension, and when she finished, they applauded seriously. Some of the audience knew how well she had performed, and they all realized that she had played the piece without a mistake.

For the moment Jane was pleased, and that was all. She had learned this wonderful new instrument in one day; she had fitted her skill to its eccentricities. She was too tired to be particularly triumphant or euphoric, though. She was simply relieved for herself and for her mother.

The concert continued. The audience was tired, with Christmas in the offing, and they were easily distracted by a stray child racing away from his mother, down an aisle, through a forest of knees. But Claudia was so enamored of the evening that she loved it all, now that Jane had played so beautifully. When the youngest children, the beginning students relegated to the lowly Red Band, finally played their one selection, Claudia was very moved by their desperately earnest expressions and their careful attention to Mr. Walters. She put her arm over Maggie's on the support that separated their seats and leaned toward her.

"Oh, Maggie! It really is exciting what these children can do! It's amazing what they're exposed to so early. It's John Cage, isn't it?"

Maggie's pale brows frowned over her program. "That's something called 'Band Room Blast.' Arranged especially for the Red Band by Mr. Walters, it says. I guess it gives all the children a chance to make some kind of noise."

But Claudia was a trifle jolted in her headlong enthusiasm.

By the time the band had finished its last number even the most temperate parents were relieved. The mothers with infants on their laps were tired of the effort of keeping them quiet and still, and the fresh air had been displaced by the breath of all those people so closely grouped. The room had become stuffy. Avery had been tense from the moment he had seen Jane come onstage with the pale brazilwood violin. He was stiff, too, from leaning against the wall, and he was glad to be able to make his way toward her as the orchestra and band members emerged in small, excited groups through the stage door leading into the auditorium. He and Claudia reached her almost at the same time, and Claudia had a quality of incandescence, she was so obviously pleased for her daughter.

"Janie, I wish you could have been a fly on the wall," she said. "I wish you could have been in the audience and could have seen yourself!" Claudia hardly ever smiled wholeheartedly; she always seemed to have her private reservations, but she smiled at Jane now, and she spoke very deliberately, choosing her words with care. "You had real poise onstage. I don't know exactly what it was . . . . You were *elegant,* not just a talented child who plays well." She wanted to explain the powerful satisfaction she felt on Jane's behalf. It was not in the nature of how the two of them were that Claudia would presume to be proud of her daughter, but she was deeply, deeply pleased. And finally Avery could not resist that pleasure either; his face lost its tension, and he smiled at Jane, too. Before he could say anything, though, the three of them caught sight of Alice approaching them slowly through the crowd, brushing aside the students who implored her to pay attention. She was determined, and her mouth was sternly set. She moved stiffly, as though she were wading through deep water. Claudia thought for a moment that Alice was moving with such restraint because she had finally realized that her little bikini underpants were sliding lower and lower over her narrow hips, but then she realized that Alice was unaccountably angry and that some of that anger seemed to be directed at her. As Alice drew nearer, that impression intensified. Claudia was especially surprised and baffled, since all during the performance she had extended to Alice every ounce of her empathy. Alice was thin and intent, and her progress toward them was inexorable, and Claudia grew agitated in spite of herself as she watched her approach.

Alice was so tiny in her flat shoes that when she stood among the three of them, even Jane looked down at her, but Alice's immense irritation made her presence loom large. Claudia was a bit indignant by now, and uneasy, and Alice stood directly before her in an obvious confrontation.

"You really don't pay attention to what people need, do you? I explained to you that it would take months for Jane to get used to a new instrument," she said to Claudia. "You really didn't pay attention. It's like you didn't even hear me!" Her voice, which was usually so inconsequential, had filled out with anger, and Claudia realized that she had always underestimated this severe little woman. She was completely at a loss, although to be attacked like this for no apparent reason made her eyes fill with tears and her chin quiver embarrassingly. It was the surprise of Alice's rage that affected her. But Alice wasn't deterred. She was not through being angry, and no one attempted to interrupt her because her quiet ferocity was so vehement. "I thought Avery was just feeling sorry for himself when he said you don't listen, but he really was right. You could have ruined this concert for Jane!"

Claudia just looked at her, astounded that she would be the object of Alice's interest right now, much less contempt. She looked to Jane, but Jane was looking away from all of them as though this were not happening; she was staring out into the crowd. Avery reached out and put his hand on Alice's shoulder.

"Well, we probably shouldn't have done it, Alice.

One of us should have told you. But you know, it really was irresistible."

Claudia turned slightly to look at him. She didn't understand what was going on. She didn't know why a note of conciliation had crept into Avery's voice or why he was smiling his persuasive, slightly crooked smile. It distracted her. He was almost unctuous, and everything he said was infused with mediation and pacification. A shudder of protective irritation for Avery's sake passed over her, because she could never bear it if he was being in the least bit foolish, and she didn't know what he was up to now.

"We gave the violin to Jane a week ago, and she's been practicing every day for hours. I know"—he held up his hand—"I know that's not enough time, and we never would have let her play it tonight if she hadn't been so good at it. You made a perfect match with that violin, though, Alice. It's exactly the right one for Jane, and I would have chosen the darker of the other two. You knew it was right instinctively. It was a brilliant choice!" Avery gestured again to hold Alice off. "I should have told you. I know I should have told you, but Jane made us promise. She wanted this to be a surprise."

Alice turned to look dubiously at Jane, who did not look back. "You haven't had a flu? That's so stupid, Jane. I thought you knew better. I could have helped you. You should have filled the auditorium with sound from this violin! You could have. It will give you more volume. And I could have explained that to you. You can't possibly figure that out if you're just practicing in your bedroom. You have to suit the sound to the environment." She was instructively earnest when she spoke to Jane about the violin, but she was angry again when she turned back to include Avery and Claudia.

"This is really not my idea of a fun surprise! I would have thought that at least *Jane* would have had more sense than that." Alice was calmer, now, but quite firm, and Claudia could not bear to have her say these things to Jane no matter how tightly strung Alice's nerves might be this evening because of the concert.

"Alice," Claudia said, and she was plaintive, because she had learned over the years that people aren't really very reasonable, "Jane was the success of the concert. Jane was wonderful!" She could not understand how Alice could be so cruel as to lessen this occasion for Jane. Jane had been valiant and careful standing beneath the lights. She had stood and looked out at the adults sitting in the audience and made it clear that she was not to be pitied. Claudia had realized that Jane had taken a great risk, and she had succeeded. She was brave and admirable and undeserving of this attack, but Claudia wasn't mad at Alice in return; she was inured to people failing to fulfill her expectations of them. And for her part, Alice only gave a small shake of her head in resignation.

"That's because she's incredibly talented," Alice said. "And lucky. Tonight she was awfully lucky." Her anger was less forthright now, and by this time her other students had found her and were beseeching her and tugging at her attention, so she turned away, and Claudia looked after her a moment, saddened a little and bewildered. She didn't want this to ruin anything for Jane.

"She's wrong about that, Jane," she said to her daughter, who might have been anyone's child, she was so apparently unconnected to her two parents and her teacher. "It had absolutely nothing at all to do with luck! I watched you all the time, and you weren't *lucky*. You had tremendous poise, and you were more concentrated than I've ever seen you be, but you weren't one bit lucky!"

Jane turned to her mother and smiled at her because more than anything, tonight, it had hurt her when Alice had counted her lucky, and she loved her mother very much at that moment. She knew her mother understood the heart of the matter, and she thought that in her own

172

vague way her mother did pay attention to what was needed, even if it was only now and then.

"Avery, why don't you come with us?" Claudia said. "I'm going to take Janie somewhere to celebrate. She hardly ate any dinner, and I think we'll go get a sundae or something."

Avery didn't reply for a moment. He stared off thoughtfully above the heads of the crowd. Then he bent down and kissed Jane carefully on the cheek in the same self-consciously guarded attitude that he had taken toward Claudia earlier. And his voice indicated a mournful resignation. He was quite serious about this part he was playing of the estranged and lonely father, Claudia thought, and she was impatient once again.

"Oh, well, I can't do that. But you ought to go celebrate, Janie. I've got a special plan for Christmas morning. We can celebrate then. The Bach was the best thing on the program. You were wonderful, Janie. You ought to feel very proud of yourself." He began to usher them in the direction of the aisle, and Claudia and Jane turned and started out ahead of him. At the end of the row they moved with the crowd into the wide central corridor toward the major exit, but when Claudia reached the top of the sloping auditorium, she looked around and saw that Avery had branched off the other way and was moving away from them toward the other end of the room.

"Oh, he really isn't coming with us, I guess," she said to Jane. "He must have parked around back. We'll see him Christmas morning." She turned back to join the crowd of people who were halted in their progress since only a few people at a time could make their way through the big double doors. Jane didn't mind at all; she was just as glad to have her mother to herself. She looked back at the stage just in time to see her father approach Alice, who was being detained, still, by several sets of parents offering their congratulations. Jane saw her father move alongside her teacher and slide his hand beneath all her brown cascading hair and press her forward gently at the waist to guide her away from the lingering parents who turned, as she moved away, and waved good-bye. Jane wasn't paying much attention, however. She was remembering that while she was standing before that audience playing the Bach, she had been briefly, absolutely, and only herself. Not her teacher's pupil or her parents' daughter or her friends' acquaintance. She had experienced a moment of undivided self-involvement. It was a heady business, even remembering it. And in retrospect it did not seem to be a state that was in the least bit dangerous, only giddy and desirable. For the several minutes of playing the "Air for the G String" she had been cast adrift from loving or caring or knowing about anyone but herself.

10

Jane stayed in her pajamas late into
Christmas morning even though whenever her
mother noticed her she urged Jane to get dressed. "Why
are you still in your pajamas on Christmas Day? We're
going to have champagne and everything. Why don't
you at least put on a pair of jeans?" But Jane turned on
the television and wrapped herself in a blanket and
watched the Mormon Tabernacle Choir. She was uneasy
and sullen and overcome by a familiar feeling of dread
which she was trying not to dwell upon. It was not as
threatening if it remained amorphous, if she did not pin
it down. With the effort not to think, her face took on a
vaguely truculent expression, dull-eyed and grimly set
through the mouth and jaw, and when Claudia looked in
on her again, she thought that Jane might be coming
down with a flu.

Claudia herself was frenetic with energy. She had
thrown off all traces of lassitude and had been up since
dawn. She had put on a dark maroon velvet dress with a
fitted shirtwaist bodice and a huge collar that framed her
face in a way that gave her features sweetness, so that
with her frothy hair she looked like a valentine. The
skirt of her dress was cut on the bias and lay closely

over her round hips before sweeping out at the hem. She liked the feel of the cloth as she moved. She swayed against it a trifle when she walked so that the luxurious fabric swung around her legs. She was alarmingly talkative and euphoric, and she was all over the house, fluffing the pillows and cleaning the counters. Everything was exactly right and in its place.

She had waited too late to cook anything. Christmas Eve Jane had gone along with her and waited at the deli while Claudia selected a sinister-looking pâté with a dark row of truffles down the center. She had bought smoked salmon, red caviar and black caviar, black bread, rye bread, four different cheeses, and two pounds of sliced Boone County ham, which Avery liked better than Smithfield, and she also chose one of the small smoked turkeys that were trussed and hanging by their leg bones one above the other on knotted ropes behind the counter.

She had rarely in her life indulged herself in such a gluttony of frivolous buying, and it went to her head. At the organic food store she bought all kinds of fruit, great spills of grapes, and lemons and onions for the caviar. She stood in the store oblivious to the many people milling about and held the grapes up to show Jane. "I hadn't ever realized how sexual this fruit is," she said to Jane meditatively as the grapes hung down heavily over her hand where she held them before her. "It's nature copying nature. My God, if you look around, though, I suppose that all this food could have a human sexual equivalent." She turned to see if Jane agreed with her, but Jane had moved away and was studying the dairy case full of imported yogurt.

At the bakery Claudia got a dozen meringues, filled croissants, and a streusel for Christmas breakfast. Jane saw that her mother was slowly—from store to store—working herself into a peculiar and flushed furor of acquisition. "Janie, this is incredible! Just incredible. I don't think I'm even a greedy person. I'm really not. But when you stand there looking at all the things you

can buy . . . and you get to choose . . . God! It's proof
that you're a grown-up. I mean, if you have the money
for it, no one is going to say anything to you at all. They
just give you what you ask for. Anything you want!''

Jane was becoming alarmed as she watched her mother's increasing elation. ''We have plenty of stuff now,''
she said. ''It's so cold. Can't we go home?''

But Claudia hardly noticed; she flashed her daughter a
smile across the front seat, and they stopped at the
liquor store, where Jane decided to wait in the car.
Claudia bought three bottles of champagne, a good bour-
bon, scotch, gin, and a bottle of Finnish vodka that had
a stalk of rye grass in it. ''Look at that, Jane!'' she said,
turning the bottle so Jane could see it from every angle.
''What an idea! It probably tastes foul, but it's so pretty,
isn't it?'' Jane didn't say anything until her mother had
settled the packages on the front seat. And even when
she did speak, her voice was without conviction or hope.
In fact, all she felt was a sort of doleful resignation.

''I don't know why you always buy this stuff when
Dad's going to be in the house.'' Her words came out
flat in the enclosed air of the car with the dullness of
coins falling on a wooden surface. But for the first time
that day Claudia fell back into her habitual passivity.
She was bending forward to turn the key in the ignition.
When Jane spoke, Claudia dropped her hand to the car
seat and leaned her head back against the headrest and
to the side so that she was looking out the window for a
long moment.

''Oh . . . well, Jane . . . it's Christmas. It's a celebration. I have all kinds of things for tomorrow.'' But she
said this to Jane without turning to look at her, and she
remained still and pensive as she looked out at the
snow-encrusted parking lot. Finally she drew herself together and started the car, but she was not as brisk as
she had been, and she was short-tempered with Jane for
the rest of the afternoon.

By Christmas morning, though, her optimism had returned. In fact, she was giddy with what was partly

terror at coming into the kitchen and seeing evidence everywhere of the risk she had taken. In the refrigerator and spread over the table were the makings of an event, and that was Avery's domain; she had taken a plunge into improvisation.

"We won't open any of the presents until your father gets here," she said to Jane. "Is that all right with you, Janie? And your main present was the violin, but I know there'll be a few surprises." Jane kept her eyes on the TV and only nodded, and Claudia wandered off.

Jane's idea of Christmas was her collective memory of all the ones before, and always her parents—especially her father—constructed it out of the most fragile material, constructed it out of his own enthusiasm, which was infectious and irresistible. For weeks before Christmas Avery would come home with mysterious boxes, and as early as August, Claudia would begin to pore over catalogues. By late November and December the UPS man would be making almost daily stops. Every year that Jane could remember, however, it had become too much for Claudia. Her mother would share her father's enthusiasm, but she also could not bear the idea of Jane's suspense. She would waylay Jane in private with this or that sealed box and furtively slit the brown tape.

"I've just got to show you this, Janie! It's magnificent. I know how awful it is to have to wait." And Jane could remember over the years that her mother had once drawn forth and unfurled from her tissue paper a spectacular doll from Sweden. A doll unlike any other Jane had ever seen, a somber-faced, stalwart, brave-hearted doll. Once her mother had let her examine all the intricacies of a two-foot-tall simulated wooden tree trunk from F.A.O. Schwarz that was cleverly hinged and opened into the most perfectly furnished home for a family of Steiff mice. "Your father would be furious if he knew I let you see this, but I can't stand it for you—not knowing. But you have to act really surprised when you open it Christmas morning." Another year she had led Jane down to the cellar on the sly to let her see the amazing old-fashioned carnival in miniature that Avery had found on one of his expeditions around the countryside. It consisted of an enameled Ferris wheel, merry-go-round, and airplane ride that all spun around in remarkable synchronization, just missing each other as they whirled. Avery had located an artist who had reconditioned it and a jeweler who had fitted into its platform the workings of a music box, so that while all the little rides circled and circled it played "The Man on the Flying Trapeze."

Christmas was wonderful in her household; it was magical, but it was also a day through which the hours followed one another with increasing dependency. It was a day made of glass, and one small fissure early-on could etch its way through the whole structure until finally the entire fabrication might shatter around their ears.

When Avery did arrive about eleven o'clock, he had an armful of gifts that he put around the tree. Jane didn't move away from the television, although she did turn her face up to her father when he came in to greet her and give her a kiss. He was looking frail and drawn and dry like paper. When Avery wasn't drinking anything at all for long stretches, his irritation was visible and rather attractive. He assumed an aggressively disheveled look. Perhaps he had shaved much earlier that morning, but perhaps it had not been since the night before. He had on an old green sweater that was transparent at one elbow and rumpled jeans, and he wore an expression of a man vexed at being distracted from doing or saying some important thing. The whole attitude was peculiarly suited to his rangy build and slightly misaligned features, and he carried himself rigidly as though he were just a little sore all over.

When he made another trip outside, Claudia came in and was upset and frankly irritated at Jane. "What's the matter with you?" she said. "You're really being a wet blanket. You'll hurt your father's feelings." Claudia's voice was hushed, as though she didn't want Avery to hear her, even though he was outside. And Jane understood that when her mother spoke in that terse undertone, whatever suggestion she made was an imperative. So Jane did get up, trailing the blanket she was using as a robe, and moved to the living room, where she settled dourly on the couch, and Claudia followed her.

"For God's sake, Jane! You could get dressed! I asked you to get dressed!" She turned away from Jane and was suddenly anxious rather than cross. "Don't ruin this." She stood for a moment looking out at Avery and opening and closing her hands by her sides; then she turned back to Jane once more, and she was angry again. "God, it's depressing to have you dragging around like this. You could be that considerate of your father. And of me. It's Christmas. You can't stay like that in those raggy pajamas!"

Jane's loyalties and the affections of her whole lifetime were frozen on this particular Christmas morning, and she wanted no part of anything Claudia was saying. She didn't answer at all. Claudia just stood there in the center of the room, and then she turned her attention back to Avery, who was approaching the house with an armload of wood. As her mother moved forward to open the door, Jane's attention was suddenly riveted to her. All her senses were alerted.

No one else would have heard her mother's footsteps on the pale rug unless, like Jane, he or she watched Claudia's feet as they left a soft impression on the plush pile in their delicate sling-back suede shoes. But Jane heard the heels of the shoes smack softly against her mother's sheerly stockinged feet in the smallest sound of flesh and leather. As her father came in with the wood, and her mother moved forward to close the door—just as her two parents passed each other—Jane was astonished momentarily to see her mother so sinuous and silky, somehow insinuating in contrast with her father's efficient conservation of movement. No grace there, today, but a lean elegance that was entirely masculine.

Jane was struck by her mother's fragile ankles and slim legs beneath the full skirt that flicked around her knees. She noticed the curve of her mother's bust and waist, and the absurd puffed shoulders of the tapered sleeves of her velvet dress. Jane was embarrassed, and filled with some other discomfort for which she had no name, to see that her mother was physically so frivolous, so useless to a winter's day. And when her mother spoke to her father, it made Jane cringe to hear the subtle modulation, the slight, soft lilt that was both condescending, somehow, and gratingly deferential.

Avery set about building a fire in the fireplace, and the labor suited him. As he knelt on one knee to crumple paper and arrange the wood, Claudia glanced over at him from across the room where she was sitting on the edge of the couch. His mood was amiable but edged with a sort of accusatory fretfulness, and it was powerfully erotic to Claudia. He exuded an air of modest suffering, and she knew exactly how that slight petulance resolved itself in slow and deliberate lovemaking that would begin with a selfish insistence on his part, so at first she would respond a little and then become irritated and aloof. Finally the two of them would become absolutely aware of the other one in lazy, self-indulgent sex that would be so leisurely and slightly grudging of the other that it would have a sullen and rather dangerous quality about it. She was so absorbed in watching him that she was not breathing for a moment, and she caught herself and got up and redirected her attention to the gifts and their arrangement around the tree.

"I'm going to get some champagne for all of us," she said. "I've got wonderful things for brunch. I'll fix a tray."

Avery was trying to get the fire to light, and he didn't turn around. "Not anything for me. I can't stay too long. Alice is fixing a special dinner." The fire would not ignite, and he didn't see Claudia stop on her way to the kitchen, for a second, like a puppet with every string drawn taut in mid-motion. But she moved forward again without comment. When she returned with the tray, however, there were three glasses of wine and three plates of heated streusel. All she did was put it down on the small table she had placed by the tree, and she didn't call it to Avery's attention when the three of them sat down on the floor to open their gifts. He took a plate and a glass without even thinking about it, and he also began to come out of his air of being put upon. Claudia made several trips to the kitchen until finally she had laid out a feast on the table before them. Avery sat down across from her and began to cajole Jane, who was still huddled in her blanket, still dressed in her pajamas. He held out a small rectangular present to her.

"Listen," he said to her, "I know that we usually don't give practical kinds of things for presents, but you've gotten so old now that I knew you'd be tired of playthings." He looked worried for a minute. "You don't already have an electric toothbrush, do you?" He handed the present across to her, and she tried to smile at him when she unwrapped it. It was an antique amethyst and pearl locket; the amethyst was her birthstone, and she meant to ask him where he had found it, because he took great pleasure in unearthing these amazing presents. She meant to tell him that it was beautiful, but she was terribly tired. In fact, it seemed to her that it was the day itself that embodied exhaustion. She felt that it was a day that had already happened so that the minutes were sticky with previous events and unnaturally slow to pass. The day had happened, but not in any mysterious or thrilling way that allowed her the wondrous sense of déjà vu. It was not at all intriguing; what lay ahead was a long, flat sheet of hours that had been worn-out. So Jane held the locket in her hand and then put it away in its box and put the box down beside her. She hadn't even remembered to say thank you, although both her parents waited anxiously. And both Avery and Claudia took her seeming sullenness as a repudiation of themselves. But they didn't say anything. They moved on to other gifts.

Claudia kept the glasses filled with champagne as they opened the beautiful packages. When she was handed a gift, she would trade the box from hand to hand, nervously strip off some of the paper, and then jump up to get something else from the kitchen. "You open one while I get the pâté." She didn't like to receive gifts, but Avery and Jane always gave her things, anyway. This year Jane gave her a tea rose weekender set she had ordered from the Bloomingdale's catalogue and put on her mother's charge. Jane was a master of 800 numbers and the American Express card. It was how she shopped for most of the gifts she gave.

Claudia thanked her in flight; she opened the package and exclaimed over it after she had put it down and was moving through the kitchen door trailing words behind her. " . . . exactly like roses . . . lovely."

But Avery had found such a perfect present that when Claudia came back into the room and opened it, it held her right to the spot. She was standing as she peeled away the paper, but she settled down on the rug immediately. With immense satisfaction she leafed through the dozen or more record albums she had unwrapped.

"God! Where did you get these? My God, Danny and the Juniors! Oh, and, Avery, look at this! The Platters. This isn't even a copy, is it? I mean, these are the real records. Bobby Blue Bland. And you found an Ink Spots album. This is incredible! Leslie Gore. She was so wonderfully awful. The Shirelles! Where'd you ever find these? I was in . . . what . . . seventh grade? You must have been in ninth. Were you still in junior high? Where in the world did you find these?"

"If you watch the late shows on television," Avery said, "They're advertised right along with the Ginsu knives and the single-hand ratchet. The same number to call, too. 'Call right now before our limited supplies run out!' I couldn't resist them. They probably are copies of the originals. The sound won't be very good. I think the copyrights run out, and—"

Claudia interrupted him; she hadn't really been listening. "Look at this, Avery! The Penguins. Oh, God, here's 'Earth Angel,' and look, The Platters. 'Twilight Time.' "

Avery was animated, too, and pleased. He sat up and rocked back and forth dramatically as he assumed an exaggerated and tremulous falsetto and sang:

> *Heavenly shades of night are falling,*
> *It's twilight time.*
> *Deep in the dusk your voice is calling,*
> *It's twilight time. . . .*

"No, that's not right," Claudia said. "What is it? Not 'deep in the dusk.' I don't think so. Let's play them. Let's put them on now."

Jane was unsettled by this new development, by all this goodwill. And she was strangely hurt and jealous. "You were probably just drunk when you ordered them," she said suddenly. "I've seen those ads. They come on real late. I bet you were just drunk."

Her parents looked at her with utterly blank faces. In this household over the years the one thing that no one ever said when Avery was sober was that Avery was ever drunk. It would be a vile, cruel, and harmful idea to hold out in the light. Avery sometimes said that he had been through a rough time. Sometimes he had been working too hard. Quite often he apologized for having been depressed. But they didn't ever say that Avery was drunk, and it displeased Claudia more than Avery. She stood up in astonishment and was too surprised to say anything right away.

"Jane! What are you doing? Why would you say something like that? Avery went all over the county to antique stores to find that locket for you. . . ." She had no idea in the world why Jane seemed determined to make them all unhappy.

Everything about Avery signified unexpected injury.

He was pained, but all the more benevolent. Far be it from him to take offense, and he behaved as if Jane had not said a word, except that in everything he did there was a little hesitancy. He quickly fell into the role of being in the house on sufferance, careful not to make a misstep.

He settled back into his comfortable position on the rug, leaning against the table with his drink in his hand. "Janie, I think that at least you ought to open that big present right there," he said. He leaned forward to push the large box toward Jane, who sat like an Indian beneath her blanket with its edges draped over her forearms and her forearms wrapped around herself as she kept an eagle eye on her parents. She looked at the box in front of her with no enthusiasm. To have attacked her father left her feeling as brittle and hollowed-out as a winter-dried reed in the meadow.

For a few moments she made no move at all, and when this registered on Claudia, who was still bewildered, she looked over at Jane slowly. Claudia had picked up two records and had been studying the backs of the album covers because she was so unnerved. Now she said to Jane, "Is there some reason you want to ruin this day?"

"Oh, Claudia, leave it alone," Avery began in an apologetic tone, a man contrite, but she didn't pause.

"Your father has gone to a lot of trouble for you. What's in that box is really a special present. I don't know why you're so sulky. Why don't you go on and open it?" Jane knew that there was tremendous anger in her mother's intention that was withheld from the rigidly civilized tone of her reprimand. In response she felt a great welling up of fury at once again being treated like a child by her own mother. She didn't make any comment at all but removed the plaid taffeta bow and the glossy green paper while her parents huddled over the box to admire the gift. It was an elaborate stereo tape and phonograph component system. Avery had been looking into it for some time, he said, and he thought he had come up with the best of the best. He had put the package together from several sources. And Jane watched him as he removed the various pieces from the box with the same care with which he had handled the Celestron telescope a long time ago. These mechanical things, so precise and carefully rendered, they fascinated him, and he talked about advanced technology, tone, the clarification of sound, and so forth. Jane thanked him, but he wasn't really aiming his comments at her or Claudia; he was simply entertaining himself.

"Avery, let's play these records. Can we play them on that machine right now?"

"I've got to get it set up. I'm going to set it up in Janie's room, but I've got two speakers for the living room, too, that can be switched on or off. It should give us a much better sound than the stereo we've got. And Jane can record herself practicing and then play it back. Or she can use it to play the practice tapes that Alice makes for her. Alice thinks that it would be great for Jane to play along with the practice tapes. It's the way Alice gets ready for her performances or auditions. But she doesn't get a very pure sound on her machine."

He took the several parts of the gift upstairs and came back to get tools from the storage closet and a stepladder from the garage. "These wires can be hidden if I tack them with brackets along the baseboards and the doorsills. It won't take very long."

Claudia had become silent again, and when Avery disappeared back up the stairs, she took a meringue from the tray and settled down on the other end of the couch from Jane, tucking her legs beneath her voluminous skirt and taking a bite of the meringue. She ate it slowly, letting each small bit melt a little in her mouth, then nibbling at the piece in her hand and musing.

"Does Avery come to your lessons at Alice's?" she asked.

"Yeah. Sometimes he's there. He usually brings me home, you know."

"But, I mean, does he stay for the whole lesson? Why didn't you tell me about this?"

Jane didn't answer. She was trying to concentrate on looking through the books her mother had given her. The *Anne of Green Gables* series, which Jane had taken out of the library and read two years ago. *The Catcher in the Rye, The Grapes of Wrath*, and a book about the lives of the composers. It was an odd lot.

"Janie," Claudia said, and Jane glanced at her in acknowledgment and then continued to leaf through the pages of the books.

"This thing with Alice. What do you think?" Her voice was not angry now; it was confidential and fairly reflective. "Do you think that Avery might have missed a time in his life when it would have been natural for him to have some sort of sexual interest in boys?" Her words dwindled off with that thought, and she sat with part of another meringue growing sticky in her hand. "I mean, we were always with each other. Maybe he missed some part of development in childhood, or something. Alice . . . well, haven't you always thought of Alice as sort of neuter? Do you think Avery might be gay? Trying it out maybe? Or trying *not* to try it out? Alice is almost like a young boy." Claudia really wanted to know what Jane thought. "He has those graduate students who sort of fawn over him. Oh, and that one . . . what's his name? . . . well, I always thought he had a crush on your father."

There was no hint of judgment in what Claudia was saying, but Jane was trying not to hear her mother. She was intently studying the book in her lap. Claudia's question was more than she could consider. She concentrated so diligently on the pages before her that she didn't quite allow her mother's voice to penetrate her senses.

"I'm very fond of Alice, of course," Claudia added, as if that explained something.

"We haven't finished opening the presents yet," Jane said, and her mother turned to look at her but didn't respond one way or another. Claudia's mind was no longer on Christmas.

The room was very warm with the heat from the fireplace, and outside the day had begun to cloud over and come in closer. When Avery came downstairs to set up the speakers, Claudia got up to turn on the lights. Avery had switched from champagne to scotch, and he looked less haggard. His color was back across his cheekbones, and he had assumed the guarded expression of careful irony that always masked his face after he had had a certain amount to drink. He was cheerful as he fitted the speakers into the bookcases, and Claudia had more champagne. Avery went upstairs to put on one of Claudia's new records. When he came down again, Claudia had slipped off her suede heels and was standing by the stairs, swaying with excessive and campy zeal to the music:

> *Tell Laura I love her,*
> *Tell Laura I care.*
> *Tell Laura not to cry. . . .*

"You have to take off your shoes, too," she said to him. "Why didn't we ever get to dance anywhere where we could keep our shoes on?"

Avery handed Claudia his drink and sat down on the stairs to take his shoes off, and he stood up and reached to take his glass back from her, but she backed up a bit, holding both of her arms up toward him.

"No, this is the basic slow dance. A clutch." And she moved forward and crossed her wrists behind his neck, still holding the glass of scotch in one hand. He was enough taller than she so that for a moment she seemed to be suspended from him, arched upward with her breasts grazing his chest and her hair falling back away from her face while he hesitated, standing up straight at the foot of the stairs. Jane saw a fractional change come over his face. His mouth relaxed at the corners just a little, and his whole face lost its irony and took on a secretive, closed-down expression. He reached down to hold Claudia around the waist, and bending his knees slightly, he inclined his torso forward to meet her body which canted backward so that she was scooped into his leaning form. Neither of them laughed, although they had meant to be silly.

Jane was stunned. She had opened all sorts of presents, and now she saw that her life was not changed in any way, nor was her future enhanced. She was sitting behind a great jumble of wrapping paper and boxes across from her parents, who fitted so naturally together to do this dance. She looked dead ahead at Avery and Claudia and understood that in spite of every single thing, nothing was ever going to change between them. She felt her muscles growing rigid in that same semi-paralysis that made her movements awkward and that restrained her speech. But she did say very loudly, "We haven't finished opening the presents!"

Then her father straightened a little and made an elaborate parody of their dancing, dipping and swaying, and their two forms seemed to lose some force that had been bearing down upon them.

Jane had a lot more presents to open, but they were just this and that. A scrapbook from Diana, a set of oil pastels from Maggie, and Avery had a good bit more scotch, and Claudia finished the champagne.

Finally Avery got around to opening his present from Jane, which she had also ordered from Bloomingdale's. He took off the gift wrap and then leaned back to look at the box. It was the medium-size model of the Cuisinart.

"Very handy," he said. He had had enough scotch so that he fell into a sort of mocking banter, and he pitched his voice to mimic a shill. "Mounds of julienne potatoes in minutes! Chop onions without tears! And look! This a-*ma*-zing machine will even slice *tomatoes* paper-thin!" He sipped his drink and became a bit more gracious in deference to his daughter. "No, Janie. No, it's very thoughtful. Very thoughtful."

Her mother was staring at her, though, and she said

very carefully and very quietly, "Jane, we already have a Cuisinart."

Jane was red in the face with some powerful and unfocused rage by now. She could scarcely speak, her mouth had become so rigid.

"*We* have one, but Dad doesn't have one. He's always coming over to use ours."

Claudia stood up slowly, pushing her skirt into place with the open palms of her hands and leaving little trails in the dark velvet where she had brushed the plush fabric against the grain. She could not understand why Jane would betray her like this. She walked a few steps away toward the window but then stopped and stood still, idly kneading the fold of her skirt with one hand.

"Alice doesn't have one either," Jane said.

Her father assumed a faintly sardonic grin.

Claudia released her skirt and opened her hands out into the air in helplessness. She held her empty palms outstretched for a moment, then dropped them to her sides. She had been content to be an observer for most of her life, but now she was filled with a slightly drunken and passionate indignation.

"I want to know about this thing with Alice," Claudia said without turning around. "I always keep thinking that people are my friends."

"Aha!" Avery said. "That's it! That's just the way you would think. Why would anything between me and Alice have anything—anything at all—to do with you?" Avery had that dangerous note to his voice, a nasty edge of distorted self-pity, and when Jane watched him uncoil from the floor and stand over her mother, she felt sick with all the memory of old fear plus the real thing, immediate anxiety.

"As a matter of fact," Avery said from behind Claudia, "Alice doesn't much like you. She thinks that you don't have 'any purpose in life,' as she puts it. A leech on civilization. Of course, Alice is awfully stern." And thinking about it made him laugh a little.

"You know what, Avery? I'm so tired," and her

mother's voice rose. "I'm so fucking tired of fools. Of little twits and fools. I think Alice is like one of those dolls you buy in the store. No humor. No sex. Just long hair that you can comb into different styles. 'Not anatomically correct' is how they print it on the boxes. Is that right, Avery? Is that right? No one you'd really want to fuck, but someone to *believe* in you? I'm getting awfully tired—"

But Avery grabbed her from behind and held one of her arms in back of her and covered her mouth with his other hand.

"Oh, Christ! Shut up! You never know when to shut up!" And it was such a perfect little domed house to exacerbate their burgeoning anger. Their own voices were scooped by the warming air currents out of the curves and corners, bounced off the glass, and thrown back at their own ears to infuriate them further.

Jane had leaped up off the couch, and her face was grotesque with alarm. "Stop it! Stop it!" She threw herself on her father's arm that was clasped over the lower part of her mother's face, and she pulled it away, screaming at them both. "Stop it! I can't stand it! Not anymore! Not anymore! Stop it!"

But as soon as Claudia was free to speak again, she turned toward Avery as far as she could with her arm still pinned behind her back.

"You're a spoiled brat! A baby! A baby!" she yelled at Avery. "I've known it all my life! I've put up with it forever! Even your mother warned me! And you know what *I* think! I think you're a borderline narcissist!"

Avery pushed her away from him so hard that she stumbled forward and fell down on one knee.

"*You* think that! You think that! You goddamned solipsistic bitch. You don't even have the remotest—not the faintest idea that there's a world out there!" He was leaning forward and shouting at Claudia as she scrambled to her feet, and the tendons in his neck stood out. "Who's the chancellor of West Germany?" he shouted straight into her face as she turned to meet him.

"Stop it! Stop it! Please stop it!" And Jane was yelling, too. Trying to get between them.

Claudia was beside herself with fury now, and she shook both of her clenched fists at him. "*Stupid!* Stupid *questions!* Don't ask me such stupid questions! What is it? Have you forgotten how to be honest? You can't even be honest in an argument, can you? You won't even talk about the things that really make you mad. How do you feel about what you do, Avery? How do you feel about women? You can hardly talk about your own mother!" And her voice had fallen into a loud and persistent taunt.

"And you *cannot* tell me who is the chancellor of West Germany! Who is it? Who is it? Have you even read a paper in the past year, or have you been too busy brooding about . . . Christ! . . . whatever it is you brood about?" All of a sudden he grabbed Claudia by the shoulders and shook her back and forth while Jane yelled and yelled at them.

"Who *cares* who it is? Don't touch me! Don't you touch me, you son of a bitch! You stupid bastard! You're an asshole of a graduate student brat! You've never changed! Nothing you can think of is as important as I am! As anyone is!"

Avery moved in closer to her, pulling her forward, so that she was standing on tiptoe, almost not touching the ground at all. "You *never* listen. You never even listen. You tell me . . . you tell me right now, *who is the chancellor of West Germany*?"

Jane began picking up the empty gift boxes that were strewn around the room and pelting Avery and Claudia with them. She threw the sturdy cardboard boxes with all her might. One hit Avery in the temple, and he released Claudia with one hand to protect his head. Both of her parents raised their elbows around their heads as Jane threw at them anything she could pick up, all the while screaming at them to stop. "Get out! Get out!" She threw an ashtray, her mother's cigarettes, which shot out of the pack in every direction like white darts. "Why do you come back all the time? Just get out! Get out!"

Avery lurched forward at her and roared as if he had been wounded. "God damn you! You get out! We can't even have any privacy! You think everything is your business. We've knocked ourselves out for you this Christmas, and you've acted like a spoiled little rich bitch all day! God knows what you've been telling the Tunbridges about our private life, but Maggie's worried as hell about you. Says you never even leave the house. Here's your chance! *Leave* it! I'd like to see how sympathetic Maggie is after she's spent a little time with you. Who are you to judge me! Or your mother! Who the hell do you think you are?"

Jane stood her ground in fury; her father had never laid a hand on her. She wasn't afraid he would hurt her. "No, *you* get out!" she said. "You left! Why can't you stay away? All that ever happens when you come over is that you get mad. You ruin everything. You get out!"

And then Claudia turned on her, too. "This is your father's house! How can you say those things to him?" Her mother was very loud, but also plaintive. "You've upset everybody today. Everybody! We were having a nice day except for you! You don't care about the trouble we went to about your violin! You don't care about the trouble your father went to to find that locket! I don't know . . . I don't know if you care about anything at all, about anybody but yourself! God, I wish I'd never had you! I wish I had never, never had you!"

Claudia and Avery were so engrossed in their own rage and the drama of it and the morbid thrill of saying the very worst that could be said that Avery didn't even notice that he was being defended, and Claudia had no idea that what she had said would not only be believed forever after, but would never be forgotten. Avery turned on Claudia again.

"How can you *say* that to a child? To your own child . . ."

But Jane had raced up the stairs to her room, leaving

them to indulge in their own gluttonously vituperative feast. She fumbled with the clasp on the violin case and tumbled the violin out onto her bed, flinging the case aside. She seized the violin by its neck and ran back halfway down the stairs.

"I *don't* care! I don't care about the violin!" she screamed into the ongoing melee. "You do everything wrong! *I* wish you hadn't had me, too! I wish I weren't even here! You do every single thing wrong! I didn't ask for a violin. I didn't ask for you to go to any trouble. I don't want it! I don't want it!" She raised the violin up with both hands, high above the banister of the stairs. She was shaking from head to foot, holding that beautiful violin that only she—only she—could play so well. That's what she knew. That's what she thought her parents knew. In a second one of them would take it safely away from her, and she looked down at them, standing stock-still below her. She had, indeed, stopped their fighting. She had caught their absolute attention, and they were standing frozen there, staring back at her. But as she looked down at them, she caught a fleeting look of interest passing over both their faces as they saw their daughter in such a melodramatic pose. And it was also a look of undisguised curiosity—so much in the world was genuinely boring to Claudia and Avery. But that one instant of dispassionate observance was more than Jane could bear. She gritted her teeth, and with a low moan of fury she brought the violin smashing down across the banister, where its back cracked in two and the strings made a flat twang.

Everyone stood completely still until Jane flung the ruined instrument down the rest of the stairs and turned and ran back to her room, where she put her jeans on over her pajamas and stepped into her boots. She pulled on a sweat shirt and grabbed her parka. She came back down the stairs and walked between her two parents without speaking to them or looking at them, and they were absolutely quiet. She went through the kitchen and out the back, not even slamming the door behind her.

She had used up the major allotment of drama in her own life.

After she was gone, Avery and Claudia couldn't think of a thing to say to each other. They stood among all the boxes and ribbons and wrapping paper utterly numb and unthinking.

"Aren't you tired?" Claudia said, without any guile whatsoever, even though it was only three o'clock in the afternoon. "Aren't you tired?" She started up the stairs slowly, stepping over Jane's violin, and Avery followed her. They got into bed, each on his or her own side, and fell sound asleep before either one of them displaced their extraordinary and slightly drunken fatigue with anything like lust or anything like remorse.

11

Jane left the house and walked straight
down the path through the meadow, and she,
too, did not allow herself to reflect. She had forgotten to
take her gloves, and she put her hands in her pockets;
but they had already become so cold that she couldn't
warm them, and she began to shiver in the frigid air. She
headed toward the Tunbridges', where all the windows
spilled a soft light out onto the dingy snow. Jane was
moving like a dumb thing, no more thoughtful than the
big turtles that migrated inland every year from the
Missouri River across I-70, where Avery and Claudia
always pulled over onto the shoulder and rushed out on
foot into the traffic to rescue them. Jane was making her
way through the meadow with the same blind instinct as
the turtles. The light ahead of her in the dismal day was
like warmth itself, puddling the yard around the huge
brick house in golden rectangles.

She went down the path past the landmarks of her
own invention and made her way to the kitchen door.
She was moving in such a risky time, too, on this day,
because for any people who celebrate Christmas, the
hours after lunch and until time for bed are the deadliest
hours of the year, filled as they are with exhaustion and

disenchantment, but also colored with some unspecified expectations.

Maggie had told Jane long ago not ever to knock at their door since she was always welcome, and Jane believed her. She went in through the empty kitchen and found the family and two friends of Celeste's in the dining room, where some of them were sitting around the table, some standing and talking. Maggie was at the far end of the long table, idly smoothing out the folds of some wrapping paper so it could be used again and talking to Mark, who was slouched in a chair next to her. He was looking glum, leaning back in his chair with his hands in his pockets. He had been genuinely appreciative when he had received an electric typewriter earlier in the morning, and now he was trying to remember that gratitude, but he was also checking it off against the list of things he remembered his sisters had received. As a middle child he always felt a trifle slighted, and Maggie glanced at him and knew it. She wasn't particularly irritated either. Mark was not a jealous or greedy child on any day but this one. She was thinking that perhaps they all should go their separate ways until dinner. The children could put their gifts away; Vince could take a nap. She was thinking about this at the very moment she spotted Jane slipping, white-faced and tense, into the room.

In one second her whole family would turn and see Jane, and it would cause a stir and a delay. She would never get everyone to disperse because Jane looked blanched with anguish. Maggie cared about Jane in a proprietary way since she was so important to Diana, and also Maggie had a simple and unambiguous concern for Jane. But not at this moment. She had three families coming for a light Christmas supper around the tree, and part of the pleasure that they would all take in the buffet she planned was that it would appear to have occurred spontaneously, without effort. Very little is more difficult to achieve. She did not want the complication of Jane's white misery, whatever its cause, although she did not think this all the way through. She was not unkind; she was only harassed, and she deftly intercepted the situation.

"Oh, Jane! Merry Christmas! You look absolutely stunned. I saw the beautiful locket your father found for you. It must have really been a surprise." And this seemed so plausible that Maggie felt very fond of and pleased for Jane at the same time. Since Avery had been away, his gift had obviously touched his daughter a great deal. "And you and Diana have to make plans for the concert. Diana got a ticket, too, you know. You'll drive in to Kansas City with Celeste. Diana, why don't you get some eggnog for both of you? You can put it on a tray with some cookies. There are all kinds. You and Jane can take the tray up to your room. Show Jane that incredible jewelry box your godmother sent you!" She had been looking at Diana, but now she turned to the rest of the room. "Jane, maybe you can help Diana carry her presents up to her room. And, Celeste, you and Mark do the same thing. We have people coming at six. I really would be grateful if you would all put your things away and get this room cleared."

And so, when any one of them noticed Jane, her strained appearance had been interpreted for them, and they were absorbed in their own day anyway. Celeste and her friends got up and began to sort through the boxes, giving Jane scarcely more than a friendly glance. Mark gathered himself together and stood up to look down the length of the table and see what he ought to remove. Only Diana looked at Jane warily. Diana had had a lovely Christmas, and she had been looking forward all morning to arranging her new clothes in her closet and putting her stickers in the sticker album Celeste had given her. Besides, Jane had hurt her feelings over the past few weeks, and she wasn't pleased to relinquish her plans to Jane's mood.

Diana had always wanted to be like Jane a little bit. She admired Jane's cynicism and wit even though it was sometimes disconcerting. She was awed by Jane's scorn, which was so wide that every aspect of their social lives was tinged by her disapproval. But for the past two months or so Jane had been so sharp-tongued that Diana was tired of trying to please her. Maggie had said that Jane would snap out of it, but when Diana looked at Jane standing rigid in the doorway, her spirits sank. She began gathering her gifts together and simply handed some to Jane, who followed her upstairs without a word. Diana didn't offer Jane any eggnog or cookies; she wanted Jane to go home, and she didn't make any pretense of graciousness.

Diana was often defensive around Jane—of her own family and their predictable domestic arrangements. Jane had a certain air of authority and chic in their small circle in her own right but also by virtue of being her parents' daughter. All the girls thought that Claudia was exotic, and most of them were a little in love with Avery, who always was careful to remember their names and never condescended toward them. He admired them— each one—on her own merits. The Parks had a strange kind of glamour. What Diana had not figured out was that glamour gets its shimmer by the possibilities it encompasses. It might lead to even greater things, a larger renown, but it is also dazzling because it may be so very brief. It also encompasses the possibilities of ruin and decay. There's nothing safe about it.

Jane put the gifts she was carrying for Diana on the bed and sat down in the big chair by Diana's window while Diana moved about, putting things away with her own face closed and set in response to the peculiar lack of animation of her friend. She dutifully showed Jane this and that. She held up a sweat shirt-skirt and a matching striped top and leg warmers to show Jane, and Jane just looked and nodded. "That's really nice," she said. And somehow that was more insulting to Diana than if Jane had assumed that faint air of contempt which would have left Diana wondering if she should ever wear the outfit at all. Once in a fit of pique Jane had told Diana that her tastes were "incredibly bourgeois," and although Diana had resented it, she had also taken down her bulletin board, about which Jane had said, "Oh, God, Diana! That's awfully *cute*." Diana had reassessed her whole wardrobe and insisted that her father detach the canopy from her antique bed.

Now, though, Diana was as tired as anyone from a morning of familial celebration, and she sat down cross-legged on the bed and opened the jewelry box that had come so carefully packed and gift-wrapped through the mail. It was quite a handsome mahogany box decorated with creamy inlaid mother-of-pearl flowers on top, but Diana was more interested in looking in the mirror fitted under its cover. She took out a tiny pair of silver unicorn earrings and put them in her pierced ears, then lifted the box to study the effect in the mirror. She shook her loose hair back from her face so she could see her ears, and she put the box down again and reached up to remove the earrings.

"Do you have some kind of problem?" she said to Jane without looking at her, and without any hint that she wanted to know about it in case Jane did. Diana was seized with what was, for her, unusual petulance on the dregs of this day. She had never been so sharp to Jane.

Jane didn't say anything, in any case. She didn't seem even to have heard Diana. It would never have occurred to Jane to reveal to anyone the things that went on in her own house. She thought that only she herself knew Avery and Claudia well enough to have the right to disapprove of them or wish that they were in any way different from the way they were. A betrayal on that scale had never crossed her mind.

Diana was fitting another pair of earrings, small enameled flowers, into her ears, and for the moment she looked quite satisfied with herself.

"You know, you're really being immature about your whole situation." This time she held her hair back with her hands and bent far over the jewelry box to see herself in the mirror. "There are lots of people whose parents get divorced. You don't have to take it out on everyone else. Vince says that everyone will be happier with your parents apart." She looked up, but Jane was still immobile in the chair, with her fingers laced in her lap and her elbows resting on the armrests. What Diana had said seemed to have floated right by her. She was sitting there completely still and gazing into the room, and it irritated Diana terribly that she had dared to be so outspoken to Jane and had not made any impression at all.

"Well, Maggie says that you're just feeling sorry for yourself, and she says it's natural. But I really do think it's immature. I mean, Maggie says that American children don't even know what unhappy childhoods are. She says that in America childhood really is the time of your life. If you were in El Salvador, you might have to stand there and watch your parents be shot to death. Maggie thinks that American children are very lucky, in a way, to be able to indulge themselves in depression. Depression is really just a luxury."

Jane sat there where she was, and Diana began to feel apprehensive about what she was saying. She had been trying out these ideas she had heard as her parents and their friends chatted over dinner or while Celeste and her mother put away the dishes. Celeste had read Joan Didion's book *Salvador* and had urged her mother to read it. Usually Jane could dismiss Diana's adopted philosophies and opinions with a superior shrug. Also, Diana didn't want Jane to repeat these ideas to Avery or Claudia or to ask her own parents about them. She lapsed into a mood of appeasement.

"I'll get us some eggnog. I think that the only kind that's left is spiked, and I bet Maggie'll let us have some. And some cookies. You stay here."

And Jane did stay there, and she did drink some eggnog and eat a cookie. But she still didn't say very much to Diana, and when she had finished her eggnog, she stood up and put on her parka.

"Didn't you bring your locket over?" Diana said. She was very worried now that she had said more than she should. "Don't go home! I'll put all these things away, and then we can do something." But Jane was already at the threshold of the doorway, and she turned back and made an attempt to smile at Diana, and she gave a stiff wave of her hand. Her face was so numb she didn't believe she could say a word, and she went quietly down the back stairs and out through the kitchen, which was empty at the moment.

She walked up the long hill toward home, but she went so slowly. It was very hard for her to move at all, the same way it sometimes is in dreams. She was having great difficulty breathing, and in the meadow each intake of breath came with a rasping short whoop, like a swallowed shriek. She turned along the path that led to the Troubled Rocks, although they were just a place to be; this landscape no longer held any solace for her. For a moment she leaned back against the familiar large boulder, trying hard to catch her breath and concentrating on the gray stones all around her and the icy pools they contained wherever they were pocked.

When she had watched Diana there in her room, sitting upon her pretty bed and talking blithely out into the air, Jane had suddenly felt crushed by the conditions of her own existence. It seemed to Jane that Diana was free in the same world in which she was not. Diana's ego and all her ambitions could expand out and out into the natural world in a great exhalation of self, not to be caught so hard against obligation, responsibility, or even love. Jane had, at that moment, been thoroughly overcome by a sensation of suffocation, and she had had to take herself away.

And now she felt that she could not breathe at all. She put her hands across her rib cage to try to press the air out, to try to force herself to exhale, but she could not do it, and she was terrified and filled with panic all alone under the low and nasty yellow-streaked clouds.

She turned toward the boulder in despair and leaned against it with her arms outstretched and her cheek pressed into the freezing stone. At last her breath was released in huge sobs, and she gasped air back into her lungs, only to expel it again in uncontrollable, deep moans. Tears slid down her face and froze against the surface of the rock where her head rested sideways, and down the other side of her face; they fell so fast that they dripped off the angle of her jaw and trickled down her neck. She was enwrapped with grief that she could not control, and while sorrow may be dependent in degree upon the source of the misery, grief is absolute. Jane was heartbroken with loss, with the small death she had caused when she brought the violin cracking down across the banister, with the loss of each one of her parents to the other. She was heartbroken with the hopelessness of loving Avery and Claudia so much for all her life, the energy it would require, the fatigue it would cause.

She wept on and on alone in the snow, but all the while she knew that Maggie was right. Jane knew that she was a fortunate child in the middle of Lunsbury, Missouri, which was itself in the middle of a rich and civilized country, and she couldn't possibly defend her own anguish in the vast realm of wickedness and cruelty extant in the world. She was lost in the universe. She was negated. She could not even take any comfort in self-pity because for this moment she had lost any idea of herself. She was a paltry thing, empty of any valid sentiment.

Nellie had heard Jane far away up the hill where she had been sitting on the Parks' doorstep waiting for someone to let her in. With her winter coat expanding all around her like a great chrysanthemum she came snuffling and shambling along the path toward Jane in abject apology in case Jane's distress might turn to anger. She burrowed her long collie nose against Jane's side, and finally Jane pushed herself away from the stone and knelt down and embraced the dog. But this, in turn, alarmed Nellie, and she rolled over on her back in even more fervent and submissive apology. Jane stood up stiffly. She had stopped sobbing, although tears still ran down her face. Nellie stood up, too, and shook herself all over while Jane brushed snow off her own clothes.

"Come on, Nellie," she said, and she made her way back to the main path and up the hill with Nellie delightedly following along or running ahead. The silly dog was delighted to have found a companion in the dull afternoon.

The lights were on downstairs, and the tree hadn't been unplugged, but the upstairs was lit only by the waning daylight through the windows. Jane went straight up to her room with Nellie behind her. She hadn't looked anywhere but straight ahead of her, and she hadn't let herself see the violin lying as she had left it at the foot of the stairs, and she didn't look for her parents.

She took two capsules from the Percodan bottle and swallowed them one at a time, without water, and Nellie thought it might be a treat. She sat back on her haunches and watched Jane alertly, wagging her tail. No one had remembered to feed the dog all day, but Jane put the bottle down on her nightstand and began to take off her cold, wet clothes. She dropped everything on the floor and put on a warm pair of flannel pajamas and crawled into bed under her covers, where she curled up and tried to warm herself. She was cold to the bone and shaking violently.

"Here, Nellie! Come up! Here, Nellie!" She coaxed the dog to come reluctantly up onto her bed, although Nellie's ears were flat against her head with uneasiness at this unusual request. Jane held her tightly with one arm and tried to stop shivering and tried to disburden herself of some of the terrific weight of all she was thinking. And a cat might have done the trick. Cats have an admirable reserve, and if one had been curled up neatly next to Jane, it might have served as a credible repository of even a little part of Jane's grief. But Nellie. . . Dogs are such trusting beasts that children know early that they couldn't possess any special wisdom. It wasn't Nellie's fault, though. The dog lay there faithfully, understanding that Jane didn't want her to move.

It wasn't anything to do with Nellie that after a while Jane reached over and took the little bottle from the night table and swallowed the last four pills, then dropped the empty vial next to her under the sheets. In fact, it wasn't anything to do with anyone, really. It was just that as soon as Jane began to become drowsy, she was seized with the fear that some strange and sorrowful thought might come upon her once more, and she was too tired to bear it. She had come to a moment, too early in her life, when she believed that there was nothing at all to look forward to. Her enthusiasm guttered and went out, but she was powerless against the horrible revolutions of her mind, that malevolent machine, unlike the stupid heart. She took all the rest of the pills because she wanted to be sure that she would not have another thought; she wanted to be sure that she would get some rest.

Nellie lay there until Jane's arm relaxed and her breathing became light and shallow and she was deeply asleep. Only then did Nellie slink off the bed and down the stairs where she happily polished off the pâté, the meringues, smoked turkey, and Boone County ham she had smelled from upstairs as she lay very still until Jane didn't need her anymore.

And Jane didn't turn in her deep sleep, but she straightened out to her full length. At age eleven Jane was five feet four inches tall and weighed 118 pounds. She had developed a certain tolerance, too, for the narcotic she had swallowed. When she finally woke up late the next evening, and in the several days thereafter of feeling sleepy and sick and hung-over, and of having Claudia murmur vaguely about her flu, Jane left behind everything of childhood. She had become old without accumulating a personal history, but the very lack of it in her life permitted her to control her destiny more than most. Jane took upon herself the task of directing her own life, and she proceeded with great caution. She had lost forever the ability to fling herself blindly into imaginative hopefulness, and she had lost the capacity ever to experience joy, because she had learned too early a hard truth: During every instant of her life that she was happy she understood implicitly that in the next instant she might be miserable. In this knowledge there was a great deal of serenity; she never doubted for a moment that the worst could happen.

12

That late Christmas afternoon while Jane
was making her journey up the hill, Claudia
and Avery slept soundly. They didn't hear Jane come in;
they didn't know when night fell; they had retreated into
sleep. They lay apart on the wide bed, and they had not
made love; but even deeply asleep each one was conscious of that other body nearby, and they lay comfortably at ease with the tall windows along the wall next to
the bed losing light in dusky gradations so that at first
they had been dimly lit, those two antagonists, and then
only their pale skin was luminous in the darkening room,
and finally the dark was complete, as if the day had
covered them over. Only sound and scent were left,
although outside, there was some moonlight that fell
straight down and did not cross the sills of the little
domed house. The house sat ominously exclusive under
the bare black trees and in the center of the snowy
meadow.

Claudia awoke first, unaware of what had awakened
her. She realized slowly, as she came awake by degrees,
that her legs were uncomfortably entangled in her wide
velvet skirt and the bodice was too binding for sleeping.
She sat up to unbutton all the tiny, covered buttons

down its front and got up to drop the dress over a chair on which she had left her filmy red robe early that morning. She took off her bra and pants and slipped the robe on in the chilly room, and she moved slowly in the dark, with sleepiness still upon her.

All she thought right away was that it must be very late, but then, almost simultaneously, she felt a twinge of regret at the muffled images of the afternoon that were emerging at the back of her thoughts, and she was relieved that, whatever else, Avery was there on the bed. But there were so many things that were hard to think about that she did not let any clear idea of the Christmas afternoon come back into her mind. She wanted to go back to bed, but first she put her hand out to touch the wall so she could guide herself out of the room in the dark and into the hall where the light filtered up the stairwell enough to enable her to see.

She went along the hall to Jane's room, and all she meant to do was to be sure that Jane was there and tucked in. Claudia stood in the doorway where she could just make out the silhouette of her daughter turned away from the door with her face toward the wall. Claudia, for a moment, ached with such a terrible regret that there was no other important thing about this day at all. For a brief moment she mourned what seemed to her to be the loss of her daughter, and she moved over to the bed and looked down at Jane's face, which was very pale and completely relaxed in sleep, just as she had slept as an infant. Claudia was afraid that Jane would awaken and that her severe features would register sweeping disapproval of almost everything that Claudia had ever done. She felt so sure that this might happen, she was so certain that there was anger in the room, that she froze there momentarily, alarmed that even a shift of the chilly air would induce her daughter's wrath. But Jane didn't stir, and Claudia didn't have the courage to lean over and kiss her on the cheek; she had never had that courage except when Jane was very young and couldn't object. She quietly left the room.

Downstairs she unplugged the tree and let out poor Nellie, who had been making frantic circles around her ever since Claudia had come down the stairs. In the kitchen she looked at the clock. It wasn't as late as she had thought; it was only a little after eleven. Finally she turned off the lights and went back to bed, stepping gingerly over the scattered boxes and the broken violin and keeping her mind empty of any implication they might have other than being impediments to her progress across the room and up the stairs.

She lay in bed with Avery next to her snoring slightly, but she was restless. She turned on her stomach and embraced her pillow with her head turned to look out at the icy driveway and far across the meadow, where lights were shining in the Tunbridge house. She looked down the hill at their windows and became drowsy, and she reversed the process in her thoughts, placing herself inside Maggie's house and gazing out over the meadow where she and Avery and Jane were warmly tucked in after a long day, and she fell back to sleep.

Only Nellie stirred in that cold landscape over the next few hours. She trotted along to the grove of pines where she customarily relieved herself, although she was abashed even then, having understood since being housebroken that this might induce anger. She went farther up the meadow to the house above the Parks', whose inhabitants thought they had a problem with raccoons. Nellie quietly tipped over a plastic trash can in which she found many mothballs and five fine bones from a standing rib roast. She settled down happily in the snow to chew on them, holding one between her paws so she could work her way down the meaty ridge that slipped away from her otherwise. In a little while, though, a light went on in the house, and Nellie made a stealthy retreat down the hill with a large rib in her mouth, moving cautiously so her tags wouldn't jangle. Nellie was a terrible coward, but that made her all the more skilled as a thief.

She carried the bone with her to her own front door, where she lay down to wait until someone came to let her in, and she dozed off with her chin resting on the well-chewed prime rib. She came instantly alert, however, and was overjoyed when she first heard the gentle crunch and then saw the lights of a car that turned from the main road and made its way slowly up the long, icy drive toward her house. Nellie was standing up and wagging her tail even before the car came to a stop behind Avery's Citation.

Inside the house the headlights had shifted fleetingly right over Avery's face as the car made the upward climb from the road below, but he woke up after the light had passed over the walls and through the room when the car leveled out in the short, flat turn to the circular parking area. He was instantly awake, however, and he knew that something significant had awakened him because he was immediately anxious. He pushed the quilt back and sat up to look out the window.

"Oh, Christ!" he said in a loud whisper of alarm. "Holy shit, Claudia!"

"What?" she asked. She was only a little bit awake, and she turned over on her back to try to see Avery through the darkness. She reached out for the light next to the bed, but Avery grabbed for her arm.

"Christ! No! Don't turn on the light! The curtains aren't even closed." He was whispering, but his voice was very urgent. Claudia let her arm fall back to the bed.

"What's the matter?" And she was whispering, too.

"Oh, shit, Claudia. It's Alice. She's right out there! Her car's out there!"

"In the driveway?"

"Right out there. She's right outside!"

Claudia slid off her side of the bed and lay on the rug by the window, peering out. She didn't say anything. It was true. Alice's brown Dodge Dart was parked directly behind Avery's new Citation. Avery rolled across the bed and slid off, too, so that he couldn't possibly be seen through the window. The two of them lay side by side, peering over the rim of the window that ran almost floor to ceiling.

"Oh, Christ!" Avery said. "I should have gone back. I told her I'd be back!" He still whispered.

"What should we do now? What if she knocks on the door?" Claudia whispered back. They had been caught out together. They had even been in bed together.

"God! Oh, God! We'll get Janie to answer it. I should have called her or something. Fucking shit! Do you know what she was fixing for dinner? For Christmas dinner? It's so awful! Shit! I should have gone back."

"What? What was she fixing for dinner?"

"There were just going to be the two of us. Just the two of us. But she was going to roast a *chicken*!"

Claudia was indignant, a little, on Alice's behalf, and she whispered back to him, "Well, Avery . . ."

"I know, I know. But doesn't it seem awful to you? I mean, it's such a pathetic sort of gesture. I didn't want her to. I didn't want her to fix that damned chicken. Christ, I bet it's sitting there sort of horrible and puckered all over the way roast chicken gets when it's cold. Oh, shit!"

They were both very quiet, watching the car warily. Finally Claudia said, "Well, even so, Avery . . . I mean, in spite of everything I really am fond of Alice, and . . ."

"Oh, God. I know. I should have gone back to her place!"

And then they both began to laugh that terrible, stifled laughter that hurts inside because it has to be repressed. They shook with panicky, breathy laughter that made their ribs ache. Claudia buried her face in her elbows on the rug and laughed and laughed, and Avery laughed and gasped occasionally to get his breath. They were hysterical on the rug of their own bedroom, hiding from Avery's lover.

Below them, though, Alice opened the car door, closing it with a thunk that was hollow and didn't reverberate in the cold air. And Claudia became completely quiet and still as she peered out at Alice, who had stepped back from her car and was looking directly up at their window with her hands in her pockets and her wool hat pulled down over her ears and her long hair streaming over her shoulders. Avery, though, still lay beside Claudia, keeping his head down, and was still racked with great silent shudders of laughter.

"Alice has such beautiful hair," Claudia said after several moments and very, very softly. "She always has had such beautiful hair." But below them Alice continued to stand and stare at the house, ignoring Nellie, who pranced all around her in a friendly greeting.

Claudia thought that Avery was still laughing into his crossed arms, but then she realized that he was stifling his own crying.

"My God, Claudia. Think of someone who would cook a chicken on Christmas Day and serve it with cranberry sauce and stuffing . . ."

Claudia looked away from Alice and turned to try to see Avery's expression in the dark. She tried to see what he was talking about, and he continued to shake with a sound of half-muffled sobbing and laughing. She could only peer at him and wait.

"You know," he said, "she had an abortion last month." He became still, too, stretched out on the floor with his head on his arms. "She didn't want a baby, anyway. And she thought I would leave her. She didn't think I would stay. But I wanted her to have the baby. I don't think she really wanted me to stay."

Claudia just looked at him through the dark where he was crying for the chilled chicken and the lost child. She just stared at him through the murky night, and she didn't move at all. She just lay there watching him.

Alice walked around her car and stood closer to the house, but she was not looking up at the windows anymore. She stood very still and straight with Nellie sitting at her side staring ahead at her own doorway.

"That's so stupid! It's so stupid, so stupid! Why did you do that?" Claudia was whispering, but she was truly anguished. "Why did you go away from me? I don't know why you go away from me. I know everything, for God's sake! I know the very worst there is to know about you, and I want you with me! I always have wanted you no matter what!" And now tears were sliding down Claudia's face, but she didn't realize it. "And you even love me. You want to be with me. You can't ever stay away from me for very long. But you do all this damage! Why do you go away from me? Why are you always leaving?" She really had to know this; it was something she had never caught on to. Avery didn't move or answer for a little while, and Alice stood silently below.

"Well . . ." Avery said, and he whispered so softly that Claudia could scarcely hear him. "Well . . . the thing is . . . you do. You do know the worst things . . . but you know the best about me too. Probably. You probably do," Avery said. "I probably can't do a fucking thing any better than you already think I can. It scares the shit out of me. It really does."

Claudia just listened to him. If she had been angry instead of so very sad, she would have torn this idea of his into little shreds with all the lacerating scorn she felt for his ambition and his vanity, but with that silent witness below them in the driveway she just heard him and made no reply at all.

They both turned their attention to Alice, who held them prisoner on the drafty floor. For a long while no one moved, although down the hall Jane shifted one arm ever so slightly in her heavy sleep.

Eventually Alice moved back around her car to the driver's side and opened the door, and Claudia let her breath out in relief even though Avery didn't look up at all. He lay as still as if he had fallen asleep. But Alice only reached inside to get her keys, and then she walked around to the trunk of the car and with some effort finally unlocked and opened it. When she closed the trunk, Claudia could see that she was holding the tire iron in one hand.

"Avery!" And Claudia put out her hand to touch his arm in alarm.

"Oh, God!" Avery said, and they were immobilized with shock in their hiding place behind the window. They hardly breathed.

Alice hefted the tire iron in her hand while Nellie watched with interest. Perhaps Alice would throw it for her. Alice paced back and forth beside the parked cars, smacking the tire iron against her mittened palm, feeling its weight. At last she stopped alongside the Citation and raised the tire iron high above her head and behind her shoulder so that Nellie reared up on her hind legs, ready to retrieve it when Alice let go. But Alice swung it fiercely down, smashing it through the front window of Avery's car, and Nellie let out a horrified yelp. Alice brought it back again and smashed at the window another time, and another, and poor Nellie ran off down the hill to turn and watch from a safe distance with her ears flat down on her head and her tail tucked between her legs.

Alice moved a little to the side and worked and worked at the passenger windows, smashing them with all her strength, until only fragments of glass remained projecting jaggedly from the frame. She walked around to the other side of the car and stopped for a moment, leaning against the hood to catch her breath, and she heaved to again, swinging at and smashing anything on the car that she could break. Finally she stopped and stepped back and surveyed what she had done for a long minute. Then with great fastidiousness she stepped carefully over the broken glass, opened her trunk once more, replaced the tire iron, and got in and drove away.

As Claudia and Avery watched the red taillights of her

car retreat down the hill, they were all alone in the dark. They no longer knew anyone else except the other one, and the illusion that they ever could had come tumbling down around them on this Christmas Day. For quite a while they lay there beside each other in utter silence.

About the Author

Robb Forman Dew was born in Mount Vernon, Ohio, but grew up in Baton Rouge, Louisiana, where her father was a neurosurgeon. She now lives in Williamstown, Massachusetts, where her husband, Charles, is a professor of history at Williams College. They have two sons, Stephen and Jack. After receiving the American Book Award for her first novel, Ms. Dew also won a grant from the Guggenheim Foundation. The first chapters of both that earlier work and the present one were published in *The New Yorker* in somewhat different form, and Dew's short stories have appeared in *The Southern Review* and *The Virginia Quarterly*.